The sexiest ice cream man she'd ever seen...

Jenny watched Nick walk toward his truck, noting the powerful muscles of his legs, how snugly his faded jeans hugged his hips. The bandanna hanging out of his back pocket swayed a little as he walked, looking strangely out of place in suburbia.

He fascinated her.

Then he reached the street, pulled out the bandanna and revealed what it had hidden.

A beeper.

Why would an ice cream man need to be reached?

Suddenly, a long, white Caddy slid to a stop next to him. Nick stuffed the bandanna away and looked around. Then he bent over the passenger door, reached into his pocket and passed something in through the window.

She didn't want to see this.

Jenny turned away. It wasn't fair. The one bright point of color in her summer, the breath of fresh air in her claustrophobic existence—and she was going to have to report him to the police.

Dear Reader,

I hope you're now used to our new look, because this month's books certainly deserve to be found in the stores. First up is Kathleen Korbel's *The Ice Cream Man*, with a hero who isn't anything like he seems. After all, what self-respecting suburban mother could allow herself to fall in love with a man who delivers ice cream for a living? Not to worry. There's more here than meets the eye—all of it delicious!

Marilyn Pappano makes a welcome return with *Somebody's Baby*, a story that will break your heart, then mend it again. At fourteen months, Katie Ryan holds her adoring parents' hearts in her tiny hand, and she knows just what to do with them. She loves each one of them so much that they have no choice at all but to love each other just as much as they love her.

Lee Magner follows up her exciting *Master of the Hunt* with *Mistress of Foxgrove*, a sensuous, soul-stirring tale set in the beautiful Virginia hunt country. And new author Marilyn Tracy spins a Southwestern web to ensnare your heart as well as those of her hero and heroine in *Magic in the Air*.

In coming months you can look for books by more of your favorite authors: Nora Roberts (who has a special treat in store), Heather Graham Pozzessere, Kathleen Creighton, Barbara Faith and many, many more—as well as a few surprises. I hope you'll be part of the excitement.

Leslie J. Wainger
Senior Editor

The Ice Cream Man

KATHLEEN KORBEL

Silhouette Intimate Moments

Published by Silhouette Books New York

America's Publisher of Contemporary Romance

SILHOUETTE BOOKS
300 East 42nd St., New York, N.Y. 10017

ISBN: 0-373-07309-7

First Silhouette Books printing November 1989

KATHLEEN KORBEL,

the *Romantic Times* Best New Category Author of 1987, has finally hung up her nurse's cap to work for herself. Living in St. Louis with her husband and two children, she writes full-time, only allowing travel and salving an insatiable curiosity—in the name of research—to interfere. She still admits to owing her success to her husband, who is her best friend and most devoted supporter.

To Kate,
the real Queen of the World.
And to Kevin,
whose dreams span galaxies.
You're *my* babies.

And to Detective John, for the help.
Thanks.

Chapter 1

No full-grown woman with two children had any business falling in love with the ice cream man. As she waited out on the sweltering street, her hand in that of her tiny daughter's, Jenny Lake kept reminding herself of that. She was a responsible adult. Responsible adults did not drool over good physiques.

The longer she stood out under a July sun in a line of giggling, preening teenage girls, though, the less she seemed to care. For some reason, in this summer of her thirtieth year, when she never seemed able to concentrate beyond the next bill, the next crisis or the newest flood of tears, Jenny was suddenly struck by a whimsy she couldn't explain. She found herself mesmerized by a good set of buns and a tattoo.

Well, she had to admit with a secret smile as she lifted damp black hair from her neck, it was more than just that.

"What can I get for you?" he asked, leveling the most mesmerizing set of whiskey-brown eyes she'd ever seen on her.

Jenny just stared. All she could think of was the movie *Picnic*. The dangerous, mysterious man coming to town. If the man in the movie had looked anything like this guy, she would have been just as foolish as the heroine.

"Mommy?"

She might have been tempted to run away or commit a crime or sacrifice her virtue....

"Mom?"

Distracted, Jenny looked down to find a set of very reproachful blue eyes leveled her way. "Bombpops, Mom. You're forgetting again."

Jenny had to grin. "Thanks, Em. I'll do better next time." She allowed one last errant thought to pass before getting down to business; she wondered once again whether fairies had, indeed, changed her three-and-a-half-year-old baby girl for a forty-year-old midget from the royal family. There should be some law against a child being more composed than her mother.

"Bombpops, please," Jenny said, lifting rueful eyes back to the ice cream man. "Two."

"What about Kevin?" Emma piped up with a tug on Jenny's hand.

"Three," Jenny immediately amended. She'd be hearing about this for hours.

"Two-twenty-five," the man answered, already bent over his freezer.

He didn't belong here, Jenny thought suddenly. He didn't look right. It wasn't the white T-shirt and low-slung jeans. Those fit. They fit too well, for several uncomfortably obvious reasons. So did the anchor and snake on his arm, wrapped around the blue *Semper Fi* proclamation. Even the way he'd pulled his dark brown hair back into a short tail made him look suspect, slightly shady. His face was angular, dark, with those hot, liquid eyes that bored holes through a person's best reserve. But it wasn't that.

Jenny thought about it as she dug into her own shorts for the change and handed it over. Maybe it was the fact that his face, for all its youth, looked too experienced. She had trouble believing he was on the shy side of thirty. And his eyes, for all their steely indifference, looked too intelligent. Maybe it was the silly fact that he didn't smell like a man who would abdicate his future to a bell and a white truck.

For all his casual disregard for appearance, he was just a little too carefully put together.

Dumb reasons, for sure. Certainly nothing even the eminently practical Emma would consider. But one thing Jenny was beginning to realize as she found herself staring now at the long, graceful fingers that were lifting bombpops out to her, was that for some reason when it came to this particular ice cream man, common sense was failing her.

Then he smiled, a grudging flash of warmth that transformed the truculence into shy sincerity, and Jenny was snagged for good.

"Mom."

Jenny was busy smiling back, and didn't hear Emma's tolerant tone of voice.

"Mo-ther." Make that disgust. The thin, reedy little voice hit two distinctive notes. "C'n have my ice cream now?"

Startled again, suddenly wondering why the air actually seemed cool beyond the scope of that man's eyes, Jenny slipped an already dripping bar into her daughter's hands.

"Let's go, honey, before Kevin's melts all over the street."

Emma wasn't quite ready to complete the transaction. Tilting her very blond head to the side, she bestowed an eminently arch look on her mother. "You forgot to say thank you," she reproached.

Jenny couldn't help but laugh. Turning a sheepish smile on the man, she shrugged. "There should be some law about your children being older than you. Thank you for the ice cream."

When he answered, it seemed that he meant it. "My pleasure."

Jenny turned back then to her house. Fifteen minutes later when she should have been paying bills, she found herself staring out the front window. There at the end of the block was the white van painted in lurid Popsicles and Drumsticks. And there alongside it was the almost constant swarm of teen and preteen girls.

And there was Jenny, seated at her desk, tapping her pen against her teeth and thinking of tattoos.

* * *

"I'm telling you it's not natural."

Poring through her cupboards in search of something better than macaroni and cheese for dinner, Jenny wished Barb would go on home. She decided against answering her ebullient neighbor, knowing from experience that the bright, perky blonde would continue on her own without any help.

"He showed up five days ago," Barb went on, just as Jenny had anticipated. "And since then this neighborhood has started to look like a cheerleaders' convention. Not to mention the fact that certain mothers I know of have been seen combing their hair before heading out for ice cream."

Jenny wondered if Barb knew that she was one of them. The new ice cream man had apparently been the talk of the few mothers who had the chance to spend summers home in the neighborhood. It was something different than *Sesame Street* and baseball, after all. And he was *so* good-looking. Being one of the working mothers, Jenny had missed most of the speculation. Being Barb's next-door neighbor, she unfortunately got it all secondhand. In detail. With enthusiasm.

"I think Donahue was right," Barb announced with great meaning.

Finally giving up on nutrition and settling for ease, Jenny ripped open the box of macaroni and set to work. "About what?"

"Oh, Jenny, not macaroni again. Why don't I send over some of the coq au vin I have? There's plenty. I was just planning on freezing some, anyway."

Jenny almost flinched. Being a divorced, underpaid working mother was hard enough. Being a divorced, underpaid working mother who lived next to the Perfect Woman was, at times, unbearable. If Barb weren't so damned sincere and nice, Jenny could find herself easily hating her.

"Thanks anyway, Barb. The kids aren't much for wine cooking. Besides, I'd hate to take food from Bill and Buffy." Jenny winced again. She did it every time she said the names Barb, Bill and Buffy Bailey. A television commercial for suburbia: surgically trimmed lawn, Christmas lights in the shape of a manger scene and trash-can lids that fit. The real life Ken and Barbie. And they lived next door to the Divorcée from Hell.

"Do you think he could be dealing drugs?" Barb asked suddenly.

Still caught in that vision of the perfect father, Jenny almost fell over. "Bill?" she squeaked. The man who if he'd been a dog would have been a golden retriever? Impossible.

Evidently Barb thought so, too. She giggled with delight, not just at the horror in Jenny's eyes but the question.

"Of course not," she said. "I'm talking about the ice cream man. I saw it on Donahue last week."

"The ice cream man?"

Barb nodded, her perfect curls not moving an inch. "Selling drugs. Evidently that's the latest thing. They get a beeper and a gun and cruise the neighborhoods selling cocaine." Taking a sip of the instant iced tea Jenny had offered, Barb pondered her own question. "The parents didn't even know it until a man ordered the triple-flavor Popsicle and got a packet of white powder instead."

Jenny went on stirring noodles. "I wonder what he would have gotten if he'd ordered a Drumstick."

"I'm serious," her friend insisted, finally getting to her feet. "You know, you could leave sun tea out while you're at work. It's cheaper than instant. We think we should go to the police."

Jenny had to smile, not just at the sincere concern on the blonde's face but the way she dispensed little household hints in the middle of discussions on neighborhood safety. "And do what? Report a man for being too good-looking? Do me a favor and invite me to the lineup."

"You don't believe me."

Jenny wanted very much to sigh. There was so much on her mind. They were trying to take her hours away at the store, and the Jerk was still holding out child support. She had to get the car fixed, Kevin was working up to a first-class case of rebellion and she hadn't had more than four hours' sleep in the last six nights because Emma had been having nightmares again. It was so difficult to worry about an ice cream man being devious just because he happened to have dimples.

He did, too, Jenny thought with unaccustomed pleasure. Big ones on either side of his mouth that stretched into the most delightful gullies when he smiled.

It was the smile that did it. That shy flash of sincerity she'd only seen once. Somehow she couldn't equate that smile with a drug dealer.

"Jenny?"

Jenny turned to find a frown on Barb's face.

"Are you all right?" she asked. "You weren't paying attention."

Jenny was embarrassed. She couldn't believe she'd drifted off into the Fantasy Zone again. In all her thirty years she'd never gotten lost like this—well, at least not in the last fifteen years or so—but especially since she'd had the kids. She didn't have time for fantasy. After the Jerk, she didn't much have the inclination, either.

Men were men. They were childish and selfish and never seemed to be around when you needed them. And then they slipped your dreams into their pockets and walked out the door.

Fantasies were for the girls who still giggled out there on the street in the afternoon. Jenny had reality.

"I'm sorry, Barb," she apologized with a rueful smile, thinking again how she was glad to have the blonde around. Maybe that little nuclear family next door wasn't quite real, but it sure looked inviting from where she sat. "I'm just tired. It's been a long day."

Barb flashed one of those prom-queen smiles that made Jen think of TV evangelists. "It's okay, Jen. I understand. You get to bed early tonight, and everything will look better tomorrow."

"Especially if I get some mail from the Jerk."

Another smile, brighter. "I'm taking Buffy to the park tomorrow. I'll pick Kevin and Emma up, too. Okay? It'll give you a little time when you get back from work to be alone."

Jen immediately felt worse. Why did she call this woman a Barbie doll when she always came through?

Because she was tired and frustrated and broke and envious. She wanted to be a professional mother, too. She wanted to be able to sit at home and rock babies and play Chutes and Ladders. She wanted to bake cookies for the block instead of selling them for a grocery store. She wanted to be able to smile and mean it.

"Thanks, Barb. Then I'll take...Buffy overnight Friday. Let you and Bill have some time alone."

Barb just nodded with another smile that was even sweeter. "I'll let you know what the officer says."

"Oh, wait a couple of days on that," Jen suggested, unsure why she was so hesitant. "Let's just see what he does first. I'm not really sure I want the esteemed St. Anthony police swarming through the streets."

"You'll sing a different tune when Kevin comes home on drugs."

Fine. Something else she hadn't thought to worry about yet. Kevin was six. "I'll buy their ice cream for them until we decide."

It's a sacrifice, she couldn't help thinking with a silly urge to giggle as she rooted around the fridge for enough milk and margarine to finish dinner. *But for my children, I'll face that very good-looking man and take whatever he dishes out.*

With her luck, it would be snow cones.

There was a crash from the playroom and both women turned toward the shrill protests that set up.

"Emma!"

"Kevin!"

"You're looking at me! Mo-o-m, Emma won't stop looking at me!"

"I thought it was too quiet," Jenny moaned.

"I'll see you tomorrow," Barb promised, heading for the back door. "Do you want me to mail these?" she asked, motioning to the small pile of envelopes on the side of the table. "You know, the police have said not to leave bills in the mailboxes. Somebody's stealing them."

Jenny swooped up the envelopes with a tight smile. "If somebody would like my electric bill, they're more than welcome to it."

"I'm going anyway..." Barb hinted, hand on the back door.

"Thanks, but no," Jen said, stuffing the envelopes into her purse. "I'll get them in on my way to work in the morning."

Barb left and Jenny headed in to break up the impending free-for-all. By the time she made it back from drying tears and cleaning up the over-ended rubber-tree plant, the macaroni had burned to the bottom of the pan and she had to start over. And, she thought, holding the blackened pot under running water, she had to deal with all those envelopes.

During the next couple of days Jenny did her best to follow Barb's instructions. When she drove by the ice cream truck she thought of cocaine. When her children begged for something cold and melting she marched out with them and tried her best to consider the purveyor a criminal.

Under other circumstances, it would have been easy. He was a central-casting dream for the part of a Miami drug runner, especially with the just-too-long hair he still wore pulled into that tail. He was a little too good-looking in a dark way, his nose bent just enough and a scar interrupting the straight line of his left eyebrow.

He was lean and graceful and quiet. Jenny could easily see him sneaking down an alley with a switchblade in his hand or imagine him lying in wait with an Uzi.

But that was the problem. Any other time of her life she would have walked right into Barb's spotless oak-and-gingham kitchen and demanded a march to the police. For some reason this summer, the idea of this dark man in her well-mannered neighborhood disturbed her in different ways. Like an exotic bird set loose in a pigeon coop, he enticed. He intrigued. Instead of shoving him away, Jenny wanted to draw him closer.

Idiot, she thought as she pulled the chugging compact into her driveway. You're just a victim of stress. You're caught in a whirlpool that's sucking you straight to the bottom, and he's like a gull soaring in the wind. That's the only reason he's interesting. He's everything you're not.

He's free. He doesn't have too many bills and not enough money. He doesn't have children who can't understand that mom can't be everything to everyone a hundred percent of the time. He doesn't have too much to do and too little time and never, never any time alone.

He drives an ice cream truck in the summer and eats his lunch listening to rock and roll.

And he's at my front door.

Jenny almost put her nose through the windshield. The vehicle jarred to a shuddering stop when she forgot to take it out of gear. What the heck was he doing there, sitting on the porch swing with the broken slat as if he were waiting for her to come home?

"Can I help you?" she asked too tentatively when she finally thought to officially turn off the ignition and step from the car.

With a languid grace that threatened to steal her breath, he unwound himself and got to his feet. There was a rip in the knee of his jeans, and he had a bandanna hanging out of the back pocket. There were sweat stains on his shirt and pearls of moisture on his upper lip. Jenny couldn't seem to take her eyes from them.

"I hope you don't mind," he apologized, strolling up. "I've tried everybody on the block, and nobody's home. I thought I'd just sit for a minute until the next car showed up."

Automatically Jenny looked over toward the white colonial where Barb lived, but she remembered that it was story hour over at the library. Barb never let Buffy miss any kind of educational entertainment, and she'd taken Kevin and Emma, as well. The rest of the neighborhood slept peacefully in the noon heat, hidden behind fully grown trees and carefully pruned hedges. Jenny had chosen her neighborhood for its privacy. Now that she stood in her driveway with a suspicious stranger and realized that even her neighbor two houses down couldn't see her, she wondered at her decision.

By the time she turned back to her surprise visitor, he'd reached the far back door and was opening it.

"Can I help you with your groceries?"

"Uh . . . what did you need?" Jenny was getting a little nervous. How did you politely say no thanks to a dope dealer to keep him out of your house? How did you draw attention to yourself when the retirees were all asleep and most of the mothers at work?

He straightened up, bag already in arm, and smiled. Again Jenny was caught by some quick hesitation that robbed the action of its glibness. She *wanted* to believe in him.

"I'm sorry," he shrugged. "The truck broke down. I need to get another fan belt over here before I lose a couple of tons of red food coloring and sugar water. Would you mind if I use your phone?"

"The phone." Surely there should be something more intelligent to say. Surely she shouldn't be standing across the car from him as if he were the Boston Strangler.

But what if he were?

This time he gave her a lopsided grin. "I can wait on the porch if you want," he offered, "if you'd call. It's just that Marco doesn't speak English."

Immediately Jenny waved the offer aside. It was silly. She'd seen this man dish out ice cream for a week now. He'd been so good with the kids, so patient with the painfully tongue-tied girls. It wasn't exactly a recommendation for the Nobel Peace Prize, but she could at least let him use her phone.

"Of course you can call. Where did you leave the truck?"

"Over on St. Vincent. It died right in front of somebody's driveway, but of course they weren't home."

Jenny leaned in for the other bag of groceries and led the way toward the porch, much too aware that he was following close behind.

"The name's Nick," he said with a little nod that would have been a handshake. "Nick Barnett."

"Uh, Jenny Lake." She smiled tentatively as she mounted the porch. Even the shade by the swing was a relief after the steam bath out on her driveway. The air-conditioning in the car had gasped its last in June, and Jenny didn't even have the money to call the dealership, much less let them get their hands under her hood. She was hot and sweaty and flushed, her hair hanging in limp ringlets around her face. She'd come home from work like this every day for the last four weeks and not thought anything about it. Today she wanted to hide.

"You work for Bennet's?" Nick asked, motioning to the cheap brown uniform that made Jenny look like an escapee from the orphanage. It had been designed by the polyester-clad wife of the food-store-chain president.

"During the summer," she acknowledged, her groceries balanced on a hip as she dug for her keys. Before she knew it, Nick relieved her of the bag. His hand brushed her hip and set up an odd static dance that startled her. "Thanks," Jenny murmured. She looked into his eyes and then glanced nervously away. "I teach—fifth-grade math."

He chuckled, completely at ease. "A better man than I, Gunga Din."

The door swung open and Jenny led the way in, the air-conditioning hitting her like a cold shower. She couldn't help the delighted sigh that escaped.

"Watch out for debris," she warned, weaving her own way through the litter on the floor. It never seemed to get cleaned up anymore before it was there again. There were two loads of laundry waiting to be folded on the dining-room table and a week's worth of unread newspapers piled by the couch. And the playroom was worse.

Alongside her, Nick was trying his best to balance the groceries and miss the odd roller skate and doll part on his way through to the kitchen.

"God," he breathed in a voice that sent the most pleasant shivers up Jenny's back. "I'd forgotten what cool felt like. You really have a nice house."

Jenny took a vague look around. "Somewhere under all this. Thanks." It was the only thing the Jerk hadn't been able to avoid. He'd kept up the payments on the upwardly mobile house he'd demanded. It was just up to Jenny to heat and cool it, to supply water and upkeep and taxes, and even that was enough to almost kill her.

Everybody saw the two-story modern and thought she'd made it through the divorce with luck. They didn't see how ratty the carpet was getting, or how many times she'd stitched up the armchair and hung pictures over the peeling wallpaper. She wished he would have left her with an apartment instead.

They reached the kitchen, which she hadn't had a chance to clean before going into work that morning, and Nick made enough room on the table to be able to set down the bags.

"There's the phone," Jenny instructed unnecessarily as she began unpacking cereal and crackers. "Would you like some iced tea?"

"Oh, yeah," Nick agreed with enthusiasm as he settled his slim hip onto the edge of her kitchen table and picked up the receiver. "It's hot out there."

How did one bring up the subject? Jenny wondered as she pulled out the instant tea and headed for the sink. Just how does one go about asking an obviously intelligent man how he got himself stuck serving ice cream for the summer? Do you have prospects? Is this what you wanted to be all your life? Or is it just a convenient cover for nefarious activities?

Behind her he was speaking what seemed like Italian into the phone, laughing with a gravelly delight that surprised her. His voice was more animated on the phone than she'd heard it in a week.

Of course, how intense can somebody get about bomb-pops and soft swirls? Not as intense as about a fan belt, evidently. Jenny heard him hang up just about the time she stirred the tea into being and turned to hand it to him.

He was still smiling, as if savoring a private joke or a special friend. Jenny handed over the glass.

"Marco," he explained, seeing her interest. "He's quite a character. Seems I interrupted a nooner."

"A . . . oh."

"His wife's a nurse. She works nights." His smile grew almost piratical. "And right now she doesn't like me very much. Marco will be over in a few minutes."

Jenny couldn't help but watch as he tipped his head back and drained the tea in one, long drink. Sweat beaded along his throat and trickled down toward his T-shirt. His hair was damp and curling. Jenny felt the heat stir in her as well, even though she was cooler than she had been all day.

Suddenly his eyes were open, and they were on her. "Thanks," he said, his expression oddly reticent. "That really hit the spot."

So do you, Jenny couldn't help but think. Embarrassed, she turned back to her groceries.

"It's Marco's truck," he explained, almost as if reading her mind. "Usually his kid Tony rides it, but he's down with strep throat or something. I'm fillin' in."

Jenny couldn't help but look up. "Then you usually don't—"

"Drive an ice cream truck for a living?" His abrupt laugh contained enough disbelief to certify the question silly for reasons patently obvious to only Nick. "Nah. Marco needed help, and I wasn't doin' anything right now. I'm in between sessions. School."

"You teach, too?"

He shook his head. "I learn." It seemed that he wasn't in the mood for elucidation. He set the tea glass down and straightened. "Thanks for the tea. And thanks for letting me use the phone. I didn't tell you, but the old lady across the street slammed the door in my face when I asked her."

Jenny had to grin. "Mrs. Warner slams the door in everybody's face. She thinks the Commies are coming over the hill." As a matter of fact, she'd also have those beady eyes glued to Jenny's front door wondering just what Jenny and Nick were doing in there. Jenny didn't know whether she felt irritated or amused. She did know that she was sorely tempted to keep Nick inside on some pretext just to see what kind of rise she could get out of Mrs. Warner. The old lady lived for this kind of intrigue.

Jenny and the ice cream man. Wouldn't that be the gossip of the year around here?

"Uh...Jenny?"

Startled, she snapped back to attention. Lord, it was getting worse. Must be the summer of her discontent, she thought with a wry smile as she apologized.

"I was just thinking what conclusions Mrs. Warner was jumping to this very minute," she told him with a quick shake of the head and a wide grin to negate the import. "Ten more minutes with the door closed, and she'll have either the police or the priest out on my porch."

He didn't seem quite as amused. He didn't do anything so obvious as look around for escape routes, but suddenly Nick was perceptibly cooler.

"Marco will be waiting at the wagon," he demurred. "I'd better be getting back."

Worried about your reputation? Jenny wanted to ask. She didn't. She walked him back to the front door, all the while thinking that for being as sweaty as he obviously was, he shouldn't have smelled quite so good. He smelled musky and dark, like a stormy night, with just enough tang to betray the lightning in those clouds. He shouldn't have looked quite so good, either. Ah, if she were only one of those giggling girls.

He turned on her porch and delivered a final grin, cocky and masculine as hell. Jenny knew it was as much for Mrs. Warner's benefit as hers. "You should think about getting new fuel injectors on your car. Yours aren't gonna last long." And then he was loping down her lawn.

Jenny couldn't manage more than a scowl. "You wouldn't fill in as a mechanic, too, would you?"

Almost to the sidewalk, Nick turned. "See me after Tony gets over his strep throat."

Feeling Mrs. Warner's hot eyes on her even through the hedges, Jenny couldn't help but smile. She smiled until Nick turned back toward the street. Then, suddenly, her smile died.

To be perfectly honest, she had been watching how the muscles on his legs shifted, how snugly his faded jeans hugged his hips. That bandanna hanging out of his back pocket swayed just a little as he walked. His loose-jointed gait was strangely out of place here in the carefully manicured streets of suburbia. It fascinated Jenny.

It didn't fascinate Jenny half as much as what she saw when Nick got to the street. Reaching back to pull the bandanna to wipe the sweat that had already gathered on his forehead, he revealed what the bandanna had hidden. A beeper. Small, square, brown, like the one the Jerk had always worn when they'd been out—just in case he'd needed to be reached.

But why would an ice cream man need to be reached? Jenny had trouble believing there were ice cream emergencies, and she doubted he wore it just in case registration opened early for a favorite class. Her heart was doing a fast slide when the situation grew worse.

Nick had no sooner reached the pavement when a long, white Caddy slid to a stop next to him. Jenny stayed at her door, watching. Could this be Marco? She didn't think ice cream dealers made that kind of money. Maybe he had a fleet of trucks and sold franchises across the country.

Out on the street, Nick stuffed the bandanna away and looked around. Jenny made it a point to close the door, and then sidled over to watch out the corner of her front window.

He was bent over the passenger door, talking rapidly, reaching into a front pocket to pass something in through the window, all the while with an eye out to the sleeping neighborhood. Jenny didn't realize that she was chewing on her thumb as she watched. She held her breath. Maybe Marco was rich enough to buy a Cadillac, but she didn't know many Italians who were black.

She didn't want to see this. She hadn't realized until now how much her funny little fantasy had meant to her. No matter their conception or import, fantasies weren't meant to die.

Nick stuffed what looked like money into his pocket and straightened, and the car slid away. Jenny and Mrs. Warner both saw it from opposite sides of the street, with polar reactions. Then, just as Nick was about to continue his walk up the street, a truck rattled into view. No logo, very little original paint, and driving, a big, burly, curly-haired man Jenny could hear laugh from inside her house. The truck pulled to a stop and Nick climbed in, laughing back.

Jenny turned away from the window. It wasn't fair. The one bright point of color in her summer, the breath of fresh air in her claustrophobic existence, and she was going to have to report him to the police.

Chapter 2

Nick Barnes had had better days. He was hot and bored and filled for a lifetime with snotty noses and whining, grasping little kids. He was beginning to dream of grape Popsicles at night, and already had the sneaking suspicion that red food dye didn't come out of white T-shirts. And on top of that, if he didn't see some action, he wasn't going to be off these damn streets anytime before he earned his first pacemaker. All in all, he'd rather spend time in the joint.

To make matters worse, just when he'd finally found something worth hanging around for, he'd had that taken away from him, too. As he watched Marco work on the overheated truck engine, Nick found himself pouting like a four-year-old over a dented fire truck.

"You can't be serious," he snarled, taking a long drag from a cigarette.

"*Paisan*, you think they send me all the way out here to pull your chain?"

"They put me out here in the first place, didn't they?"

Chuckling, Marco lifted his head from where he was considering the state of several fan belts. "Next time don't be so anxious to stand up for your ideals."

"Ideals, hell," Nick retorted, cigarette smoke curling about his head as if it were coming from his ears. "I didn't like the bastard." Taking another drag, he couldn't help a satisfied grin as he met his friend's jolly eyes across the opened hood. "Especially when he told me I couldn't ticket him because he was the police chief's brother."

Reaching over to steal Nick's cigarette for a taste, Marco shook his head in affable commiseration. "Next time such a dangerous mood takes you, remember how hot it was out here."

"It's not the heat that's bothering me."

"Remember *all* the children."

Nick leaned against the truck, looking down toward the cedar-shingled roof he could barely see through the trees. "It's not that, either."

Marco laughed so hard his head almost collided with the truck hood.

"All right," Nick admitted ruefully, casting another disgruntled glance toward the new rainbow on his shirt from the kid who just wouldn't wait until the truck had been fixed for his bombpop fix, and then had poked Nick with his prize. "It *is* that. Among other things."

Still chuckling, Marco shook his head back in among the cylinders and hoses. "You are not Captain Kangaroo, my friend."

"Captain Kangaroo only had to deal with a farmer and a moose, not this bunch of terrorists. Who says she's the suspect?"

Marco didn't seem in the least fazed by Nick's abrupt change of subject. "Tip came in sometime yesterday. Captain McGrady, your good friend, came into the squad room this morning with it."

"You mean Captain McGrady who consigned me to this Devil's Island?"

"I mean Captain McGrady who kept you from spending the rest of your career cleaning holding cells after you call the chief of police's brother a drunken, maggot-infested excuse for dog meat."

Nick grinned at nothing. "I was being polite."

Still caressing the engine with knowing hands, Marco smiled to himself. "She has twice been seen in the morning checking mailboxes. One of those mailboxes subsequently lost a check to the phone company. She is a divorced lady with two children, not enough money and an ex-husband who seems hesitant to rectify the situation. Enough, the good captain believes, to cast suspicion."

Shaking his head, Nick ground what was left of his cigarette beneath his heel. Damn. Didn't it just figure? The one person he'd found in this desert with a little life in her, and she's his primary suspect. He pulled out his bandanna again and wiped the sweat from the back of his neck, only to think of how her hair had looked, that dusty black, as if light failed to find it, disheveled and damp, curling around her neck like it was begging to be touched. And those eyes. Green, like cat's eyes.

He hadn't meant to pick her house to answer the beeper call. He'd just been hot and tired and ticked off because of the old broad across the street. He'd decided that that porch swing looked pretty damned inviting. So he'd sat, and he'd waited, knowing full well that whatever McGrady had wanted would wait until one of the denizens of this landscaped wasteland came home.

Divorced, her ringless hands had said. Skittish, her eyes had warned. Lonely and frustrated, telegraphed from every movement of her body. And with kids to boot. Even that little blond one, that little girl with the solemn blue eyes. They were still kids, and Marco had been right about that.

If there was one thing Nick wasn't, it was a kid person. He knew damned well that that was why McGrady had made him pull this little detail. Penance. Punishment for tilting at the powers that be. A gentle reminder in the idiom of police bureaucracy that he'd screwed up.

Marco had been right. Next time he'd be scrubbing toilets. But right now being imprisoned in a hot, cramped ice cream truck and surrounded by hordes of impatient, bored, shrilling kids was the equivalent of anything the Viet Cong had dished out to wash brains.

He gave in. He quit. He'd drive right by the damn police chief's brother's house and spray paint "I'm Sorry" on the garage if it could get him out of here.

Except for one thing...

"So I'm supposed to catch her pulling bills out of boxes and stuffing them into her purse, huh? Do they have any leads on a partner?" Nick considered another cigarette and then discarded the idea. It was hot enough without it. He hadn't known any place that could be as hot as St. Louis in the summer or as cold as St. Louis in the winter, which was why when he pulled undercover he did it in offices. He'd lost his knack for the streets.

"McGrady didn't say. Maybe he wants you to find out."

Nick snorted, his eyes back to that house, to the memory of cool, cluttered rooms and the smell of oranges. Damn. He didn't like setting up somebody he liked.

"And I'm smack dab in the middle of St. Anthony here," he groused. "Aren't I?"

"Your captain would rather not inform the local gendarmes," Marco informed him. "He assured me that you'll be in and out before they ever know you were here."

Nick snorted again.

The County of St. Louis, for which Nick worked, had jurisdiction within its sprawling borders, even though it was made up of a crazy quilt of local municipalities that guarded their own autonomy with zeal. Technically speaking, Nick didn't have to let the authorities of the newest of these municipalities know that he was operating in their bailiwick. In real life, that didn't always make for the best bedmates.

He knew most cops in the county. But never having worked in the southwest side of St. Louis, a good fifteen miles from his offices in Clayton, he didn't know a soul. A solidly suburban, middle-class haven of lawn services and private schools, this just wasn't his neck of the woods. Until Nick had been forced to shave his mustache and grow his hair just a little too long, his beat had been the high rises of Clayton and West County where white-collar crime was at its best.

This little caper had started with a few bounced checks. Then utility bills had gone unpaid, and an affidavit of forgery was delivered to the Special Investigations offices in Clayton. A team was working the county, but they were concentrating mostly in the five square miles of interconnecting neighborhoods Nick was patrolling in his van. One person simply pulled bills from mailboxes where lazy citizens left them for mailmen, and then got signatures and bank information from the checks. Then, using stolen checks acquired from the partner, they wrote third-party checks to the mailbox victim, endorsing them with the victim's own bank account number and forged signature. Cashed at that same bank, the checks were always cleared as long as the victim had enough money in his account to cover them. It was when the bank called the victim about bounced checks that the pattern began to appear and the affidavits roll in.

And now Marco was telling Nick that the most likely suspect for the person filching those payments and then pulling her chugging, sputtering automobile into a drive-up window to cash bogus checks was the woman he'd shared disturbing glances with over a handful of bombpops. The one he'd run to help like an overage high schooler, and who had made him want to smile with her disconcerted blush at his appearance.

So not only was Nick stuck on a creaky life raft amid a sea of kids with not even the questionable talents of the local cops to fend off sharks, he was doing it just so he could snap the cuffs on Jenny Lake. Giving in with another snort of frustration, Nick pulled the cigarettes back out. He'd definitely had better days.

Jenny couldn't really say that her first encounter with the police left her encouraged. She was seated alongside Lauren Sellers on Barb's plastic-covered early colonial couch balancing a glass of fresh brewed herb sun tea and watching as the representative of St. Anthony's finest scribbled in his notebook. Alongside Barb sat Lucy Sperring, Mrs. Warner's sister and representative at the little meeting. The four waited as the detective made up his mind.

He didn't look impressed. Come to think of it, he didn't look impressive, either. A tall man, he had the shape of one of those toys that kept rolling back up when you hit it. He wore a polyester suit that looked like it had been cut from the same bolt of cloth as Jenny's work uniform, and his mousy brown hair probably could have stood a wash. He had a too-red nose and the bored, patronizing eyes of a petty bureaucrat. Even Barb looked a bit disconcerted by him. Lauren, as usual, kept her thoughts to herself.

"So you think he's dealing drugs because he has a beeper and talks to black people," the man said with the same tone of voice Jenny's mother had used to use in talking about Jenny's imaginary playmates.

"Don't forget the ponytail," Miss Lucy chirped, bobbing her small gray head. "He has a ponytail."

Only Miss Lucy failed to see the disdain in the man's small eyes. "Oh, yeah," he nodded, scribbling. "I forgot about that ponytail."

It was up to Jenny to defend her call. "I would just feel happier if you would check it out," she said with a tight smile. "I realize that all we have are a series of inconsistencies, but there are a lot of teenagers around that truck every day, and I'd hate to think that we're letting anything slip by."

He nodded, shut the book with the information the women had imparted safely tucked inside and lurched to his feet. Jenny fully expected him to sway like the plastic clown she'd once vented her frustrations on. His expression certainly matched.

"Well, ladies," he said with bluff heartiness. "You just leave this all to me. I'll check this Nick Barnett out and get back to you. I appreciate your coming to me with the report."

"Anything we should do in the meantime?" Barb asked, getting to her feet, as well.

"No, young lady." He was, at best, five years their senior. "You just leave everything to me."

"Seems to me," Jenny mused as she watched the policeman walk toward his battered sedan, "that that was what my obstetrician told me when I delivered Kevin. I told him

I'd be happy to, but that *I* was the one having the labor pains."

Barb giggled and turned to clean out the newly filled ashtray on her oak coffee table. "Did your obstetrician dress as dreadfully as Detective Richards?"

Jenny thought about it. "His tailor probably just cost more. He had that same wonderful color sense."

Barb nodded with an impish grin. "In that case, I hope you found another obstetrician."

Jenny raised an eyebrow in amused surprise. "Sure. But how easy can it be to get another policeman?"

"We don't need another policeman," Barb decided, straightening to her full five feet and including all the women present in her statement. "We have us. We'll keep an eye on Nick Barnett. You and I and the other mothers on the block."

Jenny couldn't help but think of the sight of him balanced on the edge of her kitchen table. She couldn't keep her mind from that tantalizing rip in his jeans.

"An excellent idea," Lucy offered from her perch on the chair. "We'll see more in this neighborhood than the police ever will." The wry smile that lit her gray, birdlike features betrayed the fact that it was her sister who would do most of the watching. Miss Lucy, as she was known, was the popular one in that household, always there if help was needed, always invited to coffee and chat. It was Ethel Warner, though, who always knew more than seemed possible when just seen from her six-by-four-foot front window.

It seemed to be the signal for general support. Taking a long sip of tea from behind a meticulously manicured hand, Lauren gave her nod of approval. "I'll have Todd check with his little friends," she offered. "Warn them about this man and get information at the same time. And, of course, you can keep an eye on him, Jenny."

It took a moment for Jenny to respond. She'd often wondered how Lauren had ended up in their neighborhood. Devotedly upscale in style and appetite, Lauren spent the better part of her days doing fashionable charity work and hobnobbing in the more acceptable areas of town. She wore her heavy gold jewelry like badges, and her designer outfits like Emma her imaginary gowns. Her son Todd, just turned sixteen, was reputed to be the biggest threat to teen-age virtue since rock and roll.

As to her reference to Nick, she really hadn't meant to be mean-spirited. She just saw Jenny as *divorced*, which was somehow alien and a little unsettling. Lauren obviously be-lieved the old, she must be hungry, so she's after my hus-band, adage. Jenny hadn't seen fit to tell Lauren that her husband was a carbon of the Jerk, and therefore the sec-ond safest man in the country.

Jenny saw the other two women go still at the implied in-sult. She smiled. "Okay," she agreed with a slow nod, her mind still recalling the sudden flash of white teeth and wide-open humor Lauren would never get to see. "I guess I could keep my eyes on him."

Conflicting emotions skittered over Barb's bright fea-tures like fast-moving clouds. Jenny came back from her personal viewing just in time to catch the concern.

"Just my eyes," she assured her friend with a rueful grin. "My emotional bank account is too paltry to afford some-body like him, thanks."

"He sells drugs," Barb reminded her.

Jenny lifted a finger. "We think. Innocent until proven guilty, remember?"

Now Barb shook her head. "Only when it comes to the law. Not when it comes to my child."

For that Jenny couldn't even think of a good comeback. She'd spent too much of herself protecting her children from no more than their father's indifference to argue with that.

Just to make Jenny feel worse for fantasizing about someone who could put the Jerk in the minor leagues of sin, Emma chose that moment to grow bored with the coloring books Jenny had supplied to keep her occupied during the meeting.

"Mommy?"

Jenny automatically crouched to Emma's height, filling her sight with the sweet beauty of her little girl. "Yes, baby." She was amazed, as she was every time she looked at her children that they had been created from her gene pool. They were too beautiful. Too intelligent by halves.

Emma came to a halt right before her. "Mom," she objected with a frown. "I'm not a baby." At three and a half, it was an important point to the little girl.

Jenny could hardly argue with her. In her soft pink-and-white sundress and sandals, Emma was neater and better put together than Jenny. Emma had been dressing herself since she was just three, and coordinating her own outfits for the last two months.

Still, Jenny smiled. "But you're *my* baby," she said, reaching up to sweep a blond bang back from the little forehead.

Huge blue eyes still reproached her. With a sigh though, Emma accepted her mother's illogic. "I'm going to the Pink House, okay?"

Jenny nodded. "Okay. Have fun, and remember to clean up before you come home."

Jenny got another scowl. "Mo-o-m. Wanna come?"

"I'm afraid not right now, honey. I'm busy with Aunt Barb."

Emma nodded and headed off. The little girl had disappeared once again into the back room before Miss Lucy spoke up.

"The pink house?"

Still smiling, Jenny got to her feet. "The Pink House," she nodded with a rueful shrug. "Most little girls Emma's age have imaginary playmates. My daughter has an imaginary condo. With a hundred rooms where she has parties."

None of the three could quite decide how to react. Barb only came up with a quiet, "Oh."

Jenny laughed. "Yeah. Oh. Who says God has no sense of humor? He gave me Princess Di's kid by mistake."

Twenty minutes later, when Jenny had finished helping Barb clean up the evidence of Detective Richards's visit and been filled in on the rest of the neighborhood news, she headed in to break up the intergalactic war in Barb's playroom.

"Just a minute, Mom," Kevin objected without looking from the television screen. "I'm on the third warp zone and only have three mushroom men left."

Jenny couldn't help but scowl at the bright figures that beeped and twiddled across the screen as Kevin rolled the joystick. "Far be it from me to keep you from saving the world. We have to get home, though."

Kevin didn't even hear her. With a face that was a heart-breaking carbon of his father's and a knack for turning anything in the house into a strategic weapon, Kevin was all boy. Freckles and pug nose and chestnut hair that had been buzzed for the summer. And his best friend was still Buffy, who had yet to figure out why girls and boys couldn't be friends. She whooped when Kevin exploded something on the screen and pounded him on the back. Kevin grinned like a pirate.

Jenny decided to leave him to his mushroom men, at least this once. Especially since it would be a cold day in August around here before she could afford a similar treat for their own house. Looking around for her other bookend, she saw crayons and a Barbie coloring book open but no Emma.

"Kevin," she said, looking around yet again, as if she could have missed her behind the potted fig or something. "Where's your sister?"

He couldn't afford more than a shrug. Bemused, Jenny turned away. She wondered where Emma had holed up.

"Hello."

Engrossed in the copy of *U.S. News* he hid beneath a *Mad* magazine cover, Nick heard the piping little voice and looked up. Then he looked down.

She stood alone alongside the driver's side of the truck, clad in a pink dress, black velvet purse and a blanket. The blanket had been pinned around her neck and trailed behind the high heels that hung off the ends of little feet. The purse swung from a bent arm. She peered up at him with huge blue eyes that looked for all the world like she was expecting obeisance. Nick stifled his first impulse to laugh.

"Can I help you?" he asked, unconsciously formal as he leaned over toward her.

With a regal poise, she nodded her head. She even lifted a hand in a very royal little wave. "I," she said in arch tones, her words carefully enunciated, "am the Queen of the World."

Nick tried his best to hide a grin. Damn if this little kid couldn't almost convince him. "Pleased to meet you, Queen," he said, laying down the magazine and leaning an arm on the window. "I bet that's an interesting job."

Another nod, just as slow, just as regal. "Yes. This cape is heavy, though."

Nick found himself rubbing a hand over his face to keep from betraying his growing amusement. "Yeah, I can see that. You might try a towel instead. Be Queen of North America or something."

She actually looked like she was considering it. "Queens like ice cream, you know."

Nick nodded, unable anymore to contain the smile. "They do, huh?"

"Yes." She spent a moment scanning the side of the truck. If he hadn't known better, Nick could almost have believed she could read the damn thing. She wasn't like any other kid he'd met in this purgatory. Come to think of it, she wasn't like any other person he'd met.

"Uh, what's your favorite flavor?"

More consideration. "Blue."

Opening the door and stepping down, Nick tried to think what flavor that would be. "Blue."

"Yes. Popsicles. I'd like a blue one, please."

Now, that made more sense. There was just one other thing. "Do you have any money, Queen?"

Suddenly a little girl's giggle broke through all the solemnity. "Of course, silly. I have thirty dollars."

Nick was still too new to three-year-old math to understand. "Thirty what?" he demanded, leaning over again. He could see her tiny hand clenched before her like one of the magi carrying a gift. "Where did you get thirty dollars?"

The little girl looked at him as if he were very slow. "The Pink House, of course."

Nick felt more confused than ever. McGrady didn't say that this job should come with an interpreter.

"The Pink House."

"Where I have parties. And a hundred jewelry boxes."

Nick was rubbing his face again. "Where's your mother, Queen?"

"Busy."

"Oh. Uh, can I see your thirty dollars?"

He should have known. When the little girl reached up and opened her fingers, Nick saw the three pennies nestled inside and sighed.

"Uh, kid, you wouldn't—" One look at the earnest little face showed that this, indeed, was the extent of her outlay. Nick vacillated. He could just see what the crew back at the station would have to say about this. He couldn't help it. Giving in, he gravely accepted the three pennies and walked back to swing open the doors for a blue Popsicle.

"What's your name, Queen?" he asked as he handed it over.

That seemed to break through the little girl's reserve. For the first time she looked unsure. "I'm not supposed to talk to strangers."

"But I—" Never mind. He shook his head, completely left behind. He couldn't really argue with her on that one. Just because he was the ice cream man didn't mean he was a good guy. It didn't even mean he liked kids, he thought with a private grin.

He was leaning against the back of the truck watching the little girl peel the wrapper from her treat when he heard the footsteps. He wasn't that surprised when he looked up to see that it was her mother.

Today she wore khaki shorts and a pink T-shirt. Nick could develop a real fondness for pink T-shirts. Especially if they looked like that. She was running, her brows drawn with worry, her hair tumbled again so that it looked like she was always dragging her hands through it. Nick guessed she was about five-four, with pale, freckled skin that dewed up like a peach in the heat. His tongue itched for the taste of it.

"Hey, Queen," Nick whispered in warning. "I think you're about to do time in the Tower."

"What are you doing here, young lady?" Jenny demanded, coming to a stop in front of her daughter.

Emma looked singularly unruffled. "The man gave me my sicle."

"You're not supposed to get sicles from 'the man' by yourself, Emma," she chastised. "Now, you get on home. We have some serious talking to do."

Still maintaining that regal bearing, Emma turned up to find Nick watching her with a delighted grin. "Excuse me," she said.

"Yes, Your Highness."

She giggled again, delivering a killer smile beneath a coyly tilted head. Nick wondered where the hell she'd learned that.

"Thank you, man."

"You're welcome, Queen."

"Mom," she piped up, turning up to Jenny. "Is it okay if I tell him my name's Emma?"

Jenny dispatched a look that betrayed as much amusement as exasperation. "Yes, Emma. I guess you can."

With that, Emma turned for the royal proclamation. "My name," she announced, "is Emma."

"My name's Nick," Nick said just as formally. "It's been a pleasure."

Without further ado, Emma tottered off down the street on her heels, Popsicle clutched in her hand, blanket trailing in the dust, purse swinging with her unsteady gait. Left behind, Jenny could do no more than shake her head.

"I'm sorry," she apologized, motioning to the sandwich Nick had been working on when Emma had interrupted.

"No problem," he assured her with a wave of his hand. "I've never served royalty before."

Jenny chuckled, a pleasant throaty sound. "Don't encourage her. Next thing I know she's going to be assessing taxes. Did she have money?"

With a nod that was just as sincere as Emma's, Nick plucked up Emma's booty. "Thirty dollars."

Jenny started. Then she saw the copper in Nick's palm and grinned. "Put it on my tab. I'm sure once Kevin finds out Emma got a Popsicle and he didn't, we'll be back."

"Don't worry about it," Nick said with a wave of the hand. "I think Marco can stand it."

She should really do something about that poker face, Nick thought. The mention of Marco sent clouds scurrying over the bright, pert features. It made Nick wonder what was wrong.

He could smell oranges again. Tart, fresh, mouth-watering. Just like Jenny Lake. Jenny Lake, his prime suspect.

Nick guessed that a cloud or two passed over his own features.

"How's that car of yours?" he asked, needing some kind of way in, unhappy with himself for using it. "Did you get the fuel injectors fixed?"

Again the cloud, the hint of unease beneath those bright, open green eyes. "Oh, uh...I'm waiting for a check to come in pretty soon. That'll cover the car, thanks."

"Alimony's comin' through, huh?"

At that, she did a credible imitation of his snort of disbelief. "When pigs fly," she retorted. "No, this is...something else. Thanks again, though."

And before he could get off another shot, she was headed back down the street.

Nick watched from where he stood at the back of the truck, cataloguing the various reasons he shouldn't be appreciating her retreating view so much. She was a suspect. She was a divorcée with kids. She had black hair. His thing had always been blondes.

She had the greatest little tush since Marcia Sternberger in junior high.

And then, just as he was going to pull back where he belonged, Nick saw her run up to the little queen and sweep her up in her arms. Even from where he stood, almost a block away he could hear the unbridled delight in her husky laughter counterpoint the shrill giggles of the little girl. The two continued down the street wrapped around each other and telling each other secrets, and suddenly Nick was assailed by a sense of loss he couldn't explain. He just knew that he didn't want to bust Jenny Lake. He wanted to make her laugh like that, too.

He wanted what he couldn't have, which was the story of his life. With a sigh that sounded much too final, Nick pushed himself from the back of his truck and went back to business.

Chapter 3

Do you know how tired I am of hearing this song and dance?"

At that, it was all Jenny could do to keep her temper. "Do you know how tired I am of singing it?" This was the worst part of a divorce, the constant begging. Please, honey, just a few dollars for shoes, for dentists, for school. Please help me out.

"I told you before. My cash flow is a problem right now. I'll have a check to you the beginning of September."

Sell some of Amber Jean's jewelry, Jenny thought with justifiable spite. "I have school expenses in August, and the car's about to go out. It needs fuel injectors. And Kevin wants to play soccer like his daddy. Only it'll cost us $38 to join."

"In September."

She'd been hearing next month for the last six. "Sign-up is in two weeks. Please help me out on this."

The acid roiled in her stomach; the shame of it reddened her face. There was nothing Jenny hated more than these much-too-regular phone calls. Nothing except denying her children.

"All right. I'll try. Now, stay off my back."

"Mom, ask him about the video game."

Startled, Jenny turned to find Kevin at her elbow. "Not now, Kev. Want to talk to your dad?"

"Jenny, I really am in a hurry here. I have an appointment."

Jenny felt renewed resentment for her son. God, she was tired of seeing his eyes light up only to die again.

"Say hi and then goodbye," she told Kevin with a grin. "Dad's gotta run."

Kevin barely got that out before handing the phone back to her. "Did you ask?"

"No," she told him, hanging it up and pulling her tough, independent son into her arms. "I didn't. I didn't have time for anything but the necessities. We'll have to wait a while longer, hon."

"But you promised."

Jenny sighed. "I promised I'd try, Kev. Now, if memory serves me, you were in the middle of cleaning your room before dinner."

"Aw, Mom..."

It was as easy as that...sometimes. Jenny laughed and rumpled his hair. "No more excuses, bud. You're growing enough mold in there to supply a hospital. Go on."

The huge kiss Jenny planted on Kevin's cheek only intensified his heartfelt scowl. He was well on the way to whining when he was interrupted by the clang-clang, clang-clang call of the migrating refrigerated truck. Immediately his head came up and his eyes grew wide. Pleading, begging, throwing himself on his mother's mercy.

"Please, Mom," he groaned as if she'd just grabbed his last canteen of water on the Mojave.

"Kevin, you've had ice cream every day this week."

He gathered every ounce of pathos he could muster. "Ple-e-e-a-s-e."

With a sigh of capitulation, Jenny let him go and pulled herself to her feet. "Don't give me Bambi eyes. I can't take it. Get some ice cream. Get a Ferrari, I don't care. Just don't give me Bambi eyes."

The supplication on his face dissolved into giggles as he hopped to his feet. "Works every time."

"Don't be so sure. There's more to life than ice cream."

Like money, she thought, checking her cookie jar for loose change, and I don't have any. There was enough for a couple of "sicles," and that was it. She wasn't getting paid until Monday, and she had to still get through the weekend. Macaroni and cheese time, again, she thought with a sigh.

Oh well, today there was ice cream.

Clang-clang, clang-clang.

"Mo-o-o-o-o-m!"

"Yes, Emma," Jenny answered with a grin as she followed the herd to the door, not even wanting to admit to herself that it was her treat, too. "I know. Let's go get ice cream."

By the time Nick pulled to a stop there was already a swarm of girls waiting by the curb. He gave a couple extra tugs on the bell and shut off the engine, sighing at the crescendo of giggles that met his arrival.

He wasn't going to last much longer on this detail. It was getting more difficult every day to put up with the cloying, giggling attention of so many self-conscious teens. That was almost worse than the little kids. At least they just whined. The girls flirted. And they flirted with an enthusiasm and expertise Nick had sure never noticed during his own high-school days.

It was easy with the little kids. When they got too obnoxious, you treated them like cats. You pulled them off your pant leg and shooed them in the right direction. If he tried that with this bunch, he could end up behind his own bars.

He wanted to tell them to all go home and wash their faces and trade in the miniskirts for baggy jeans. He wanted to tell them that growing up wasn't as much fun as they thought, that they should enjoy the safe years they had while they were still tucked securely away in their comfortable, reliable houses.

But he didn't. He got out of the truck and tried his best to smile and tease and play his part.

"Yo, Mr. Ice Cream Man."

Nick looked up to see a male head in that female crowd. Oh, yeah. Todd. The neighborhood lothario, out, he guessed, to treat his herd of fillies. Tall, too good-looking for his own good and very, very into latest fashion with a spike cut and a tiny gold stud in his left ear. Nick refrained from grinning. Surely he hadn't been so patently obvious when he'd been that age. Surely he'd never even been that age.

"Yo, Todd. What'll it be?"

Nick swung the door open and basked in the escaping chill. God, he was hot and tired.

"Hey, dude, whatever these ladies would like. I'm buying."

Nick wondered how long it would be before Todd tried that line out at the local bars. All the same, he acquiesced with a nod. At least if Todd were keeping them busy they wouldn't brush up so close to him or give him the honey-I'd-like-to eye flutters.

Nick was in the middle of counting change for Todd's conspicuously presented twenty when he happened to look up and see Jenny. She was standing in the street across from her house, almost hidden from his sight by the overgrown bushes and trees between. Nick handed off the change, his eyes still down the street, and didn't notice Todd's attention follow.

A mailbox. She was standing by a mailbox which wasn't hers. Nick couldn't see what she was doing. She was in between him and the box. But she was looking around her as if she didn't want anyone to see what she was about. And her two kids were coming his way at full tilt.

Damn. He didn't want to see this. He'd spent the entire night before trying to sleep through some pretty vivid dreams about her, dreams that weren't made any more comfortable by the cold shower he'd finally gotten up to take.

"Oh, yeah," Todd breathed with assured delight. "Jenny Lake."

Startled, Nick looked over, managing a dry appraisal just in time to miss Todd's keen eye. "Know her well, do you?"

Todd flashed a big grin. "Hey, like, not well enough, ya know? I, like, have this thing about older women."

"To-o-o-dd," one of the girls objected.

"Oh, man, Lacey," he objected with raised hands. "I'm kiddin', okay?"

He waited for no more than another man-to-man leer with Nick before herding his fan club away.

Nick's attention was already back down the street. So, he had Jenny at the mailbox looking nervous, and he had a possible informer, depending on how much he wanted to trust Todd around her. He should have felt better.

The problem was, he didn't feel better. He felt like he was slipping down that damn slippery slope, his perspective lost to a set of bright, teeming, wounded green eyes. And if he had any sense, he was going to go back in and ask Mc-Grady to take him off the case.

Watching that little blonde run for him and knowing that her mother wasn't far behind, though, Nick knew he wouldn't do that.

"Well, if it isn't Queen Emma," Nick greeted her.

Emma pulled up before him with a smile that was suddenly shy. "Hi, Mr. Nick," she greeted him, head down, hair falling into her eyes.

"So how's the world today, Queen?"

"I'm not queen anymore," she said. "I'm a taxi driver."

It was all Nick could do to keep from laughing all over again. Now that Todd and the cheerleaders had dispersed, he was back to regular business, and he had to admit he was relieved. He was uncomfortable with all that, and he didn't want to have to deal with it in front of Jenny. Hell, he was having trouble dealing with *Jenny* in front of Jenny.

"A taxi driver," he said, nodding sagely, his eye on Jenny as she turned toward the truck and followed her children around the corner. "I bet that's exciting." Where would you hide an envelope in shorts that short? he wondered. Maybe inside that crisp cotton camp shirt, nestled safely in her bra.

"I charge a thousand dollars a ride," Emma informed him, bringing him back with a start. "Except for Mom and Grandma. They're free. It's so I can pay for my Pink House. Would you like to see it?"

It took Nick a moment to connect Emma's statements. "Sure. Where is it?"

"Emma," Kevin broke in, exasperated by the wait for his ice cream.

Nick immediately looked up. "Hey, Kevin, how's things?"

"Great," Kevin assured him. "Can I have my Drumstick? *Ninja Turtles* is on, and I have to watch before Mom finds out."

Nick nodded, turning to the truck. "Good cartoon. I know. I'm a connoisseur. Ever watch The Roadrunner?"

"Aw, sure." Kevin accepted his Drumstick with a look that betrayed the fact that six-year-olds didn't believe adults really watched cartoons. "My favorite's Johnny Death, though."

Nick just shook his head. "No finesse. Now, you want class, you turn on some of the older cartoons. Sylvester and Tweetie, Bugs Bunny and the good old Roadrunner. My favorite was still the time the Roadrunner dropped the safe on Wile E. Coyote's head." With a conspiratorial grin, Nick slowly shook his head in appreciation. "Pancake city."

He saw Kevin waver and then fall, his eyes lighting like a pirate, and knew he had an ally.

"Nick?" Emma piped up, impatient with sharing her new friend.

"Yeah, Emma. Let's see. I bet you want a bombpop, right?"

"Yes, please. Are you coming to dinner to see my Pink House?"

Nick handed over her ice cream with a frown. "I don't know. Am I?"

"Tonight," she nodded with a perfectly sincere face. "My mom said so."

Nick took another look up to where Jenny ambled nearer, still out of earshot, and found himself smiling almost as broadly as Kevin. "She did, huh? Well, I guess I'll just have to come then. You tell her I'll bring the wine."

* * *

It was worse than macaroni and cheese. It was tuna-noodle casserole. Jenny hated it, the kids hated it and the cat hated it. But it was all she had left in the house, and they were just going to have to choke some down. At least she'd found a can of mandarin oranges for dessert, which would go a long way to appeasing the kids' palates.

It didn't appease her sense of outrage or her frustration. By this time of her life she should have been able to attain some kind of stability: a home, a husband, a growing family. Jenny had always wanted to fill her rooms with children and nurture that special, loving madness that comes only with big families. She had it with hers, all seven siblings. She'd grown from child to teen to woman anticipating the same thing—a big, close family that could fend off any of the world's disasters.

Jenny hadn't wanted a huge house or a membership to the country club. She'd wanted family. She'd wanted simplicity, certainty in her life. What she'd gotten was a bad sit-com.

Her husband, that bright child of charm and drive, had grown into a superficial man of drive and drive. He'd left Jenny in the dust when he'd decided that the giggly secretary at work with the assets that bounced would fit his upwardly mobile life-style better than a Phi Beta Kappa who thought that there was more to life than being an arm ornament at social functions. So the Jerk and Amber Jean lived in the upper reaches of Ladue, with a pool, a membership to the country club and a lot of superficial friends. And Jenny was left to struggle alone on a too-small paycheck, child support that never seemed to be available and even less attention from her children's father.

And tuna-noodle casserole for dinner.

"I bet *Amber Jean*'s not having tuna-noodle casserole for dinner." She sighed, pushing damp hair from her forehead as she slammed the oven door. Even potato chips crushed on the top hadn't incited any wild interest in the dish from the kids. She couldn't blame them. Godiva chocolates crushed on the top wouldn't have made her want to eat the damn thing.

"What is she having?" Emma asked, as always too handy with an ear when Jenny didn't want her to be.

Jenny turned to see Emma decked out in her best dress, a little green-and-white pinafore her grandma had gotten for her. "Honey, why are you so dressed up?"

Emma blinked up at Jenny as if her mother needed to think more. "For dinner."

Instinctively, Jenny crouched to her daughter's level. "Emma," she objected as evenly as she could, "you don't usually come out of your room for tuna-noodle casserole, much less dress up."

"Of course I do," Emma smiled grandly. "When Nick comes to dinner."

"Nick?" It took Jenny a moment. She had to get through imaginary playmates before she attached the new name. "Oh, Nick. He's coming to dinner tonight?"

Emma nodded. "I invited him."

"I see. Do I have to set an extra plate?"

Now Jenny could tell that her daughter thought her extremely silly. "Of course."

Jenny just nodded. Taking a quick look down at the paint-spattered shirt and cutoffs she sported, she thought that this was just the night she'd like to entertain a handsome man with a tattoo. Maybe he'd come in his good white T-shirt and they could compare ponytails. Or maybe she'd ask him to pop the hood of her compact.

Suddenly Jenny found herself wishing for more than another night alone with bedtime stories and overdue bills. But Jenny knew what good that kind of wishing did. Abruptly she regained her feet and turned back to her dinner. "Well, go ahead," she said lightly. "Just make sure he washes his hands before he eats."

"My face, too?"

Jenny almost burned her hand on the oven when she whipped around.

He didn't have on his best white T-shirt. He had on an oversized linen jacket and pleated pants and a mock turtleneck. And he'd taken out the ponytail. Suddenly Jenny couldn't think of anything to say. Nick was leaning in her kitchen doorway, one hand resting high against the door frame, the other holding a wine bottle. And he was smiling that cocky, crooked grin again that told her just how much he liked to catch her off guard.

"Oh, my God..."

Pulling himself up straight, he extended the wine bottle. "Emma said that you'd invited me. She wanted me to see her pink house." He took a moment to scan the cluttered kitchen before returning his regard to Jenny. "It doesn't look pink to me. But then, I'm not a kid. Does that make a difference?"

For a moment all Jenny could do was stand and stare. This might just come under the heading of worst nightmare in her life. She had the feeling it was even going to beat out the time she got the hem of her dress caught in her panty hose at a formal party and walked around with her underwear showing for ten minutes.

No, this was definitely worse. She'd realized how good-looking Nick was. It was, after all, hard to miss in those tight jeans and negligible shirts. The first time she'd seen him walk, she'd realized he was sexy. What she hadn't realized until now was how classy he was. Tonight he looked like a completely different person, a powerbroker or an actor on hiatus. Definitely dangerous. And he carried the style of the outfit with an easy grace that threatened to take Jenny's breath away.

Damn. And she looked like she'd just been rat-hunting in the attic.

Jenny made an abortive reach for the bottle and then changed her mind, wondering if she had to invite him to stay if she accepted the wine. She ended up with her hands in her cutoff pockets. "I guess you haven't figured out yet that Emma has a rather formidable imagination," she said, trying in vain to pull her eyes from the way that just-too-long chestnut hair framed the angles of his face. God, it made her hungry.

He just shrugged. "Beats reality all to hell." Then he set the bottle on the kitchen table and turned back to Jenny with a grin. "Hey, Kevin!" he yelled. "Come in here a minute!"

Nick did something Jenny hadn't accomplished since Kevin had turned three. He got him unpeeled from the TV with one shout. Jenny found herself staring again.

"I think your mom doesn't trust me," he told the little boy with a smile that betrayed just what kind of silly women mothers could be. "So I figured I'd let you frisk me for weapons. Make her feel a little better, ya know?"

"Why doesn't *she* frisk you?" Kevin asked.

Nick's answer had to wait for the lightning that sparked between his eyes and Jenny's. His was deliberate, taunting, testing. Hers was an uncomfortable surprise, sizzling all the way to her toes.

Nick ended up holding his hands out to his sides in a classic position. "I think she thinks I'd feel better if a guy did it."

Kevin shrugged, but performed the service anyway with a professional air that told Jenny he'd been watching too many police shows.

"He's clean," he pronounced finally. Jenny groaned.

"See?" Nick countered, hands still up, that cocky grin back on his face. "No knives, no guns. No loaded weapons of any kind."

Jenny almost laughed. She knew better than that. She'd seen the fit of those jeans. Just the thought sent her whirling back to the sink, a blush suffusing her face. She didn't need this. Not now. Not ever. Not when this guy was supposed to be the new neighborhood drug dealer. Not even if he weren't, she knew.

The Jerk had taken his mid-life crisis right over to old Amber Jean. Jenny wasn't going to make the same mistake and drop hers in the lap of Mr. Softy.

"I'm not going to bite," he said softly from just behind her.

Jenny whirled again, this time backed right up against the sink. Nick stood no more than two feet away, and his aftershave preceded him. It was that tang, the one that smelled too much like lightning, that tickled her nose and crept in beneath her good sense.

And his eyes. Those eyes the color of brandy, laced with sunshine and nightfall. Those eyes that seemed to melt right through her.

At least Kevin had escaped back to the tube. Jenny was having enough trouble without having to worry about his much too inquisitive little ears.

"Do you really think this is a good idea?" she demanded, trying her best to assume the pose of an outraged mother.

"What's wrong with it?" Nick asked. "Emma invited me to dinner. I accepted. I promise never to come between you and the telephone so you can dial for help if necessary. If you'd like, I'll even call Mrs. Warner across the street to let her know I'm here. That way we'll have a witness to everything."

"Why?" Jenny asked.

He shrugged, that self-assured gleam back in his eyes. "So you stop looking like I'm going to murder you all in your beds and run off with the silver."

Jenny shook her head. "Not that why. Why go to all this trouble?"

This time when Nick smiled, Jenny saw the assurance slip a little. There was just enough surprise beneath to convince her he was telling the truth.

"Because I haven't liked anything about this job except for you. I've been watching for you every day, you know."

"No," she admitted, wondering if she should tell him the same. "I didn't."

He nodded. "You think I eat my lunch up at the corner because I like warm soda and hot vinyl seats? You usually get home from the store right about one, and I like to watch you walk into the house."

Jenny wasn't sure just how she was supposed to react to this. "I don't think I want to hear that."

Nick shrugged. "It's true."

"It's . . . *weird*."

That made him laugh, and that did even more damage to Jenny's self-control. It was that raspy laugh, the one she thought was reserved for his good friends. Its sound settled in her chest and warmed her where she'd been cold for so long.

"No," he finally disagreed, his eyes holding hers with purpose as he lifted a hand to brush the tangle of hair back from her forehead. "It would be weird if I *didn't* stop to watch you."

Jenny saw his hand approach, felt the brush of his fingers, as sweetly coarse as the sound of his laughter, and couldn't seem to find her objections. She couldn't even seem to locate her suspicion that this man was doing something illicit. She just knew that he incited something in her she thought had been mortally wounded too long ago. That gull she'd watched so far over her head now dipped lower, almost close enough for her to touch, its cry the taste of freedom, of the open sky and the sun. As much as she wanted to be frightened by it, Jenny couldn't be.

"I wanted to be able to talk to you without feeling like I had a telescope at my back," Nick admitted. "I wanted to prove to you that I'm more than just what you see out there every day. And," he added with a sudden grin, "I wanted to see what a real home-cooked meal could taste like. I've been eating bachelor food for too long."

It was Jenny's turn to laugh. Looking up at him with eyes that sparkled with wry humor, she gave in. "Well, you sure came on the right night for that." Only her own little devil kept her from elucidating. Instead, she took him by the shoulders and turned him toward the playroom. "You go on out and watch TV with the kids while I change. After all, if Emma wore her best dress for you, I should be able to at least get out of this stuff. You can baby-sit while I shower."

That goading grin firmly back in place, Nick turned his head back toward her. "I'm a great back scrubber."

This time Jenny gave him a good nudge in the right direction. "I believe Emma's your date this evening. You can have a sparkling conversation with her over drinks while I change. Apple juice for her, beer in the fridge for you if you'd like. I'll be back."

By the time Jenny got back, she felt cleaner if not any less confused. She'd just invited a possible drug dealer to her house for dinner, and she hadn't even told the police about it. She didn't even want to. In fact, she'd gone to the trouble of pulling on the only pair of stockings she'd worn since church last Sunday just to look good for him. A dependable peach-jersey shirtwaist had been called into service, and she'd even gone to the extent of adding a little makeup for good measure.

Nobody would believe it. Jenny hadn't so much as dated since her divorce two years ago. Her family, especially her two sisters, had gone to great and tortuous lengths to rectify the situation, but Jenny had been adamant. She'd also been pretty bitter, but that had to be normal. Especially after the Jerk came to her in Emma's hospital room, while the child was battling with a surprise bout of pneumonia, to tell her that he'd been sleeping with his secretary and suddenly found himself more enamored of *her* back rubs than Jenny's demands for participation.

Since that day Jenny had learned all there was to learn about putting on a brave front and putting off prying questions. She'd also discovered a lot too much about court systems, especially ones presided over by judges who'd just had their own wives take them to the cleaners. And she knew about the tight little fraternity of lawyers that played racquetball together and dealt deals that only excluded ex-wives with children to try and raise.

Jenny had precious little trust left for anyone but those sharing her own gene pool. To put some of that rare commodity into a man who was being investigated by the local police didn't seem terribly sound, even to Jenny. But she had a gut feeling that they were all wrong about Nick. She just couldn't get past the fact that he had a smile that seemed to surprise emotions in him that he didn't even recognize. Honest emotions. And that had been something, she'd realized two children too late, that the Jerk had never had.

Or, she thought with a wry smile as she reached the bottom steps and headed into the playroom, it could be a matter of hormones. Maybe hers were finally just rising from the dead.

They were certainly setting up quite a clamor in her every time Nick looked her way with that lazy, assessing look of his. She felt tingles in places she'd forgotten she had. She found herself overcome with the desire to comb her hair and straighten her clothes, just like all the little girls who lined the streets waiting for the ice cream man to appear. Now that he was here in the house, she felt the first stirrings of anticipation, a feeling that seemed for all the world like the first breezes of a hurricane.

It felt so good. It felt *too* good, after all this time.

But if it were only that, she wouldn't let Nick into her home. Jenny had fought too long and too hard for her children to let anything or anyone jeopardize them—even a man she felt attracted to.

Especially a man she felt attracted to. She'd already seen what a disappearing father could do to a child. She wasn't about to watch it happen again.

Which was why, she supposed, she was so surprised to find Emma chatting so comfortably with Nick. Nick, of course, looked a little more than bewildered, but that was normal when faced with an alien being like Emma. One had to get used to her gradually, kind of like non-euclidian geometry.

What surprised Jenny was that Emma had her hand in Nick's. Emma didn't take to people. She saw it as her karma to rule them. Familiarity only bred contempt. Emma even held her grandparents at a proper distance, bestowing kisses rather than slobbering and hugging like most three-year-olds. She'd been three before she'd even let Barb give her a hug. Emma just wasn't like that.

And here she was looking up at Nick as if he occupied the throne on the other side of hers. Jenny couldn't quite take it in.

Maybe her instincts, rusty as they undoubtedly were, were right. Maybe this guy wasn't the criminal she'd helped paint him out to be. Maybe he was just a student who was finishing school a little later than most and driving an ice cream van for a friend. Jenny found that in that moment she wanted more than anything else in the world to believe it.

Jenny made it a point to use the dining-room table, centerpiece and all, but in the end there was only so much she could do to make tuna-noodle casserole look palatable. She stood looking down on her table and found herself wishing once again for something intangible. Something...more than just subsisting for the rest of her life.

That was where Nick found her, still looking down at the sparsity of food on the table, running her finger absently over the sleek teak of the Danish table, her eyes just a little distant and sad, her hair tumbled around her head like smoke and the dress poured over her sweet figure like honey.

Nick was surprised by the pang of longing the sight set up in him. He saw the empty place in this room, in this home where this bright young woman held her family together by her fingernails. He saw the patches and the twelve-year-old car in the driveway, and heard her shove that all aside with a challenge. He also saw more security, more love here than in even the best, most prosperous places he'd inhabited on his way to adulthood, and missed it all over again for never having had it.

"I hope the wine's appropriate," he said, stepping in.

Jenny looked up, and Nick saw her quickly shunt her frustration aside. She straightened with a grin and tilted her head just a little. "I'm not sure. Just what wine goes with tuna-noodle casserole?"

Nick knew she couldn't miss his instinctive reaction. His heart hit bottom almost as fast as his stomach. He wasn't sure what he'd been anticipating, pot roast, maybe even meat loaf. But not tuna-noodle casserole. Of all the gastronomic nightmares from hell, that was it.

With the greatest of efforts, he offered a smile. He guessed he shouldn't have been surprised when she laughed back.

"You asked for it, pal," she goaded with great delight. "Next time Emma invites you over, make sure you ask what's on the menu first."

"Oh, don't get me wrong," he instinctively apologized, stepping closer so that he could catch the elusive citrus in her perfume. "I mean, I really..." In the end, though, his voice faltered over so bald a lie.

"Hate tuna-noodle casserole," she finished for him, still grinning. "Don't feel like the Lone Ranger. So do we. Unfortunately, that's what's in Mother Hubbard's cupboard. Next time, get yourself invited over to Barb and Bill's next door. Now, she can cook. She personally knows thirty-seven different things to do with a duck.''

Nick couldn't help laughing at the wicked glint in Jenny's eye. He couldn't imagine what she'd say about him behind his back. "I guess when it's a choice between food and company, I choose the company every time."

Jenny's grin just broadened. "Fool."

Nick challenged her eye-to-eye, his own smile infected by her sharp humor, his taste heightened by the sight of her wrapped in that peach dress. It softened her, highlighted the outrageous green of her eyes, the curious black of her hair. "I'd rather not know how to do *three* things with a duck, if it's all the same to you," he said more quietly. "Ducks aren't my style."

Jenny became very still, the smile still hovering deliciously. "She's also very good with chickens."

"Are you trying to tell me you can't cook?"

Jenny motioned to the table. "You're looking at my ability to stretch out a meal on a shoestring budget."

Nick felt a flash of discomfort from her words. He'd nudged just a little too far. Maybe because he understood their import better than she thought. Maybe because he'd seen the ache in her eyes as she'd looked down on the meager fare. He didn't want to hurt her any more than she already had been.

"Jenny, I didn't mean to imply anything."

Jenny looked up at Nick in surprise. He leaned against the dining-room doorway, beer still in hand, for all intents and purposes still exuding that same flirting sensuality that had taken discussions of poultry to such new and interesting heights. But she heard the caution in his voice. The sudden sincerity that gave her back her distance if she needed it, and afforded privacy and respect. All in one sentence. He left her breathless.

"Nick," she said, her eyes sharp and bright, wanting least of all that he should be uncomfortable in her house after he'd brought such surprising life back into it. "My situation is hardly secret. My mother sends care packages, my sister sends hand-me-downs. Barb sends leftovers. The old ladies across the street send the lawn service. I think that's just because they can't abide the sight of grass tall enough to lose small animals in, but there you are. I've been divorced for two years, and I've been paddling like hell to stay upstream the whole time. So trust me, there isn't anything you could say that could insult me.'' She had already turned away to introduce her corkscrew to Nick's wine when the afterthought hit her. ''Unless, of course, you called me a lawyer. *That* would insult me.''

From behind her she heard Nick take a drink of beer. ''I take it you don't get along with lawyers?''

''Euphemistically speaking. Right now I'm on Shakespeare's side.''

''Shakespeare.''

''Uh-huh.'' She screwed the implement in, thinking how symbolic the act was and grinning. '' 'The first thing we do,' '' she quoted with a flourish of the free cork, '' 'let's kill all the lawyers.' I always did like Shakespeare's sense of priorities.''

Jenny looked over to see that Nick wasn't quite sure how to take her spiel.

''Well,'' he said with a half grin. ''I guess that means a long-term relationship is out of the question.''

She was still feeling reckless enough to be his straight man. Wine bottle in hand, she shrugged. ''Why? You're an ice cream dealer.''

''An ice cream dealer on his way through law school.''

Jenny didn't know whether to laugh or cry. Didn't it just figure? The first man she'd let in her house with the exception of the refrigerator repairman and he turns out to be one of *them*. Well, after all, it was only par for the way her life was going. Next he'd tell her that he knew the Jerk, and oh, he respected him so much for his talents in corporate law. And then she'd have to hit him.

''You're right,'' she said instead, bending over to pour the wine into the two crystal glasses she'd pulled from her long-unused set. ''I've used up my lifetime allotment of lawyers.''

Nick didn't move. ''Do I leave now?''

Jenny looked up and smiled, wishing she really felt like it. "And miss a dinner like this? You'd never forgive yourself. I'm just afraid that I can't invite you back again."

And that, she thought with a feeling in her too much like shattering glass, was that.

Chapter 4

You have to invite him back."

Jenny sat quite still in Barb's blue-flowered armchair and balanced a glass of tea on her lap. She would have definitely preferred to throw it, but this was, after all, Barb's house. It wouldn't go unnoticed as long as it would at her own. The meeting today, called on such quick notice, only included Barb and herself. And, of course, the ubiquitous Detective Richards.

"Don't be ridiculous," she snapped at the offending party. "I told you it would be...unwise. Besides, I really don't think he's who we think he is."

Detective Richards did a neat trick with his left eyebrow that packed all his disdain for housewives into it. "Oh?" he asked. "That's a pretty sudden turnaround for you, isn't it, Mrs. Lake? What changed your mind all of a sudden?"

"I've been talking to him, Detective."

"And I've been researching him. Just like you ladies asked. And I've found that Nick Barnett does not exist. Not at the License Bureau, not in any of the local schools, not even in the Marines."

"He had a tattoo," Jenny retorted, knowing how perilous her footing was even as she defended Nick. "Not dog tags."

"Well, he's gotta be drivin' that truck on something more than a tattoo, lady. And it ain't in our computers."

"Which means what?" Barb asked from her corner of the couch.

"Which means that Barnett seems to be an alias. And since you were so anxious to find out if he's sellin' drugs—which, by the way, are on the uprise in the area, just like you thought—I figured you'd like to help us find out what his real name is. Or what he's up to on that truck."

Jenny leveled a freezing glare at the detective, who this very minute looked like he had her in the pincers. "By inviting him over."

Richards gave her an elaborate shrug. "Well, you did it once."

Jenny opened her mouth to explain, once again, and then realized that a concept like Emma just wouldn't register on the good man. "And I told him I wouldn't do it again. What's he going to think when I change my mind?"

"That you got the hots for him, probably. Which is fine, 'cause maybe you can find something out about him."

Jenny set her tea on the table, putting it just out of her reach so that it wouldn't be such a temptation. "Why don't *you* talk to him, Detective Richards?"

"Because," he said as if he were explaining to a very small child. "I don't want one penny-ante drug dealer. I want his supplier. If I can get you to loosen him up, I might come up with something. Besides, I bet he'd be a lot happier talkin' to you."

"Shouldn't this be handed over to the county narcotics bureau?" Barb asked diffidently.

That seemed to be something the detective definitely didn't want to hear. "We don't need them pokin' their busy noses in down here. I'm on line with a guy from DEA who's investigating the rash of ice-cream-truck traffickers, and he assures me this is the way to go." Lowering the level of his tea with a long, loud gulp, Richards seemed to take the time to dredge up a modicum of tact. "Look, ladies, this is a hard neighborhood to stake out. The guy's got a run of about five miles, and all of it's heavily wooded. There aren't all that many responsible adults home during the day to help us keep an eye out for him. It just makes it a lot easier on us if we have a contact already set up.''

''He's not dealing drugs,'' Jenny insisted.

''He's doin' somethin','' Richards retorted. ''And we gotta find out what.''

Rustling in her chair just enough to betray her agitation, Barb finally put in her vote. ''Jenny—''

Jenny didn't even need to look over to read it. She'd known what the outcome of this little chat would be from the moment Richards had brought up Nick's name. She was going to let Nick right back into her house. She was going to encourage it. And she was going to suffer for it.

''All right,'' she sighed, feeling the weight of her words settle on her like a sentence even as she tried to think of a way to lighten the impact on Nick. ''But you owe me a lot of coq au vin for this, Barb.''

''And don't try and warn him, or say somethin' like, 'So, why are you usin' a fake name?''' Richards said. ''You do that and he disappears before we can find out anything.''

She hadn't even thought of that, but it was the best option of all.

Except that she wouldn't do it.

''Nice to see you could take time away from the high life to visit your friends.''

Nick gave the dispatcher a grin and headed toward his office. He hadn't been in for about a week, but of course everybody knew what he was doing. His continuous run-ins with McGrady were the stuff of legend around here.

''Hey, Barnes,'' one of the bomb-and-arson guys greeted him. ''What's new on *Sesame Street*?''

''Big yellow bird shoots frog. Film at eleven.''

The Special Investigation office was grouped with the other detective bases, so that Nick worked a particleboard wall away from the guys in narcotics, burglary and bomb-and-arson. Greetings floated in from each of the different branches as Nick made his way into the cubbyhole that housed him along with four other special investigation detectives.

"Like the outfit, Nick. Makes you look ten years younger."

"After this, wanna pull some undercover time in school?"

"High school?"

"Grade school!"

Nick curled his lip in response. He'd never been terribly thrilled with his face. Too off-center-looking for the places he usually had to work. The fact that nobody was questioning his place on the ice cream truck proved it. He wanted his mustache back.

His attitude slid further when he opened his door. A bell jangled, and the anticipation could be heard in every laugh along the hall. He looked up. A bell from an ice cream truck. Wonderful. It looked like nobody was going to let him off easily.

And then there was the box of crayons and coloring book on his desk. Much as he didn't want to, Nick found himself grinning. It was good to be home.

"Baker," he said, sitting down and pulling out one of the crayons. "What do you have so far on the Lake woman?"

Baker, a short, sharp woman of thirty with a military taste in clothing and a buzzed blond cut strode over and handed him the file. "I missed you, too, honey," she retorted with a dry, toothy smile that portended more to come.

Nick just stuck the crayon behind his ear and set to work.

Jenny Lake, the file reported, thirty years old, graduate of St. Mary Magdalen School, Nerinx Hall High School, St. Louis University with B.A. in mathematics and education, Phi Beta Kappa, graduated magna cum laude, went to work teaching at West Vine Elementary School to put husband through law school at Washington University. Three pregnancies, two live births, Kevin Barton Lake, Jr. and Emma Louise. Divorced two years. Husband remarried to Amber Jean Wilson (*Amber Jean?* he thought. Sounded like a cheerleader.) Present address 12 Summerset, Ladue. Pays child support in amount of $250/month, in arrears six months (*Two-hundred-fifty? Who was he kidding? That was highway robbery. And the bastard couldn't even get that in on time. Probably in too deep to his pool service.*) To support herself, Jennifer Lake taught fifth-grade mathematics at Mary Mother of Eternal Patience and rang up groceries at Bennet's during the summer.

"Who can blame her for trying to make ends meet?" Baker had been reading over his shoulder.

"Yeah," Nick retorted. "All you divorced women stick together."

"Nobody else is gonna do it."

"Tell you what," he suggested, opening his drawer for a notepad. Instead he found a family of Smurfs, two teething rings and a box of animal crackers. This time he allowed a laugh.

"Hey, you guys, this is great!" he yelled for the benefit of every listening ear. "You gave up all your toys just for me! I especially like your teething rings, Washington!" Washington had just gotten his first set of dentures. The laughter rippled all the way down the hall. Nick broke open the box of crackers and shared them with Baker, who had perched on the side of his desk. "Now, find out the make and model on the car this Lake guy drives. And the license."

"Why? He's not stealing out of mailboxes."

Shrugging, Nick jotted the information down in brick red and replaced the crayon. "Because I don't like the bastard."

Nick's words brought a big smile to the policewoman's face. "I love to hear you say that."

Nick just smiled back. "I'm sure he's doing *something* wrong out there."

Baker tapped the file. "What about her?"

Looking back down at the evidence of Jenny's need, Nick still found himself shaking his head. "I don't think so. She just doesn't look like she's bringing in any extra income. All the same, I'll keep hunting."

"Yeah," Baker retorted in a too-knowing voice as she headed down to the computer. "Right."

The dry tone of that voice made Nick lift his head. There was no way Baker could have known. He hadn't even been in the office since he'd met Jenny. Her reaction was just typical sarcasm. Even so, it unsettled him.

It struck too close to the truth. Nick *was* interested in more than just the case here. He hadn't lied to Jenny when he'd told her she was the high point of his job. He did position the truck just so he could watch her walk up to her porch while he munched on peanut-butter-and-jelly.

And he was getting in too deep for his own good. He should walk in to McGrady right now, beg forgiveness and ask off the case. Maybe he should even tell the truth, that he was fantasizing too much about the suspect, making himself too comfortable in her house and actually talking to her kids.

And maybe McGrady would bust a gut laughing.

Everybody in the place knew about Nick's solitary nature. He lived alone because that's the way he preferred it. He socialized only a little, and that with other cops. And as for women, he hadn't been able to find one without an overactive biological clock. And as everybody within shouting distance of McGrady's office knew since Nick had been assigned to this case, Nick didn't like kids.

He had no patience for them. They were noisy and troublesome, and he'd never seen the good side of them growing up. Of course, that was the wonder of the foster-care system, that it popped you out without a secure base or a real regard for another human being, but what the hell. He'd made it through, escaped to the Marines and made it a point not to look back.

Except for odd little moments, like when he'd been invited in on family prayers over at the Lakes'. Jenny had looked at him when he'd suddenly gotten up and stalked out, but she hadn't asked. Nick had taken himself back to the kitchen and the last dose of wine, seeking some kind of antidote to all the love and support in that little pink-and-white room of Emma's.

God, the woman had no husband, she had no money and she was pulling enough hours between her kids and work to lay out a drill instructor. And she knelt on that floor and thanked God for what she had, and meant it. She'd taken the time to tell her kids that because they had each other, they didn't need anything else. *And meant it!* All the screwed-up families in the world, and he had to stumble onto the real thing.

Nick slapped the file shut and got to his feet. He popped a cookie into his mouth. Looked around for some coffee. He'd been closing his eyes to that particular void too long to give in to it now. Nick Barnes was a survivor. He didn't need that homey garbage, with little blond girls asking you how elephants dance, and bright-eyed boys comparing cartoon preferences with you. He didn't need the scent of oranges waking him in the dark. What he needed was some coffee.

In the end, he knew he'd go back. He didn't think Jenny was the thief, and if he weren't around to find the real one the department would just as easily tap-dance all over her in hobnail boots. And she deserved better than that.

What he deserved was a shrink.

"Don't you think you should dress up a little?"

Jenny looked down at her uniform and then back up at Lauren, who was assessing her with a definitely uncomfortable eye.

"What would you like," Jenny retorted. "A bikini and gold body paint?"

Lauren fluttered a distressed hand, setting up a jangle among her bracelets. "No, of course not. It's just...do you really think he'll be attracted by that outfit?"

Jenny couldn't help but laugh. She was standing with Lauren and Barb in the Bailey kitchen planning the Barnett Assault, as Jenny had taken to calling it—more to keep the considerable butterflies at bay, than for any better reason. She'd just pulled six hours at the store and was sporting a throbbing headache. She'd locked her keys in her car and had then fried when she'd finally gotten inside. She hadn't had lunch. And she hadn't even faced her children yet. She might as well deal with Nick now, while she was still too uncomfortable to care.

"Lauren," she said. "You're talking like I'm preparing for an espionage assignment or something. I'm going to ask him to help fix my car. I really don't think silver lamé is appropriate for that, do you?"

Barb grinned, but Lauren was taking her part of this seriously. "Of course not, Jens. But, well, I'm afraid that your uniform just isn't . . . well, becoming."

Jenny grinned. "Well, if worse comes to worst, I'll pull one of the shoulders down real low and sing to him."

Barb burst out into giggles. "That would send him screaming in the other direction, Jen."

Jenny offered a heartfelt scowl. "Thanks for the support, hon. After all, this was *your* idea." Just because she couldn't hit a note in a bucket with a barrel of double-ought shot, it wasn't something Jenny considered a laughing matter. Especially when everybody laughed.

Barb giggled again. "I'm just trying to offer constructive criticism."

"Wonderful," Jenny retorted. "So far, the only instructions I've gotten for this caper are take off my uniform and don't sing. That kind of leaves me a lot of leeway, doesn't it?"

Lauren finally worked up the enthusiasm to grin along. "We're right here behind you, Jens. Go out and get him."

Jenny just shook her head, foregoing the urge to tell Lauren that she really hated Lauren's idea of a nickname. "Richards was right. I am the only man for this job."

Lauren got in her last shot. "In that uniform, you *look* like the only man for the job."

"You're just jealous because you have to wear that heavy new tennis bracelet and I don't," Jenny retorted with an easy grin.

Lauren never knew just how to take Jenny. She lifted the offending arm, an arc of diamonds glittering in the sun that streamed through Barb's spotless windows and then, uncertain, glanced up at Jenny.

"It's beautiful," Jen assured her. "But it just wouldn't go with this smashing brown polyester. You might as well be the one to wear it."

Lauren smiled. "A girl should be able to treat herself now and again, don't you think?"

"Lauren," Jenny retorted, "Häagen-Dazs is a treat. *That* is an orgy."

"Speaking of which," Barb interrupted, eyes on the bracelet. "That ice cream truck isn't going to sit there all afternoon."

Even Lauren laughed. "Jens is a bad influence on you, Babs."

Jenny didn't think that either woman saw her wince.

Jenny was all set to follow Lauren out of the house when Barb surprised her by pulling her aside. "You really seemed convinced that he's not guilty," she said, the gravity in her voice matching the concern in her eyes. Barb wasn't one to pry, but she knew better than most what was going on where. "Why?"

For a moment, all Jenny could do was look out onto the peaceful shade of Barb's yard. The neighborhood was quiet at this time of day, when the heat took over and even bored the birds to silence. The trees rustled listlessly in the breeze and set the shadows to a slow dance.

Jenny couldn't help but think of how much the peace of this neighborhood meant to her. The huge old trees, the deep lawns and constant neighbors. She didn't want anything to happen that would hurt it.

And then she thought of the raw pain she'd surprised in Nick's eyes the night before when he'd stumbled from Emma's room. He'd avoided facing her, but what she'd seen had reminded her of a little boy looking into the lighted rooms of a warm, noisy house on a cold night and knowing he didn't belong. How could a man break her heart without so much as a word?

Still feeling the chill even in the summer wind, Jenny shook her head. "Because Emma likes him, Barb."

It actually took Barb a moment to answer. "Emma?" Her surprise couldn't have been greater if Jenny had said that the Queen of England danced topless.

Jenny nodded, her smile as good as a shrug. "Had him upstairs introducing him to all her animals. She even held his hand."

Still Barb faltered. "Emma?"

Emma didn't even let the Jerk hold her hand, which said quite a bit about Emma's discriminating taste in people. Those great blue eyes of hers saw more than most adults. Those patient little ears heard what Jenny swore hadn't been said. And Emma, who held most of the world at arm's length, had a special affinity for life's casualties. A silent pat to trembling hands, a smile to bravely passive faces.

And she'd found Nick.

"Emma likes him," Jenny said again in some wonder. "And I like him." This time she did shrug. "But then, at one time I liked the Jerk."

"It's not the same, at all," Barb insisted, instinctively defending her friend.

Jenny grinned. "You're right, there. I can't see the Jerk sporting a Marine Corps tattoo on any part of his body. Nor, come to think of it, would I want to see it if he did. Now, on the other hand, Nick . . ."

"Is up there eating his lunch," Barb interrupted with a tolerant smile. "The perfect time to discuss cars, if I'm not mistaken."

"I know," Jenny retorted, with an upraised hand. "'Jenny, act your age.' That does get boring after a while, though, doesn't it, Barb?"

Wrong person to ask. Barb couldn't imagine any reason to prevent one from accepting her responsibilities. Jenny just laughed and offered a conciliatory pat on the arm and acted on Barb's suggestion. She walked out the door.

Jenny started down the street with at least a modicum of purpose. She wanted to find out one way or another just what Nick Barnett was up to. She wanted to get Detective Richards out of her hair. She wanted to get this conversation over with and rediscover the joys of air-conditioning and aspirin.

She'd made it about four houses down when she noticed the envelopes sticking out of the mailbox. They distracted her.

"Damn!" she sighed, heading in that direction with a look over her shoulder to make sure she wasn't in Mrs. Warner's line of sight. The trees effectively shaded her.

Opening the box a little, she checked the contents. "Aw, now why don't they listen to advice and mail these?" she whined, taking another look around and shoving the envelopes into her pocket. "They're just asking for trouble." Turning back to her original purpose, she gave her head one last shake and rubbed at the growing throb at her temples. "Not to mention somebody else I know."

Nick had spent the last few hours convincing himself that this was the only thing he could do. He'd debated the fact that he was too involved and countered it with the obvious answer that it was better to have somebody who cared investigating Jenny than somebody who didn't.

He challenged the wisdom of trying to get back in her good graces after she'd all but thrown him out the night before. He'd even considered telling her that he was really resigning from law school. Instead he was going into a really respectable field. Teaching or accounting or...oh, hell, the priesthood.

No, he'd decided with the first wry smile of the battle. You can only strain credibility so far. Besides, that wouldn't allow for any unforeseen opportunities in the emotional expression department. Just in case any came up.

So here he was girding his loins, so to speak, sweating more from the turmoil of what he had to do than from the hundred-degree temperatures, and suddenly Jenny was walking his way. Alone. Smiling.

So, just what was wrong with this picture?

"Hi," she greeted him, bobbing her head almost shyly, the sunlight making her squint a little.

Grinding out his cigarette and setting down his can, Nick nodded back. "Hi. Thanks again for dinner last night."

"Oh." Again that little bob sent her hair trembling about her head. "Don't think anything of it. It wasn't like I cooked real food or anything."

There was a moment of silence, taut, brittle, as if each of them was waiting for the other to speak. Not knowing quite what else to do, Nick opened his door and slid out. He felt absurdly like a high-school boy meeting his date at the drive-in.

"Popsicle?" he asked, heading toward the back of the truck.

Envelopes. There were three envelopes in her pocket. His heart faltered. His eyes strayed. He couldn't see more than a first name on the return addresses, but that was Frank. Unless Jenny had some bigger secrets than even the police department knew about, she wasn't a Frank. Nick wanted to throw something.

"Actually," Jenny said, sounding terribly stiff. "I was going to ask for a...favor."

Nick turned to face her, his surprise showing. Did this mean he didn't have to pretend to be a priest?

"A favor?" he countered as easily as he could, especially downwind of that perfume. "What kind? Does Emma need to run a tab? Financial crisis in the kingdom?"

"Don't encourage her," Jenny warned with a grin. "No, it's not Emma. It's...well, it's my car. You said you thought the fuel injectors were going bad."

Leaning against the back of the truck, Nick frowned in bemusement. "Yeah. One of these days you're gonna be driving home from Bennet's and they're just gonna quit on you. Why?"

"Would you have a set of metric tools?" she asked. "The car needs to be fixed and I'd give it a shot, but I don't have anything metric to my name except a prescription for ampicillin."

Nick couldn't help but betray his surprise. "Fix the car? You know how?"

"I know how to do a lot of things," Jenny assured him, with more pique than pride. "A repairman charges forty dollars just to ring your doorbell."

There was a whole new understanding of Jenny in Nick's expression. "I hear ya. When do you want to do it?"

Jenny shrugged. "As soon as possible. I, uh, can't afford to be without a car. Especially with school coming up soon."

"Well, sure. But...do you mind my asking what changed your mind? About having me around."

He saw that he'd hit a live nerve. Again, that poor poker face, the emotions skittering over her face faster than cloud reflections on a lake. Frustration, resentment, anger, discomfort. She turned her head, just a little, as if it could better hide the truth behind her answer. But when it came, she had the guts to give it all.

"Sure. I had an unproductive session with the Jerk yesterday. The funds I'm short of aren't coming, from him or anyplace else right now. It doesn't mean I've changed my mind. It means that I'm using you. The pay is beer and chili."

"The jerk?"

She flashed him a quick, wry grin absolutely devoid of guilt. "The lovely ex-Mr. Jennifer Lake. Don't ever tell my children I call him that. But it helps stoke the fires of self-righteous indignation a little when I need the energy to do things like fix my own car."

For a moment Nick just looked at her. She looked so independent, so self-sustaining, with that challenging fire in her eyes. He could only imagine the price she'd paid for that strength. No apologies, no retreats. She did what she had to for herself and her children. And if that meant robbing from mailboxes, Nick wasn't sure she'd apologize for that, either.

"Beer and chili, huh?"

"All you can eat."

"Deal. How 'bout Sunday? I'm off."

"Sunday it is." For a moment, it seemed that Jenny deflated a little. "Thanks, Nick. I really appreciate the help."

Nick took a second to run an appraising eye over the pink, flushed cheeks, the wide, sparking green eyes, the full, brassy mouth. Even in that androgynous lump of material they called a uniform she had the ability to raise his blood pressure twenty degrees. When he finally answered, it was a smile free of all the tortuous deliberations he'd gotten snagged in earlier in the day.

"My pleasure," he assured her, and realized that he meant it.

It wasn't until Jenny was halfway down the street that Nick realized he'd forgotten to ask about the envelopes.

                                    * * *

A sainthood, Lord, for the man who invented air-conditioning, Jenny thought. And a severe talking-to to the God who thought up children.

"Mom!"

"Mom!"

"Mom!"

"I've changed my name," Jenny informed them both as they danced impatiently by her elevated feet. She'd stretched out in the playroom, trembling with effort, exhausted with heat, crabby with headache. And there, like little human magnets, they'd found her. "Until you guess it, I'm not answering."

"Aw, c'mon, Mom."

"You heard me." She didn't even bother to open her eyes. She did purse her lips, though, and both of them fought to get the first kiss.

"Bill?"

"Wilma?"

"Eleanor?"

"Ralph?"

"Ralph?" Jenny retorted, eyes opening, body refusing to move no matter what she commanded. "You guessed! What can I do for you?"

Kevin beat Emma to the punch by a nose. "Mrs. Warner has my ball," he said, his face a struggle between distress and outrage. "The soccer ball Dad got me for my birthday."

The soccer ball Mom got him and put Dad's name on, when it looked as if he wasn't going to remember again. "Kicked it in her yard, huh?"

Outrage won out. Nothing provoked indignation like older women who didn't understand the vagaries of soccer. "I didn't mean to, but Buffy and Dustin were blocking the other side of the goal."

"Wasn't Miss Lucy there?" Jenny asked, carefully closing her eyes against the light, her arm around Kevin's waist as he stood alongside the couch.

"No. I think she was out walking. Mrs. Warner said we couldn't have it back again. She said she was tired of picking it out of the ivy."

"Okay," Jenny sighed. "I'll see what I can do. A little later."

"Mom, now," he whined. "She might throw it into the fire or something."

"I don't think so, honey. Now, go on out for a while so Mom can get rid of this headache."

"But I don't have a ball!"

"Go do something..." Her abstracted search for inspiration was interrupted by the front doorbell. "Go answer the door. That'll keep you busy. If they want money, tell 'em I already gave."

Both kids pounded down the hallway through to the foyer to win first place at the door. The sound of their race echoed through the rooms and reverberated through Jenny's skull. She groaned.

Then she heard the excited babble, which meant that it wasn't Barb, and it wasn't the Jerk, and it wasn't the mailman.

The mailman. Oh, God, she had to remember to get those envelopes taken care of again. They weren't something that could just lie around the house for days. And then she'd have to put a stop to it.

Jenny was giving serious consideration to getting an eye open for the surprise visitor when she realized she didn't need to. She smelled him.

Her heart stumbled. Butterflies swarmed in her stomach, and her headache set up a fresh pounding. Nighttime and lightning. Leather and denim. Danger and attraction.

Nick.

"I thought we said Sunday," she said without opening her eyes.

It wasn't hard to hear the humor in his voice. "How'd you know it was me?"

"I'm a mother," Jenny assured him. "I know everything."

That got a laugh out of him. Jenny wished she felt as jolly.

"Are you okay?" he asked, suddenly sounding serious.

"Fine. I've been cooking a headache all day, and it's finally well done."

"Anything I can do?"

Jenny still didn't get her eyes open. He was nice enough just on the other senses without facing all that light yet. "Wanna go over and beat up an old lady for me?"

There was a polite pause. "What?"

Jenny managed to get her eyes open and grinned. He did look just the least bit confused. "On the other hand, you'd scare the hell out of her if you just showed up on her doorstep." It was something about the glisten of sweat on his throat, the hair falling into his eyes and the indecent fit of those faded, ripped jeans. And he had a Deadhead shirt on. That clinched it. He was scaring the hell out of her, too. "Mrs. Warner took Kevin's ball and he wants retribution."

Nick took a quick look over his shoulder, as if he could really see the house. "The neighborhood FBI? *That* Mrs. Warner?"

"The chief of police's aunt. That Mrs. Warner."

She heard the hesitation in his voice. "Oh, brass, huh? Well, that'll cost you extra. What do you want, your basic roughing up or a little arm-twisting for good measure?"

"Arm-twisting!" Kevin piped up with relish. "Make her stop taking my ball."

Jenny afforded herself another groan. "Thank you, Nick. I'll send him to you when he needs bail money."

Nick stood by the foyer wondering what he should do now. Jenny really did look pale, her face drawn from the artillery attack going on in her head. He had the urge to go over to her, to take her hand and run a soothing hand over her cheek. It amazed him how suddenly protective he felt of this woman who wouldn't allow anyone to protect her.

"Why don't you guys go on outside for a while?" he said to the two little ones who flanked him. "Let your mom get some rest."

"Don't be worried, Nick," Emma said with a patient mother's smile. "Mommy does this sometimes. Then she takes a nap and gets better. We're used to it."

Nick still wasn't really sure how to answer that kid. Especially when she sounded older than he did. "Yeah, well, thanks. Now, go on out."

He really thought his idea was an inspiration until Kevin slammed the door on his way out. Nick winced. Jenny winced.

"Did you take aspirin or anything?" he asked, heading into the playroom.

"I'm just going there now," she assured him without moving a muscle.

"Where?" he asked. "I can get them."

"Kitchen." He didn't say anything, but she answered him anyway. "I figured I'd save time by keeping them in the place that causes the most headaches."

"Right next to the tuna, right?"

That got a smile out of her. "You're catching on."

Nick should have been relieved at the chance he'd been given to check out her place. For some reason he felt like a heel. It didn't keep him from sorting through the piles of paper on the kitchen table when he went in search of aspirin and water.

The kitchen wasn't as messy as it had been the first time he'd been through. This time he took a moment to notice the refrigerator art, construction-paper flags and little handprints, imaginative renderings of warplanes and big, scrawling figures that probably only meant something to three-year-olds and their mothers. Nick wondered how the hell she got the fridge door open without knocking half that stuff off.

And then there was the collection of jelly glasses and mismatched Tupperware that took up her shelves. Nothing matched in this house—not towels or plates or silverware. It was as if she replaced things as they broke, never having enough money to invest in a whole new set. There was *Sesame Street* dinnerware and *Star Wars* glasses, and a sign over the kitchen sink that proclaimed, "Children need love. Especially when they don't deserve it."

Nick found himself smiling. A pragmatist, this woman. An idealist who lived in the real world. She had sun-catchers in the window that spilled jewels over the walls, and a collection of tiny frogs in a shadow box on the wall. Suddenly Nick wished somebody he'd lived with had had enough whimsy to collect frogs. He wished he'd been hung in a mother's art gallery, his work collected in a huge box to be preserved for the day he'd moved away. When Nick had moved out, he had gone with a driver's license and a high-school diploma, and that was it.

Suddenly he was shaking himself again, fighting the pull of this house, this family. He had to find out about the forgery and then get the hell out.

Picking the aspirin bottle off the windowsill and filling a glass with water, Nick took another moment to sort through bills and school notices and snapshots without any luck.

No envelopes. No evidence. Just a very attractive lady stretched out on the couch rubbing her head and a quiet, cool house. Nick walked back in, gave Jenny the aspirin and settled himself on the edge of the glass-and-teak coffee table well within the perfume perimeter.

Working her way up to a sitting position, Jenny popped the tablets in and swallowed with a huge grimace. It was only then that she was able to get her eyes open and focus on her benefactor, only to find him no more than a foot away. Her eyes just a little too wide, she flashed a tired grin.

"Thanks. Again. I appreciate it."

Feeling suddenly foolish, Nick shrugged. "Anytime."

"You never told me."

"Told you what?"

"Why you came over."

"Oh." He flashed her a sheepish grin. "Sunday. What time?"

Jenny grinned back. "Would two be okay?"

"Sure." He didn't think about what he did next, he just acted. "Why don't you get some sleep?" he asked, his words unaccountably quiet, his hand up to brush her hair back from her forehead in a way that would have reminded anyone else of a parent comforting a sick child. "You look like you could use it."

Jenny's answering smile faltered a little. Her eyes grew wide with his touch. "A rank play for sympathy," she assured him in a curiously small voice. "My mother used to call me Sarah Bernhardt."

Still Nick hesitated, uncomfortable with staying, unwilling to go. He'd liked that touch of her, the silk of her hair, the velvet of her skin. He liked making her smile, especially that hesitant, sweet smile that said she was feeling more than she wanted. Nick could have stayed all day and coaxed that smile out of her. He could have even seen his way to stroking his hand across her forehead, her cheek, her hair, soothing, quieting.

But he knew better. That just invited involvement, and that wasn't possible. For more than one reason, the main one being Frank, whoever he was.

Or was the real reason the false security he felt with this woman? Nick knew better than to trust that. He'd been proven wrong too many times.

She was forging checks. It was his job to find out how. That was all. And when this was over, he'd go back to his apartment in Clayton and reclaim his solitary life. And by God, he'd like it. Because right now, Nick couldn't see how he could do any different.

"Young man! Young man, let her go!"

Nick turned to the sound of the quavering voice, wondering what the hell was up now. He didn't get as far as his feet. He didn't even see the intruder. What he did see was the afternoon paper as it slammed into his head.

Chapter 5

"Miss Lucy, no!"

"Hey, lady!"

Nick and Jenny collided on the way up. Nick had his arms up trying to ward off the flurry of slaps he was getting with the business section and sidestep enough to get over the table and at his attacker. He only succeeded in knocking Jenny back down.

"You get away from her, do you hear me?"

Nick got a quick impression of wrinkles and gray hair and a big straw hat with a wilted flower on the crown. And gloves. Good God, he was being whaled by Grandma Walton. He was never going to hear the end of this down at the department.

"Miss Lucy," Jenny objected, shoving her way back up again. "It's all right. Nick was getting me some aspirin. It's all right!"

The old lady didn't hear in time. Nick had just made it around the table when she came out of a backswing with a huge purse Nick swore was carrying bricks. It caught him square in the side of the head and sent him reeling.

Suddenly, though, as if she were on a three-second delay, she gaped. The paper dropped, her hand flew to her mouth, and Nick came to an uncertain halt.

"Oh, dear," she stammered, her watery blue eyes lifting way up to Nick's face. She couldn't have topped five feet, dressed in organdy and thick shoes. She looked like somebody Nick would find in Shaw's garden sniffing the roses and talking to the birds. "Oh, dear, dear, dear."

"Nick? Are you okay?" Jenny asked, a hand to his arm.

Nick realized that he must have looked a little wild, because when he turned to answer her Jenny was fighting a huge grin.

"Couldn't you have a German shepherd, like everyone else?" he demanded, rubbing at the side of his nose where the purse's zipper had left a new crease.

Jenny stifled a laugh and gave him a pat. "I'm sorry, Nick. I haven't introduced you. This is Miss Lucy Sperring. She's Mrs. Warner's sister from across the street. Miss Lucy, this is Nick Barnett, the ice cream man."

"Oh, it's a pleasure," Miss Lucy piped up as if the introduction weren't at all out of the ordinary, a hand demurely extended, the purse back over her arm.

Not knowing quite what else to do, Nick shook hands.

"It's just that the children said that you'd thrown them out and, well, you were bent over Jenny like that..."

Jenny leaned over as if she were sharing a secret between girls. "My virtue is safe, Miss Lucy. My paper?"

"Oh, yes, dear. I thought I'd drop in with it. Especially..."

"Yes, Miss Lucy."

"Well, dear, then I'll drop dear little Barbara hers. Good day." Resettling her purse and giving a proper little tug on her gloves, Miss Lucy shot Nick a smile straight out of a Tennessee Williams play. "And you must stop in and visit with us, Mr. Barnett. We do so enjoy company."

Jenny shot Nick a warning glance. When Miss Lucy had cleared the room on her way out the door, Jenny allowed in a straight voice, "Set foot in that yard and Mrs. Warner will have the police helicopter circling."

"That's what I thought." Nick couldn't quite pull his gaze from the empty door where Miss Lucy's presence still remained like a well-mannered ghost. "She's the ball warden's sister?"

Standing alongside, Jenny considered the same view. "Amazing, isn't it? Like having the Queen Mum and J. Edgar Hoover sharing the same train berth."

Nick just shook his head. "Lady, you got some neighborhood."

"They take care of me," Jenny defended them.

"Yeah," Nick retorted, rubbing at the side of his head where the memory of something very solid inside that purse still lingered. "I know."

Jenny chuckled. "I'm sorry. Really. I'm used to Miss Lucy just walking in. She does it to everybody. She's harmless."

"She's an ozone commando."

"Broaden your horizons a little, Nick. You might get to enjoy it a little."

"Anybody else I should know about?"

Easing back down on the couch, Jenny propped her feet on the coffee table and thought about it. "Well, Mr. Ventimiglia writes letters to the president and Libby Vilhels balances crystals on her forehead looking for enlightenment. And Bill Hobbs on the corner is trying to make *The Guinness Book of Records* for having the most ailments in one body."

Almost by unspoken consent, Nick joined her on the couch, propping his feet alongside hers, a hand still testing the sore spot at the side of his head. "A fairly normal bunch for south county."

"Don't be smug," she retorted, leaning her head back against the couch. "Where do you live that the people are so different?"

"Clayton."

Jenny snorted. "Of course. The center of the universe."

"I live in an unair-conditioned efficiency off Skinker, so I can be close to school. Is that a crime?"

"I bet people balance crystals on their forehead in Clayton, too."

"They don't carry plates and napkins out to get Popsicles."

Now Jenny laughed, eyes closed, comfortably quiet, headache subsiding. She sat alongside Nick as if it were the most natural thing to do, and she didn't know how to stop it.

"Don't make fun of Barb," she asked. "She's six of the most sincere people on the face of the earth."

"She's gonna be buried in a Tupperware container."

That took care of the subsiding headache. It flared when Jenny started laughing again. "Stop that," she begged, giving him a smack. "Now I'm not going to be able to look in her cabinets without thinking of somebody burping the lid over her."

"I bet she's got a kid named Muffy."

"Buffy."

Now he was laughing. "And a golden retriever?"

"And a compact station wagon."

"You were right," he admitted, leaning back next to her. "I should have gone over there for dinner."

Half an hour later Kevin ran into the house with the ball he'd sweet-talked out of Miss Lucy to find his mom and Nick asleep side-by-side on the couch. With a disgusted scowl, he intercepted Emma and took her up to his room to play.

At first Jenny thought it was the alarm. It was six-thirty and she had to get the kids up for school. She sighed and stretched and tried to reach over to shut it off. That was when she realized she was on the couch.

The phone. It wasn't the alarm she heard but the phone, relentlessly ringing out in the kitchen. Jenny opened her eyes and realized two things simultaneously. She'd been asleep for at least an hour, and Nick was still asleep next to her.

Sitting up, she looked over at him, stretched out in an identical position, head against the cushions, feet up on the coffee table, one arm on the couch back, the other over his stomach. His chest rose and fell in an even, deep rhythm. His eyes were closed and his face so relaxed Jenny wondered if she'd been wrong about his age. He looked curiously young in the half-light in the playroom, his hair tousled over his forehead and his mouth open just a little as he gently snored. He looked vulnerable, and that was something Jenny had never thought she'd say about Nick Barnett.

She was just sitting there staring, wondering at the urge to reach out to him, the sweet ache in her chest at the sight of him, when the phone finally stopped ringing. Jenny looked up, surprised by the silence, completely unnerved by the fact that she'd been comfortable enough with Nick to fall asleep alongside him. Stunned by the fact that he'd been comfortable enough with her to do the same.

What made it worse was that looking at him now made her realize just how tired he'd looked before. He must have been putting in long hours to fall asleep on a stranger's couch in the middle of the afternoon.

"Is Mr. Nick coming to dinner?"

Jenny looked up to find Emma in the doorway, the cat clutched in her arms and dressed in Cabbage Patch clothes.

"No, sweetheart. I don't think he could survive it twice. He just fell asleep."

"Kevin said we should be quiet so you wouldn't be crabby."

Edging off the couch, Jenny held out her arms. The little girl trotted over and snuggled into Jenny's embrace.

"Well, thank you both. I'm feeling all better now."

"Did Mr. Nick have a headache, too?"

"I wouldn't be surprised after Miss Lucy got through with him. Now, why don't we be quiet for him so he's not crabby, huh?"

Emma took a moment to consider the sleeping man on her couch. "He doesn't do this a lot, does he?"

Surprised, Jenny looked from her daughter to the sleeping man. "No," she admitted softly, more troubled than she could say by Emma's observation. "I don't think he does."

It wasn't the phone that got her attention this time but a knock at the back door. Hopping to her feet, Jenny tugged Emma after her. She wasn't exactly sure what she should do about waking Nick up. He might have something to do, somewhere to go. But looking down at him now, so quiet and peaceful, she couldn't bring herself to wake him.

She should have known it was Barb. By the time Jen got to the door, the blonde was peering in through the curtains with the kind of look that preceded the calling of police.

"Hi, Barb," Jenny greeted her. "Aren't you supposed to be cooking something?"

Barb didn't consider the situation a laughing matter. Still looking carefully around as if expecting a sudden rush from a weapon-wielding intruder, she stepped into the kitchen, her arms loaded with food containers. She must have decided that she needed a plausible excuse to visit.

"Are you all right?" she asked, setting the booty down on the countertop by the sink. "You didn't answer your phone."

Jenny couldn't help but grin. "I take it Miss Lucy told you about my surprise visitor."

Barb shot Jenny a meaningful look. "The ice cream truck's been in front of your house for over an hour."

Jenny gave in to a groan. So much for the neighborhood network. By dark the word would be around that Jenny was doing unspeakable things with the ice cream man. She wondered whether Lauren would be relieved that Jenny was interested in somebody other than her husband or outraged at Jenny's aberrant behavior.

"Who's called you so far?"

Now Barb offered her own version of a sheepish smile. "Mrs. Warner, Mr. Ventimiglia and Patsy Deaver. It's turning into a great story."

"Did you tell them I was working undercover?"

Bad choice of words. Jenny could see the double entendre strike home and fight for expression in Barb's carefully controlled face.

"The question came up."

Jenny afforded herself a grimace. "Go see for yourself what happened. He's in the playroom. Want some tea or something?"

Now Barb allowed just the least bit of doubt. Jenny could see the suspicion flick across the blonde's mind that Jenny had somehow done the man in and left him in with the *TV Guide*.

"He fell asleep," Jenny offered with barely controlled humor.

"He was crabby," Emma added with a knowing nod from her perch on a chair. The cat now sat in her lap.

Barb actually crept in through the French doors and stood there, looking down as if watching a sleeping lion. The expression on her face mirrored all her distrust, distress and uncertainty. Jenny grinned at her and turned to clean off the table for dinner.

Barb walked back into the kitchen to find Jenny frowning at an envelope she held in her hand.

"He doesn't look quite as dangerous lying on the couch," Barb admitted, looking at the envelope, then Jenny. "What's wrong?"

Jenny shook her head. "I've been looking for this for three days, and I just found it right on top of a pile of mail on the table. Lord," she sighed in exasperation, "if I were organized, I'd be dangerous."

Barb was still Barb. "You have a lot on your mind," she assured Jenny with a passing hand on the shoulder. "You do have room on your wall here for a mail organizer, though. You can get them at the crafts store. Did you find anything out?"

Jenny had to suppress a grin at the sudden, conspiratorial hush in Barb's voice. Excitement was a rare commodity in St. Anthony. It seemed that when it struck it even had the ability to infect Barb.

"No," Jenny answered in a voice just as hushed and then turned to the fridge for something to drink. Soda, she thought, with lots of chemicals and preservatives. Just the kind of thing that made old Barb wince. "How 'bout a soda, Barb? Diet, of course."

"No, thanks," Barb demurred, her expression just as carefully noncommittal as Jenny had anticipated.

"Spot says she would like a soda for us," Emma piped up, lifting the placid tabby she'd named herself. Spot was evidently getting weary of looking like a furry kindergartner. Her tail was beginning to switch.

"Tell Spot that she's not old enough for soda," Jenny answered, popping the can and taking a long swig. "And tell her also, please, not to wear my lipstick anymore."

"But she wants to look lovely."

"She's lovely already, Emma. She has to stay out of my things, please."

Emma exhibited one of her patented pouts. "Okay," she acquiesced and headed out.

It didn't occur to Jenny that the little girl was headed back toward the playroom. She had dinner to cook and about a week's worth of laundry to catch up on and Kevin to talk to. And that didn't even take into account the situation that placed Barb in her kitchen and a near stranger asleep on her couch.

In point of fact, Nick was no longer asleep. He hadn't been since the cat had run up his chest. For a long moment he sat straight up on the couch, trying to understand what the hell had happened. Somehow he'd ended up sound asleep on Jenny's couch with her daughter curled up alongside him and a cat now staring malevolently at him from atop the television. A cat in a dress. Nick shook his head.

He remembered stopping in the house to get a line on those checks. He remembered the sight of Jenny lying on the couch, eyes closed, looking as fragile and vulnerable as a tropical flower in winter. And he remembered Miss Lucy.

Had she knocked him out? He couldn't really remember. The side of his head sure ached, but he didn't have the queasy, concussed feeling. He looked down at Emma, thinking maybe to ask, but she was engrossed in the letter P, her eyes already glazed by the bright, flickering television. Since it was a cinch the cat wasn't going to tell him, the only option was to look for other life.

Rubbing ruefully at the tender ache in his left temple, Nick lurched to his feet and headed toward the sound of the voices. Maybe Jenny would explain.

One look at the two in the kitchen brought it all back. He'd been talking. Sitting alongside Jenny as if he belonged there, talking about her neighbors. And then, as subtly as nightfall, the two of them had drifted to silence, to easy comfort side-by-side. To sleep.

Nick couldn't believe it. He couldn't imagine it. He wished suddenly, with a yearning that surprised him, that he'd woken up before she had.

Barb noticed him first. Jenny had her back to the play-room door as she retold Miss Lucy's surprise attack.

"I'll tell you something, Barb," she was saying, using the soda can for punctuation. "That old lady has a mean swing on her. I thought Nick was going to be down for the count...Barb?"

But Barb's attention had drifted, her eyes widening as they focused beyond Jenny's shoulder. Curious, Jenny turned to look. Then she found herself staring, too.

No wonder Barb had been distracted. Nick stood in the doorway, looking rumpled and a little disoriented. He was running his hands through his hair as he stretched out the worst of the kinks, and his eyes still had that soft, sleepy look about them. Jenny couldn't help the smile that crept all the way up from her toes. It was all she could do to keep from saying, "Aaaw."

"Hi," she greeted him, not realizing how soft her voice sounded. She didn't see Barb transfer her wondering look to Jenny.

Nick smiled back, his eyes a little sheepish as he leaned a hip against the doorway. "I seem to have made myself right at home. I'm sorry."

Jenny just shrugged. "Hard for me to kick you out since I was asleep, too."

"How's the headache?"

"Well," she admitted. "That one's gone, but we might just have another one brewing. Barb just showed up to tell me that the neighborhood grapevine is all a-twitter about your van being here so long."

Nick had a very impressive scowl. When Jenny saw it she realized how Miss Lucy could have felt the need to defend her. His presence in the neighborhood probably had those two old ladies locking up everything but their police scanner.

The problem was that to Jenny his scowl just made him look more enticing. There was such a dark set to his features, a hidden place that added shadows and meaning to his reactions. She wanted to know what that was. She wanted to know why Emma had realized that he wasn't the kind of man who relaxed enough to fall asleep around other people.

"And don't say typical south county," she warned, keeping her tone deliberately light. "Gossip is part of the human condition everywhere."

"Thanks for the sociology lecture," he groused, pushing away from the door and approaching. "I'll bear it in mind when I punch out that old guy with all the diseases for calling you loose."

Jenny flashed him a wry grin. "And they said chivalry was dead."

When Nick smiled back, it was with a sensual promise that left Jenny's knees weak. "Thanks for the couch. See you Sunday?"

Jenny nodded. "Sure." Silver-tongued devil, she thought in despair. The man was making her into an idiot.

"By the way," he added when he came alongside Barb, who was just as suspiciously quiet as Jenny. "Do you always dress your animals?"

Jenny responded with a slow, dry smile. "Don't you?"

She could hear Nick's chuckle all the way down the driveway.

"What are you going to do about him?" Barb asked, the hush in her voice more wonder than conspiracy.

"Enjoy him," Jenny answered automatically. When she saw the stunned distress on Barb's face, she offered a smile and a pat on the arm. "Calm down, Barb. I'm talking basic fantasy here. Do you know what kind of school he goes to?"

Barb seemed unable to do more than shake her head.

"Law school." Jenny waited for the understanding to dawn, and behind it the relief. Then she nodded. "That's the problem with having been married to the Jerk," she said. "I can only think with my hormones so long before reality interferes. Even if Nick isn't a drug dealer. Even if he's selling ice cream to support his work for Mother Teresa, he's still going to be a lawyer. I've danced that tune one time too many. I'll watch this one from the wings."

Barb smiled. "I think I'm glad."

Finishing off her can of soda, Jenny tossed it in the trash and turned to her neighbor with a piratical grin. "Although, come to think of it, I would like to see Mrs. Warner's face when I started dating a man with a ponytail."

As a rule, Sunday morning at the Lakes' was a madhouse. Jenny had long spent her Saturday nights dreading the alarm clock the next morning, living for the minute she walked back in the door from church.

When she opened the door this Sunday, though, it was no relief. For the first time in days she had time to notice just how much of a mess the house was. There were toys and clothes everywhere, bits of cutout paper and stick weapons of all sizes. Not to mention the dirty dishes that lurked behind those French doors in the kitchen.

Usually Jenny had a great amount of patience for the mayhem children wrought on a house. As she stood in the front foyer on this particular day, though, she suddenly decided that it was just too much that Kevin had draped kite string all throughout the playroom to make an "art project."

"It's cleaning time," she announced, bringing both children to a stunned halt.

"What?"

"This house is a mess," Jenny told them, hands on hips for extra emphasis. "We're cleaning it up. Right now."

Tilting his head to the side in an expression of supreme distaste, Kevin considered her. "Who's coming over?"

"Nobody," Jenny answered automatically. "Do we need somebody to come over to clean the house?"

"Usually."

"Don't be a snot. Just get started dismantling your spiderweb."

He gave it one more shot. "Are you *sure* nobody's coming over?"

Jenny just glared. It was enough to get Kevin moving.

Somebody coming over, she thought with a scowl as she headed up for her room to change. Where did I get such smart alecks? You'd think a woman didn't have a right to a clean house.

For some reason she didn't notice that her room wasn't much better than the rest of the house. She'd long since gotten used to filling the other side of the king-size bed with clothes to be folded or projects or books she was working on in bed. It seemed to keep it warmer that way. This week's work included preparations for school. Her clean clothes lay folded over the bench at the bed's foot and her dresser was piled with clutter.

Jenny slipped out of her church dress and stood in bra and panties looking for something to wear. Of course, there was somebody coming over today, but that wouldn't put her in such a cleaning frenzy. After all, she wasn't doing anything but keeping an eye on him for the police, getting license plates or something for Detective Richards. It wasn't as if she were trying to seduce him.

No, she thought, picking through a pile of shorts and jeans, I'm not doing anything special—but all the same, that just doesn't look right. That doesn't fit right. That makes me look fat. But it doesn't make any difference. After all, it's only Nick coming over.

Unable to resist, she took a quick look up at the mirror.

There she was, stretch marks, love handles and all. Well, not exactly a lot of stretch marks, just a few silvery threads creeping up the side of her belly that were her children's gift to her. And, well, the love handles weren't as bad as they used to be. Just enough to keep her from being too skinny.

She still had good breasts, she thought, doing her best to make her assessment objectively. Even after nursing the babies, she was still firm and full. And when she took the trouble anymore to wear her good underwear, the lace and satin that had once seemed so important, she could compete with the best of them.

The only reason she was wearing lace and satin today was because it had felt so nice beneath her dress. Even so, she didn't change it when she slipped on her slacks.

If she'd really thought about it at all, she would have admitted that ecru slacks and a pink sweater weren't the things to fix a car in but, well, she always had time to change. Casting a quick glance at the clock, Jenny found that the minute hand had only inched forward a couple of numbers. She still had plenty of time to get finished before Nick showed up. Hours. Months. Years. Too much time, and not nearly enough.

Not that it made any difference.

Cursing, Nick threw another shirt into the corner. He knew he was just going to have to come home later and clean it up, but the growing pile gave him some satisfaction.

Surely a cop should have something better to put on. After all, he spent most of his time in the high-rent district. A person would think he'd have something appropriate to put on for an afternoon in suburbia.

Undercover, of course. On the job.

All the same, if he drew too much attention to himself he couldn't blend into the neighborhood enough to see who else might be slipping envelopes out of mailboxes. He couldn't get the chance to ask Jenny what she was doing with Frank's mail in her pocket.

So far, there hadn't been any action on a victim with the first name of Frank, which relieved Nick. Baker was going through Jenny's bank-account figures to see if there was any unaccounted-for money coming in, and they were waiting for her credit-card statements to verify overspending. Which meant that Nick didn't have much time to try and ferret out somebody else.

He still couldn't believe that Jenny had offered him the perfect opportunity to spend time at her house, especially after he'd gone to such lengths to try and come up with something himself. If he was lucky, he could stretch out the afternoon to late evening. Between fuel injectors, beer, chili, talking, he figured he could get her pretty relaxed.

For the case. So he could collar whoever was doing this and get the hell off dingdong duty.

Even so, he couldn't figure out what to wear. He didn't want to go back in his workday outfit. Those jeans were becoming his trademark. On the other hand, it was counterproductive to try and fix an engine in an Armani suit.

Damn, the apartment was hot today. He was sweating and it wasn't even much past noon. It would be hard to get Jenny to relax if he couldn't. Not like the other day. Standing before his closet in his briefs, Nick found himself shaking his head. He was still baffled. Uneasy. He couldn't figure how he'd come to fall asleep on Jenny Lake's couch. What's more, he couldn't understand how she'd managed to treat the whole thing as if it were normal.

Nick Barnes didn't fall asleep on the job. He certainly didn't fall asleep in front of strangers. That left you open somehow. Vulnerable to attack. And Nick had never to his knowledge let his guard down enough to be in that kind of danger. He just figured, standing there looking through clothes that suddenly looked ill-fitting and strange, that the tight discomfort in his chest was from the heat, from the pressure of the job, from having to go back to that five-by-five icebox on wheels in the morning.

That tight ache in his gut at the sight of windblown black hair and huge green eyes was one thing. The constricting emptiness in his chest at the idea of never getting the chance to fall asleep on Jenny's couch again was quite another. Nick didn't allow that kind of thing.

He only ached to get out of that apartment and on with the job.

Looking over the shirt he held out before him, he shook his head and threw it in the corner.

Nick pulled into Jenny's drive on the stroke of two. The neighborhood was quiet, with only a few kids skateboarding down the block and Todd entertaining a knot of teens by his car. Nick had waved as he'd driven by, and Todd had waved back, signaling his approval of Nick's vintage GTO.

His own car, Nick noticed, was a late-model Firebird. Red hot and bad, the stamp of an overprivileged suburban youth. Nick had seen the boy's father laboring over the surgically manicured lawn and the guy didn't look quite as nonchalant as his freewheeling son. Maybe the gift of expensive new cars wasn't as easy for the old man as the son would believe.

There were a lot of secrets behind those fancy doors; a lot of problems that never came to light until the lawyer or the police showed up. Nick figured that Jenny was probably more in the majority with her money problems than either she or the brass over in Clayton thought. It was just a matter of finding out if it was Mr. Sellers or Mrs. Bailey or maybe Mr. Hobbs, with all those medical bills to pay, who was sneaking envelopes out of boxes.

Or, like McGrady thought, Jenny.

The compact wasn't in the driveway when Nick pulled up. He decided Jenny must have left it in the garage overnight. Pulling out the bag he'd decided to carry his work clothes in, he opened the door and stepped out.

Across the street, a curtain slid back from the window. Nick saw it and grimaced. Well, he thought as he mounted the steps to Jenny's porch, can't have everything. He guessed he should have known he wasn't going to have a nice, comfortable afternoon with Jenny without an audience.

At least the old battle-ax wouldn't get in the front door for a helping of chili. The last thing he needed was a confrontation with the police chief's aunt. He couldn't even imagine what they could do to pay him back that would be worse than what he was doing now.

Nick opened the screen door and balanced it against his hip. It sounded awfully quiet around here. Usually Jenny's kids came barreling out of that door at the vaguest sign of life. Nick raised his hand to knock and prepared himself for anything.

Well, almost anything.

Before his hand even hit the door, it swung open. A good thirty people crowded into the foyer with balloons and party hats. The minute they saw sunlight, they began jumping up and down.

"Surprise!"

Chapter 6

Swinging the car around the corner, Jenny checked her watch again. Damn. It was already ten after two. She just couldn't believe she had a sister-in-law who insisted on running out of gas within twenty minutes of the time Nick was supposed to show up. A sister-in-law who was also pregnant, which made turning down the mercy mission nigh unto criminal.

Of course Kate had been penitent. And of course she'd had to make it a point to notice that Jenny was wearing makeup and nice slacks. The kids had just egged her on by mentioning the housecleaning binge.

So, now Jenny was ten minutes late, and Nick was probably sitting out on the porch getting hot and crabby. Kate was on her way back to her house in the city, filled with gasoline and gossip. Sometimes Jenny couldn't believe how screwed up her life could get.

His car was in the driveway. At least, she guessed it was his car. It looked like something he'd drive, an old '68 midnight-blue Goat that had been painted and shined to a gleam. A lot of power under an understated hood.

Jenny caught herself grinning. Kind of like its owner, she couldn't help but think. Pulling up behind his car, she switched hers off and waited for it to stop chugging. And then she went about looking for Nick.

He wasn't on the porch swing, waiting in that languid slouch that had taken her breath that first day. He wasn't pacing the yard, and he didn't have a key to her house. She could always ask Mrs. Warner where he went, but Jenny wasn't really sure she had the patience today to put up with all that disapproval. She just hoped Nick hadn't gone across to ask after her. Mrs. Warner would just as soon lock him up in the basement as say hello. Then nobody would see him again, Mrs. Warner would have all the ice cream she wanted and her nephew, the police chief, would end up dragging her away.

"Mom, are we going in?"

Jenny shook her head. Too much Stephen King, she decided, and opened the doors.

She couldn't see a note on the front door. She didn't see any sign at all that Nick had been there—except for his car. Maybe she should go across and see if Mrs. Warner was fixing any extra lunches....

Jenny had her key out and aimed at the door when suddenly it opened. She jumped back. Emma shrieked. The crowd in Jenny's foyer yelled surprise. Caught right in the center, Nick just lifted his beer can in salute.

"You didn't tell me it was your birthday."

"You knew!" Kate accused the minute she showed up.

Still struggling with the frustration of wanting to kill her family for being so thoughtful, Jenny could do no more than shake her head. "No, I didn't. Trust me."

She already had a party hat on, and had been handed a rum-and-Coke by her brother Tim. The house echoed with the tumult of twelve Gardner grandchildren and the babble of seven Gardner siblings plus spouses as they finished setting up the party they'd brought along with them. Squeezed in among all the relatives and looking for all the world like a man caught in a crowded elevator with a lot of strangers, Nick sipped at his beer and flinched at the noise.

"You did, too, know!" Kate insisted, her voice rising accordingly. "You were dressed up and your house was clean."

"So what?"

Now more than one of her family scowled. "So when was the last time that happened?"

Joey and Claire had made it a point to come in from out of town for her birthday. Jenny really appreciated all the care that had gone into their surprise. She just wished they'd done it on a different day. Or better yet, that they hadn't done it at all.

Thirty. She hadn't really thought she'd react so badly to it but she was. She didn't want to face the passing years anymore. Their scope had grown too limited of late. And here was her family rubbing her face in it.

On the other hand, she had to admit that she was getting more than a kick out of watching her brothers' reactions to Nick. He'd worn his hair back again, and with the polo shirt he wore the Marine tattoo was amply visible. Jenny's brothers were all religiously white-collar and obsessively protective. It didn't take much to know that Nick wasn't exactly what they wanted to see show up at Jenny's house.

The women, on the other hand, reacted more to the scar at Nick's eyebrow, his out-of-line nose and the biceps that sported that tattoo.

"So," Joey said, throwing an arm around Nick's shoulder. "Are you dating our little girl here?"

His little girl was four years older than he.

"He's fixing my car," Jenny spoke up. Poor Nick was looking more and more bemused all the time.

"Fixing your car?" Tim demanded. "Why didn't you ask us?"

"Because the last time one of you clowns tried to fix my car, it ended up in the shop for two weeks."

"Do you play whiffle ball?" Joey asked Nick.

Jenny groaned.

Nick stared at Joey as if his hair were on fire. "Whiffle ball?"

"Family tradition," Joey assured him. "On birthdays."

The other boys nodded right alongside.

"We're gonna go out and play later. Wanna come on out?"

"Yeah," Nick shrugged, still unsure. "Sure."

"This is a special game," Joey continued, taking another long drink of beer without taking his eyes off Nick. "For Jenny's thirtieth birthday. We figure we'd better let her play before she's too old to lift a bat."

Jenny answered instinctively. "Eat snakes, Joey."

"Just trying to make your friend at home, Jen."

"Eat *big* snakes."

Jenny knew better than to explain. She'd been through this too many times already. The famous Gardner manhood-and-patriotism test. Anybody who seriously dated one of the Gardner girls had first had to pass the whiffle-ball test, the theory being if they could handle a bat they could be trusted to handle a sister. She just took a long drink of her rum-and-Coke.

"Feel free to run for your life," she grinned limply. "Nothing is more terrifying than a Gardner-clan rally in full swing."

"No," Nick said with a private sparkle in his eye that more than one of the Gardners caught, "I think I'll stay for cake and ice cream."

"Busman's holiday," she warned.

Joey had just detached himself to get another beer. Hearing that, he turned. "What do you mean?"

Jen took great pleasure in telling him. "Nick is the ice cream man in the neighborhood."

Jenny wasn't the only one to laugh at Joey's stunned reaction.

Actually, Jenny had to admit that the party went off better than she'd feared. She loved her family, and usually couldn't wait to get together with them. They were a noisy bunch, preferring to express their love in a bickering, challenging fashion some people wouldn't recognize. She even liked the four in-laws in the bunch, three wives and one husband. All had ended up passing the whiffle-ball challenge and now played mean family sports up at the Michi-

gan cottage where the family vacationed every year. Usually
Jenny couldn't ask any more than having her family around
her again.

Today, all she'd wanted was Nick.

At first she'd been really worried how he'd deal with all
the nonsense. Joey's challenge was just the beginning of the
outrageous ribbing, and Jenny was afraid Nick wouldn't
know how to take it. She'd been relieved to see him hold his
own with that dry, quiet humor of his catching everybody
off guard.

Of course it hadn't hurt at all when Emma had trotted
into the kitchen where everyone was gathered to take Nick
by the hand to introduce him to her cousins. The astonishment among the gathered family had been genuine and
heartfelt. When all the questioning gazes turned on Jenny
for suitable explanation, all she'd been able to do was shrug.

Ah, and then there was the whiffle-ball game. Jenny had
had a sneaking suspicion all along that those biceps and tri-
ceps weren't just there for decoration. The first time Nick
stepped up to bat she had her proof. Joey lofted the ball in
over the plate and then hit the dirt when it almost took his
head off on the return trip.

Jenny knew for a fact that she wasn't the only woman on
the street, much less the family, who stopped whatever she
was doing when Nick stepped up to bat. He had such a nice
stance, loose and fluid, with those arms and shoulders rip-
pling and that little tush wiggling as he set up. She saw Claire
smile more than once, and Kate, swollen with her third
child, rolled her eyes from the sidelines.

By the time she snuck away from the party to quiet her
newest niece up in her bedroom, Jenny had to admit that she
felt happier than she had in months. Her house was noisy
and full. Her family was home. And Nick had gotten a
grand slam off Joey and ended up sharing a beer and views
on the Cardinals. There was a symmetry to her day that had
been missing for too long—even if it had to happen on her
thirtieth birthday.

* * *

The telegram came amid the horseshoe tournament. All of the Gardners were in the backyard laying down bets, and Jenny had disappeared somewhere. Since Nick had been corralled by Emma to "see something" (her cat riding in the handlebar basket of her tricycle out in the front yard), he was the one who ended up with the job of handing Jenny her message.

He made a quick recon of the backyard, only to see that the competition had gotten fierce. Two of the men were pitching, and three were wrestling by the swing set. The women were taking bets on both ventures. No Jenny. When asked for ideas, Kevin just shrugged.

"Probably playing with babies," he said and headed back out, purloined cookie in hand.

Nick was sure that answer made sense to someone. He hadn't seen any babies, but then that wasn't something Nick watched out for as a rule. He took another quick look around the first floor just to find kid debris and diaper bags, and decided it was time to breach the second floor.

He climbed the first step shaking his head. Nobody at work would believe this day. Nick Barnes surrounded by kids—screaming, shrilling, laughing, fighting kids. Nick Barnes stuck smack in the middle of suburbia's answer to the storming of the Bastille. Nick Barnes not scratching and kicking to get free.

To be honest, he kind of liked Jenny's family. They acted a lot like the cops he knew, carefully cloaking their camaraderie beneath some of the most elaborate insults he'd ever heard. Outrageous to a fault and protective as hell. He could just imagine what Jenny had gone through when she was dating.

He could imagine, having heard the way they tap-danced around the subject of her ex-husband, what she'd gone through with her divorce.

They were a family that had judged him quickly and then cavalierly set their judgment aside and welcomed him like a sibling within the space of a well-hit whiffle ball.

He shook his head again and found himself amazed when he realized he was smiling.

Nick found her in the first room he searched. It must have been her room, all feminine clutter and refrigerator art, the big four-poster bed covered in a peach, gray and black comforter as thick as snowfall and the bedside table topped with books and stuffed toys and clumsy art projects.

She sat before the window, a nimbus of sunlight outlining her and turning her hair to smoke. Curled into an old rocker, she gently rocked back and forth, her head down, her finger caught in the hand of the tiny baby nestled in her lap, her eyes wide as she talked to the child. Entire conversations, as if the baby were answering, her own reactions magnified on her mobile features. Her smile was a radiant one, as if the sunlight suffused her as well, her eyes liquid and soft looking down on the child.

Nick saw her and stopped. A great silence filled him. There was nothing more one could add to the scene, the perfection as rare as a madonna by a master. And then he noticed what could kill him.

That face, so exquisitely beautiful as she smiled and sang down to the baby, that face that radiated a joy Nick had never known, had tears streaming unchecked down it.

Struck, shaken, he stood without moving, unable to take his eyes from her, unable to break the fearful spell she was weaving. And then, just as Nick was going to leave—to run—she looked up.

"Sometimes," she admitted in a voice that spoke of cherished secrets and wonders, "I forget just what I have."

Maybe it was the way the light glinted off those tears, but Nick thought that her smile had a hollow edge to it, a place missing. She smiled for what she dreamed as much as for what she had, he thought. And that was why she refused to apologize for the tears.

The baby reached again for her, a blind, uncoordinated movement with hands so small they seemed unreal. Nick saw her turn back, instinctively feeling the communication and returning her attention to the bundle in her lap.

"A...telegram," he offered diffidently, feeling the usurper in this woman's room, this place of motherhood and belonging. "It just came."

Jenny's head came up, fear briefly flaring. Old superstitions reared and died. Just as quickly she rose to her feet, carrying the baby with her as easily as if it had been a part of her, and approached Nick.

He handed the telegram to her. She responded by handing Nick the baby.

"Don't..." But before he could protest, a set of wide, unfocused blue eyes were turned his way and that tiny, insistent hand was seeking him out.

Nick looked up, instantly panicked, searching for help. Guidance. Deliverance. Jenny was already tearing into her message.

What did you do with a kid this small? he wondered, turning his attention back to the weight that seemed so ungainly in his hands. What if he dropped it or hurt it? Weren't you supposed to hold its head some kind of way? Couldn't you break its neck or something? And they had that soft spot. If you touched it wrong, the kid could die. Quickly he looked around for someplace to set it, thinking that ten pounds had never felt so heavy. He wasn't sure where Jenny had found it, but there wasn't any sign of where to put it back.

When she laughed, he jumped. She looked up, quickly brushing leftover tears away with the back of her hand and brandishing the telegram.

"Could a person have better parents?" she demanded with glee, the momentary loss polished over with her news. "'Jenny,'" she read. "'Stop. You're getting older and we're not. Stop. We love you almost enough to come home for your birthday. Stop. Love. Stop. Mom and Dad.' What warmth, what sincerity."

"Come home?" Nick echoed, holding the baby out a little as if in offering. Jenny didn't seem to notice.

"They're in Beijing," she acknowledged. "Isn't that neat?"

"Sure. Now, will you...uh..."

With another laugh that looked suspiciously superior, Jenny took the baby back and fitted it against her hip like a tight end running back a football. Nick looked at it and wondered just how women managed to do that without dropping the kid. And how the kid managed to look so comfortable. Jenny started swaying back and forth and the baby cooed.

"Not familiar with the equipment?" she asked, that laughter still lingering in her eyes in a way that lightened her whole face. She didn't seem to think she needed to explain the swaying. Nick wondered if she even knew she was doing it.

He shrugged his answer, trying to find something to do with his hands now that he had nothing to fill them. "It's not really my line of work."

"I think that's what you call an understatement, Nick," she grinned. "You looked suspiciously like a whore in church standing there with that baby." For a moment she studied him, indecipherable emotions skittering across the soft fields of her eyes. Then it seemed to Nick that she actually braced herself, even though her smile was brighter than ever. "Just what are you doing on an ice cream truck?" she demanded, finally slowing to a stop.

"I told you," he answered, trying his best to sound sincere. "Marco needed some help. And . . . well, I like kids a lot, ya know?"

Now the smile looked suspiciously self-satisfied. "Yeah, and I like tuna-noodle casserole."

He was getting all set to protest, wanting to say something complimentary about the baby that even now was wriggling unnoticed in Jenny's grip, when he saw that it wouldn't do any good. Kind of like telling God you believed in him with your fingers crossed. She had him pegged.

"All right," he admitted, eyes briefly down as he searched desperately for plan B. "I owed him some money. I was available and he decided it would be really funny to watch me out on that wagon with *all those kids.*" Well, stick as close to the truth as you can. At least he could give that lie some weight.

Still supremely delighted, Jenny nodded. "Well, if it makes you feel any better, you're handling it like a pro."

Feeling absurdly complimented, Nick gave her a stiff little bow in return. "Thank you."

Finally tiring of all the adult conversation, the baby voiced an opinion of her own. Jenny moved with fluid comfort and swung the baby neatly up into her arms.

"This is Amanda Jane," she said, her eyes on the baby's, her finger stroking the dewy cheek. "Tim and Nancy's little girl. Doesn't she look just like Tim?"

Nick actually looked, but came to his usual conclusion. "She looks like a baby."

Jenny offered a scowl. "Romantic. Well, I'd better take her to her mom. She's ready to eat, and I'm afraid all I can offer is a dry well."

Flashing Nick a more distant smile, she shoved the telegram in a pocket and headed for the stairs. Before Nick turned, he got a look at the other corner of her room and bit back a grin, his attention suddenly stolen away from kids. As a cop, he lived for evidence, and he'd just spotted some that belied a lot of Jenny's breezy nonchalance. There, by the closet, was a pile of discarded blouses.

Claire didn't look in the least bit happy. With an apron tied around her khaki-silk jumpsuit she was washing up the barbecue dishes and sharing the leftovers with Jenny, a custom kept since childhood when the two of them had been sole executors of kitchen detail.

"I can't believe you allow him in the house," she snapped, her voice quiet just in case the men out in the driveway would hear them. The fuel injectors were in the process of being replaced, all her brothers kibitzing.

Taking a deep breath, Jenny took stock of her younger sister. Taller than Jen, slim and professional-looking, the real working woman. The redhead in the crowd, Claire had spent a nervous few years wondering whether her brothers were telling the truth when they told her she was adopted. Claire was the rebel, the one who couldn't tolerate being compared to Jenny, who had made it her life's work to be different than the older, resented, revered sister.

And now that sister had betrayed a sacred trust by rebelling herself.

"He owns a suit," Jenny countered, wondering at the outrage in Claire's eyes. Claire hadn't liked the Jerk any better.

"He sells drugs," Claire snapped, shoving a dish into the rack with enough force to set the glasses to tinkling.

Taking a quick look to make sure they didn't have any eavesdroppers, Jenny leaned against the counter and faced her sister. "Who've you been talking to? Mrs. Warner?"

Claire couldn't keep the betrayal from her mirror-green eyes. "I haven't paid attention to Mrs. Warner since she told me she thought Tim was working for the KGB. I was talking to Barb."

Jenny's heart sank. Barb. The woman whose word didn't need a Bible. She wondered if Claire would ever believe her now.

"He isn't."

Her frustration bubbling over, Claire came to a halt and faced Jenny's challenge. "Then who is he? And why is he selling ice cream when he goes to law school?" That sent her off on another tirade. "*Law school*, for God's sake. Don't you learn your lessons?"

"Claire," Jenny said in a carefully controlled voice, holding her sister's hot gaze with deliberate eyes. "He's here so I can help find out if he's legitimate. He's here because the police asked me to invite him over. I agreed. But since I've gotten to know him I've decided to help prove that he's innocent."

"Innocent."

Jenny nodded. "I don't think it's possible. Not Nick."

One hand resting on a slim hip, Claire glared. "That's what they said about Ted Bundy, baby. How can you take that kind of a chance around my godchild?"

Now Jenny's eyes sparked a little on their own. "Around *my* children, Claire. Do you really think I'd hurt them?"

For a minute the challenge was fought in silence. Neither woman had practice backing down. Neither could have loved the other more. Laughter drifted in from the front, the men's having the ring of dirty jokes and locker rooms, children's squealing with excitement. In the living room Amanda Jane was mewling to her mother for more lunch and outside one of the neighborhood jocks was revving an engine. In the kitchen, the wall clock ticked.

It was finally Claire who backed down. "No," she admitted with a hesitant grin. "You're the official poster child for Mother's Day. That's why I couldn't understand it when Barb admitted what you were doing."

Jenny nodded, not expecting apology or explanation, just glad for the returned equilibrium. Along with the excitement in her family, came the fights. All that energy, all that emotion, all those opinions. Fights flared and then died as fast as sun storms, but they bothered Jenny more than they did most.

"Besides," Jenny offered with a wry grin of her own. "You said it. He's in law school." She was turning away when a thought came to her and she gave her sister one last glance. "Although I would buy tickets to watch him swing a bat."

Claire's answering laugh assured her that in at least that they were both agreed. Taking one final moment before returning to the dishes, Claire bobbed her head just a little, her way of emphasizing a sensitive point.

"I just wanted to be sure you hadn't—" even in the silence of the kitchen she faltered "—sold out."

Her arms full of bowls to be washed, Jenny smiled for her sister, knowing what her answer meant. Knowing now how worried Claire had been. "I'd love to be married again, Sassy," she admitted, deliberately using the name the family had long ago pinned on their individualist. "I'd dearly adore to have more babies and stay home and knit." She saw Claire's inadvertent wince and her smile broadened. "But all I *need* is enough money to take care of my children. If I could get the Jerk to come through, I'd spend the rest of my life working overtime and be thankful for small favors. I'm not the kind of girl to court a man for his stability."

"At least not anymore," Claire agreed, her eyes purposefully swinging out toward the party in the driveway.

Jenny laughed. She couldn't wait to see what kind of man Claire finally settled on. If she didn't miss her bet, Claire would be more surprised than she.

"Want to come test out your high-performance vehicle?" Nick asked only minutes later, appearing at the door in his favorite Deadhead T-shirt and jeans. He was wiping the grease from his hands and brushing the perspiration from his forehead with his forearm, one foot into the house, one hip holding the door open.

Jenny saw Claire inadvertently stiffen and smiled. "You mean one of my brothers hasn't electrocuted himself on the car yet?"

"You can't electrocute yourself on a car engine," Nick assured her dryly.

Jenny shook her head. "They could." Quickly drying her hands on the apron Claire still wore, she followed him out the door.

Night again, even while the sun was shining. Jenny could smell it as she followed Nick, and it made her want to curl up and purr. As a matter of fact, she was enjoying everything about this walk down the drive. The view was fine, the scent and sound of his swinging walk, the one that still seemed so alien to the sidewalks and zoysia around here. He walked more like one of the Jets from *West Side Story*, loose and agile as if watching for trouble, as if ready for anything.

The only thing waiting for him were her brothers, leaning over the hood of the compact and looking like a high-school shop class. Jenny had to admit that she hadn't seen anything to match it in a long time. She hadn't had as much fun as she had this afternoon, licking barbecue sauce from her fingers and sharing a beer with Nick as he argued baseball and local politics.

This was the real world, she thought. Beer and chicken and diaper bags in the living room. Whiffle-ball games in the street with a family that yelled and fought and laughed all in one breath. A man who looked like sin and didn't know how to talk down to a three-year-old. Jenny didn't know what the Jerk thought he could get out of that fancy address in Ladue, but she bet he never sat in a lawn chair in his backyard and bet on how many times he could throw popcorn up and get it in his mouth.

And the more she thought about it, the more she realized that she was the lucky one, after all.

She should have known it couldn't last. There was just something about her luck that prevented her from holding onto an optimistic mood for more than twenty minutes without disillusionment.

It wasn't the ride in the car. That went well. Jenny drove, and every one of her brothers did their best to pack in along with Nick to make sure that the two of them didn't do anything suspect on the ride. They ended up looking like one of those circus acts, the kind with all the clowns piling out of the little fire engine. Jenny laughed so hard that she killed the car three times at a stoplight. And of course, heard about it from not only the brat pack in the back but from Nick, who had proved an uncanny knack for meeting her family word-for-word in the insult-and-tease category.

By the time the car was officially pronounced fit and the families began gathering their paraphernalia to leave, Jenny had almost managed to forget that the electric bill still waited to be paid, that she had to get up at four in the morning to go into work, and that she'd vowed never to develop an interest in Nick because of his law-school aspirations.

That seemed to be the mistake. Because when she and Nick stood by Tom's car wishing him and Diane a safe trip home, Tom suddenly reached into the glove compartment.

"Oh, hey, Nick, I forgot to give you this."

When he turned back to them, he held a card between his fingers like a conjurer. Tom was the entrepreneur in the family, the one who kept his finger on financial pulses and prided himself on his money-making acumen.

"Like I said," he was telling Nick, who accepted the card. "This guy has done well by me. Sharp mind, quick on the move when you need it. He'll start you at any level you want and grow with you."

"Thanks," Nick acknowledged with a nod and a quick shake of the hand. "I appreciate the help."

Tom just shrugged with that big, hungry smile of his. "You'll need a place to squirrel away those fat fees when you start getting them, counselor."

Nick nodded, a little smile lighting his features. "Your next arrest is on the house. Just try and wait until I get out in June."

Jenny barely heard the rest of the salutations. She stood on the sticky asphalt of her driveway feeling the heat take her in waves, fighting the sudden nausea that swept her.

Counselor. All those fat fees.

She wanted to run. She wanted to shut the door and never come out, hide herself again in the mountain of minutiae it took to raise children so that she couldn't possibly have the energy to look at another man.

She just couldn't go through this again. She couldn't watch another man suck her dry and then pitch her on the trash pile.

Suddenly she didn't care that Nick was holding Emma's hand, or that he played the best game of whiffle ball the family had ever been witness to. She just wanted him gone before he hurt her. Before he hurt Kevin and Emma.

Standing out there with Kevin and Emma and Nick, looking for the world like a real family waving relatives goodbye, Jenny couldn't help but think that she had actually been lulled into envisioning something this domestic. She should have known better. She'd been the only one fending for her family for two years and that just wasn't going to change.

At least, not with Nick it wasn't.

Chapter 7

We have a new victim!"

Printout held high, Baker charged into the office sounding more like a game-show host than a civil servant.

"And who is the lucky contestant?" Nick asked, secretly dreading that his first name would be Frank.

Coming to a halt before Nick's desk, Baker took a moment to officially read the name.

"Mr. Melvin Waterson," she announced. "And he promises never to leave his mail in the box again."

Nick plucked the paper from her hand and read the details for himself. "What a good boy. Too bad he didn't think of this before they cashed four hundred dollars' worth of checks against his account."

Grinning with anticipation, Baker leaned close. "I saw McGrady in the building," she warned. "I imagine he's going to tell you to step up the investigation."

"I step any higher," Nick retorted without looking up, "I'm gonna look like the Rockettes. Which reminds me—" his smile was purely lascivious "—get out your steno pad, little girl, and prepare to sit on my lap. We have some work to do."

Baker gave him the glare he deserved. "Don't practice for that fancy law office on my time, chump."

Nick grinned. "Just think," he taunted her. "This time next year, that'll be *Mister* Chump."

She grinned right back. "A pleasure."

Finding the top of Nick's desk more comfortable than any of the chairs, Baker crossed her legs and handed Nick the file she'd compiled on Jenny.

"What are your thoughts?" Nick asked, paging through bank and credit-card statements.

Baker never batted an eye. "That all men are slime."

Nick slowly scanned numbers, knowing how much it cost to live in St. Louis County and seeing what Jenny brought home. She was definitely walking a delicate balance here. He also spotted something else amid the charge accounts, and checked again. "Have we learned anything about this particular slime?" he asked.

Baker had been saving her best smile for this answer. "That he has a nasty speeding habit. In a red Porsche, of all things."

Nick clucked. "So easy to spot."

Baker nodded. "Patrol said to say thank you. They haven't had so much fun in ages. They especially enjoyed the useless threats."

"How many?"

"Four, to be exact."

Now Nick smiled. "He should be sufficiently softened up for a little soul-saving message in another week or so. Don't you think?"

"If he's not broke."

"He'd better not be. He owes his wife a lot of money. And he's about to find out that he's gonna owe her more."

"Barnes," Baker said with just enough caution to tell Nick she meant it. "I really appreciate the blow you're striking for divorced mothers everywhere."

"But?"

"Do you think you should be doing it for her?"

Nick looked up to see the carefully camouflaged concern in Baker's eyes. They had been partners for almost two years, wasting hours on stakeouts, tap-dancing through undercover operations and just slogging through paper-work. Baker knew him. She was the best friend he had. Nick figured that the least she deserved was an honest explanation.

"All right, Chris," he conceded, setting the file down before her. "I don't want it to be Jenny. I've developed a soft spot for her and that oddball little family of hers. I don't want to pull the rug out from under her feet when I see how hard she's working to keep it there."

"What else?" Baker demanded. Leaning forward she tapped the bank statements with a polished nail. "She's living right at the limit, Nick. She's been putting money into her checking account that doesn't correspond with pay-checks. Usually in amounts of about a hundred dollars or so; and if you'll look close, she shoved another two hundred in just yesterday. It's not lottery winnings, and she doesn't belong to any office pools. Where's it coming from?"

"I'll find out," Nick promised, looking back down at the evidence Baker had so painstakingly compiled. "I have a gut feeling on this one, Baker."

"Are you sure you're not thinking lower than that?"

Nick's head came up. He saw that his partner's concern was honest, a cop's concern for his objectivity. And well she should have been concerned, he couldn't help but think. He wasn't objective. Hadn't been since that moment when he'd found Jenny in the rocking chair.

He'd spent the last two nights tossing and turning, waking from vague dreams that had wandered through long, empty hallways and cold rooms. Looking, walking, never knowing just what he wanted but knowing that he couldn't find it.

He'd spent yesterday compiling snapshots of neighborhood joggers, strollers, visitors—anyone who would have the same chance Jenny had at the mailboxes.

He sat here now trying his best to deny the evidence Baker had brought him, trying to find some way to prove that no matter what, Jenny wasn't the one he was after. If Frank had been the victim this time he might have wavered, maybe crumbled in his conviction. But Frank was safe. Jenny was

safe. And Nick still walked silent halls in his dreams, looking for the way out.

"We only have one person's word that she saw Jenny at
a mailbox," he argued, his voice sharper than he'd intended.

Baker wasn't one to back down. Especially to Nick. It was
what made them such good partners. "And a disaster of a
bank statement, three credit cards bobbing right up at the
limit and no foreseeable help from the ex-husband." Leaning very close now, Baker faced him nose-to-nose, her
chocolate eyes sincere. "I think it stinks, too, Barnes. But
if she's doing it, she's gonna be collared."

Nick nodded. "If she's doing it, Baker, I'll snap on the
cuffs myself. But until then, I'm not counting out any of the
other people I see wander around that neighborhood. Now,
are you gonna help me or not?"

Straightening, Baker offered him a bright smile that betrayed why so many of the cops jostled for first place in her
line of suitors. "My pleasure, *Mister* Chump."

"Don't you realize that this is illegal?" Jenny demanded. "We could both go to jail."

She was seated at her kitchen table, a stack of envelopes
piled before her. She tapped at them with a finger, trying her
best to keep her temper. This was all getting to be too much.
If she didn't stop it right now, somebody could get into real
trouble. She was just amazed that old Mrs. Warner hadn't
caught on a long time ago, with that eagle eye of hers always focused out the front window.

"They really wouldn't put us in jail," Kevin argued
without much conviction. "Would they?"

Jenny looked at her son, who wore a smart-alecky grin
tugging at the corners of his mouth, and she wanted to
scream. That was just the way the Jerk had looked when
she'd told him she knew he was cheating on his law-school
exams. Nothing could really happen to me, he was saying.
I'm above all that. I'm too handsome, too popular, too
charismatic. For the Jerk, it was still working. The last thing

Jenny wanted for Kevin was to develop that kind of attitude.

It was time for some real threats here.

"Kevin," she said, struggling to keep her voice even. "You have been taking people's mail out of their mailboxes. That is a crime. They put people in jail for that. The police are looking for someone right now who's doing that kind of thing, and when they catch them, they're going to put them in jail. Would you *like* jail?"

Wrong tack. He screwed up his face as if she'd just asked him to kiss a girl. "No."

She nodded, lifting the envelopes she'd pulled out from under his bed. "Well, then, this time you can put them back."

"Aw, Mom," he whined, squirming in his seat. "I was playing mailman. I needed some letters to deliver to Buffy."

Jenny supposed she should have been thankful. At least he didn't want to play doctor with Buffy. That would probably come later.

"That's why God invented paper and pencil, darling," she said instead. "You make your own envelopes. Now, after you've put these back," she went on, "you can sit in your room for half an hour or so and think about how you're not getting television today or tomorrow, and that if I catch you doing this again you won't see a lit screen until you take computer class in high school. Do I make myself clear?"

Now came Kevin's version of the pout. "Dad wouldn't make me do that."

Two, three, four, five...Dad wouldn't come to any of his soccer games, either, but Kevin managed to conveniently forget that at moments like this.

"I asked you a question," Jenny said with great restraint.

He hung his head, knowing how very much Jenny hated the TV time he put in, and how close he usually skated to losing it anyway. "Yeah."

"Pardon?"

"Yes, ma'am."

Doing her best to keep the smile off her face, Jenny handed over the evidence. Kevin walked to the door as if the guillotine waited on the other side.

Jenny probably would have gone easier on him if she felt better. But today she was making yet another stand at the lawyer's office, trying to get services she couldn't immediately pay for. She figured that if she could get Mr. Whittier to get the Jerk to cough up a little more money, she could pay *him* off as well as her charge accounts. She might even have enough left for school clothes for herself.

She had to admit that the birthday party had been a more generous gesture than she'd imagined. After everyone had taken off she had found several packets of money in her purse from brothers and sisters who knew of her pride, her need to stand on her own feet, but her need nonetheless. The total had reached a little over two hundred dollars, with some gift certificates thrown in from Kate who had insisted that Jenny be prevented from spending all her birthday money on something practical.

So she'd managed to pay off her electric bill, after all, and had treated herself to a baby-sitter, a walk in the mall and the first nice new purse she'd bought in two years. It had been the best present of all.

The problem was, of course, that she was stuffing her purse in preparation to go see Mr. Whittier, and confrontations about the Jerk just gave her indignation.

Suddenly unsure again, Jenny checked her watch. She had time. She didn't have to be in Clayton until three. Still the butterflies collected, unwanted companions, her little reminders of all the times she'd faced humiliation in lawyers' offices over the last two years. She'd rather go to the dentist and have all her teeth pulled. It felt better.

When the doorbell rang, Jenny pounced on it. Anything to take her mind from her impending appointment. Her heels clacking on the foyer parquet, she straightened the skirt she'd donned for the meeting and wondered who wanted her.

Kevin hadn't been outside very long. She hoped Frank Patterson hadn't caught him slipping his overdue mail in his box and was even now standing on the porch holding her recalcitrant son by one ear. She couldn't have had such luck.

It wasn't Frank. It was Nick.

It seemed to Jenny that he swept all the summer heat in before him. She didn't remember it being quite so stifling outside, so that just the touch of the humid air took her breath. She didn't remember enjoying the feel of it so much, either.

"After Sunday, I figured you'd stay as far away from here as you could," Jenny said, suddenly at a loss.

Nick smiled, shoving his hands into his back pockets and making Jenny think of a truant teenager. A sexy truant teenager. He'd worn another old T-shirt today, this one boasting the original Rolling Stones logo, and another pair of impossibly erotic jeans, the glint of the gold belt buckle pulling her eyes in objectionable directions.

"Takes more than a little whiffle ball to scare me away," he assured her.

Jenny looked up to see a wry glint in those whiskied eyes. She saw the sum of the hours they'd shared, the simple pleasures of an afternoon barbecue, and it warmed her even more. Why couldn't she keep her mind on the fact that this man was climbing onto the Jerk Express? All she could seem to concentrate on was the attraction that warmed those incredible eyes, the seductive smell of him, the way he stood with one leg up on the doorsill like he owned the place.

"How's the car running?" he asked, bringing her abruptly back.

"Oh, fine," Jenny said with a distracted nod. "Just fine. Thanks." She was letting the summer in, the air-conditioning out. She was flushed and hot and had to get ready to face the lions, and still she didn't want to move.

Nick was nodding, his eyes never straying from hers, his smile at once suggestive and sweet. Jenny couldn't pull her eyes away, either. His dimples were back, and suddenly her tongue was restless against the roof of her mouth.

"I was on my way back home and I thought I'd check in," he was saying with a quick nod over his shoulder. The white truck waited at the curb. Several teens had gathered, and the activity was drawing attention from across the street.

"Looks like you've brought your business with you," Jenny offered diffidently, hand still on the door, undecided, increasingly uncomfortable.

Nick took a look and grimaced. "Pied Piper, that's me," he acknowledged dryly.

"The teens have really started coming out of the woodwork," she offered, an eye to the back of his head before he turned back to her, her expression torn. She didn't want to ask. Didn't want the answer. And yet he was turning back to her.

"I have the only game in town," he grinned, and her heart sank.

Unable anymore to meet that inviting gaze, she let her own slide away. That was when she noticed the activity behind the tall fence across the street. Mrs. Warner was stirring. It wasn't a good sign. She never ventured from behind that fence without a complaint.

"Biddy at six o'clock," Jenny warned.

Nick swung around again. "My cue to leave. I don't think she wants a Popsicle." Turning back to Jenny, he leveled one of those hesitant smiles on her that threatened her pulse rate. "Before I go, I'll get my payment."

Jenny blinked. "Payment?"

He nodded. "I never got that chili."

Jenny scowled. "You did load up on chicken and potato salad like the famine was coming."

Nick lifted an excepting finger. "But no chili. The offer was for beer and chili."

Out of nowhere, a short, freckled missile shot through the door, sending Nick stumbling to the side.

"Hi, Mom. Hi, Nick." And Kevin was clattering up the stairs before Jenny could greet or recriminate.

Nick looked a little like he'd just been hit by a car. Jenny eased up for a laugh.

"The best way to avoid further punishment is to be unavailable for it," she explained. "A wonderful diversionary tactic."

Nick couldn't help casting a nervous look up the stairs, obviously wondering when the return trip was planned. "Okay. Well, about that chili."

"Mrs. Warner has met the teens and they are hers," Jenny warned, not sure what he was going to say but sure she didn't want to hear it.

Nick turned to see the little knot disperse and Mrs. Warner cast her cold eyes toward his own backside. "Then I'll just make the date. Since you won't have the time to turn me down, that'll be that."

Now it was Jenny's turn to blink. "Date?"

Nick swung back on her, eyes bright, smile broad and certain. "Dinner. I decided that since I didn't get my chili, and I didn't get you a birthday present, I could take care of both problems with one invitation. Friday night, seven o'clock. I'll be here."

"Friday?" she objected, desperately digging for an excuse. "Oh, no, I—"

"Don't have anything to do." He flashed a triumphant smile. "I checked your calendar. The only excuse I'll accept is a note from a doctor stating that both kids have bubonic plague."

Mrs. Warner had reached the sidewalk, her short, plump stride purposeful. Nick cast one last look her way and leveled a parting grin Jenny's way. "Dress up. This is going to be the best damn chili in town."

"But, Nick . . . !"

She didn't have the chance. Before Jenny could object, he was loping back down the lawn, nodding a greeting to the blustering Mrs. Warner and flashing by her before she could get a single warning off.

Suddenly as Jenny watched, the truck screeched off, bells tinkling like a runaway sleigh, Mrs. Warner staring after empty space, her face still screwed up in righteous indignation. The old lady had barely had time to consider turning her wrath in Jenny's direction before the door to the cedar-sided two-story home shut firmly and the bolt could be heard sliding home.

* * *

All in all, Jenny had to admit she had a lot to be grateful
to Nick for. After all, she'd spent the last two hours so ad-
dled by his sudden invitation that she'd made it clear
through her appointment with Mr. Whittier without once
wanting to throw up. Even when he insisted that the court
schedule was just too tight to expect action anytime soon,
that the original financial arrangement was almost impossible to break, that the idea of penalizing the Jerk for po-
tential income was still too alien to conservative St. Louis to
consider. Then he'd patted her hand as if she were a six-year-
old in the big, fatherly lawyer's office and told her that she
could take all the time she needed to pay him off. Especially since he hadn't managed to get her enough money to
live on, much less pay off her lawyer.

But now she found herself firmly wedged into rush-hour
traffic in downtown Clayton, the near hundred-degree heat
and humidity making a joke of her makeup and hairstyle,
the sun glinting brutally off the glass-and-steel buildings, the
other cars and her own hood. The traffic was moving in
spastic fits and starts, and with her windows down in lieu of
air-conditioning, Jenny was the beneficiary of clouds of bus
exhaust.

Now, she felt as if she were going to throw up.

She was going to have to pay off Mr. Whittier. Then
somehow she was going to have to find another lawyer. This
was absurd. She knew better than to think that she had no
recourse against an ex-husband who refused to live up to his
responsibilities just because he was such good friends with
the legal community in town.

The Jerk had his office right here in Clayton, a cool, gray-
and-mauve haven up about fifteen floors. He was probably
looking down at the rusted roof of her car right now and
laughing. Try and beat the system, Jenny, he'd said when it
had all begun. I'll have you for breakfast. And he had. He'd
played the judge like a symphony and walked out with
everything but the furniture.

There just had to be something she could do.

That was when she decided that God really had a warped
sense of humor. Jenny was in the middle of figuring out

ways of breaking through the Fortress Lake when the car died. Again. It happened in the heat. Evidently the manufacturers just weren't used to constant hundred-degree temperatures. It was the only problem she'd had with the car, the heat. Unfortunately, this time she couldn't get it started again.

She tried everything, waiting, pumping the gas, not pumping the gas, cursing, checking fuses, even praying. No one seemed to be home. The rather long line of people behind her wanted to get home, though, and they communicated that with her in no uncertain terms. So when she finally unsnapped her belt and slammed the door open, there was a crowd of people ready and willing to help push her out of the way.

And that was when she looked up.

Somehow, she had managed to kill the car right in front of the Jerk's building. Leaning in to pull out her brand-new purse, Jenny shut the door without enough force to do damage to locks. She pushed her hair out of her eyes and picked her sticky silk blouse away from her stickier torso. Other than stepping into traffic and flagging down a car phone, she had no other option but to step into the building and ask for help.

She'd rather land facedown in a bucket of mud. Unfortunately, she had a baby-sitter who had to get to her job at the movie theater, two small children waiting for dinner and about forty cents in her purse. Letting loose with several choice expletives that caused a few heads to turn out on that shimmering, stifling street, she stalked into the building.

Inside the cool marble-and-glass foyer, the guard lifted his head. His thin white eyebrows quirked. "Can I help you?"

Just the sudden blast of climate control sapped some of Jenny's rage. "My car died. May I use a phone?"

He inclined his head and lifted the receiver. "Who can I get you?"

"A man named Nick Barnett," she snarled. "He's the one who fixed it."

Now the muscles on either side of his mouth twitched. "Number?"

For a moment Jenny just stared at him. She came to a stop, her shoulders sagging as the realization hit her more forcefully than it should have.

Number. She didn't know. She'd invited Nick into her home, shared enough chemistry to satisfy a college course and been caught anticipating a dinner date with him, and she didn't so much as know his phone number.

For some reason, the realization stunned her. She suddenly felt as if she'd lost her footing. How could she feel as if she knew him so well, when she didn't even have enough of his trust to know his phone number? The only thing she knew was that he lived off Skinker somewhere.

And that Detective Richards claimed that Nick Barnett didn't exist.

If it was possible, Jenny felt even worse.

"Never mind," she smiled limply, dropping her purse and running a hand through her hair. "I have brothers."

"Yes, ma'am."

Fifteen minutes later she had to admit defeat. There was no one available to help. Her baby-sitter was getting frantic, and Jenny had run out of options.

"All right," she announced, pulling out her driver's license. "I didn't want to do this, but I'm Mrs. Lake. I need to see Mr. Lake. The Wellerby, Cline, Phillips and Phillips law offices."

The guard's face was a study in composure. "Of course."

The Jerk's secretary didn't have quite as much facial control as she considered the disheveled state of her surprise guest.

"Mrs. Lake?" she echoed, trying to keep the disbelief polite. "Excuse me, but I've met Mrs. Lake."

Her head pounding again and her stomach roiling with the fact that she had to ask the Jerk for help to his face, Jenny took another swipe at her hair and flashed the probable third Mrs. Lake a chilly smile. "The ex-Mrs. Lake."

"Oh," said the carbon copy of Amber Jean, with a smile that betrayed a lot of orthodonture. "Of course. I didn't think you were Amber."

Jenny stiffened. "Bite your tongue."

"Was he expecting you?"

Now Jenny's smile broadened with some relish. "Oh, I don't think so."

He wasn't. Cushioned behind a desk that cost more than her kitchen appliances, and privileged to a view that encompassed every square inch of office space in downtown Clayton, the Jerk took Jenny's surprise appearance badly.

"Your timing stinks, Jenny."

Jenny did her best to maintain control. There was something about that razor-sharp Brooks Brothers suit and salon hairstyle, the manicure and matching tie and handkerchief that grated on her.

"So does the car you left me with," she retorted, dropping into one of the plush leather chairs he kept for paying customers before he could object. "If you'll take a close look out your west window, you'll see it parked at the front of the building. Well, parked isn't really a good description. I guess lying inert would be better."

He couldn't keep his eyes from where he just knew she was getting sweat stains on his good furniture. "Get to the point."

"A sign from God, dear," Jenny smiled. "It seems he wanted me to see you today. He killed my car in front of your building."

"Well, get one of your hundred brothers to come pick you up."

"No one's available."

"Get a cab."

Now she counted for control. "I have forty cents in my purse. Cab drivers resent being asked to drive twelve miles for forty cents." Another sweep through her hair, another deep, controlling breath as she fought amid her discomforts for tact. "I'm sorry. I really don't want to be here, either. I need some help getting home, and I didn't know what else to do."

He began to pace. "Jenny, why don't you ever take care of things?"

Jenny stared. "I've been trying," she retorted, her voice carefully quiet. "Even an automobile has a life expectancy."

He didn't seem to be listening. Still measuring the thick, gray carpet in his Italian loafers, he addressed the view. "All I wanted was a new life. Some peace, some support. And you keep turning up, dragging me back. Dragging me down."

"Please..."

"I suppose you want a new car," he snapped. "Or maybe a chauffeur."

"I need enough money to get home."

"Why should I, dammit?" he demanded, turning on her then, his face a mask of fury. "Why should I forever be giving you more? You got the house, Jenny. You got *my* house. I worked for that house. It was my goal, the symbol of everything I fought for, that first step up. You *know* what it meant to me. And you grabbed it, lock, stock and alarm system." Working himself up to a fine state of indignation, he ended up leaning over her. "Well, what else do you want, dammit? My law license?"

For a minute Jenny could only stare at him. Who said divorce got easier with the passing months? It had been a long time since she'd seen him this worked up. If he wasn't careful, he was going to be cleaning off his shoes. Her stomach couldn't take much more.

There were so many ways she wanted to answer him. She wanted to ask him why the hair-pulling routine when he was in the process of putting in a new sauna. She wanted to tell him that what she wanted was some return on all the years she'd busted her own buns to get him that damn law license. But by now Jenny knew how well this man listened. He'd already turned away, stalking over to watch Clayton empty out on a Wednesday night.

"All I want," she said as deliberately as she could, her hands clenched atop the soft linen roses on her skirt, "is enough money to take care of our children."

He whirled on her. "Don't give me that, now. Those kids were your idea, not mine. I'm tired of you trying to make me feel guilty for something that isn't my fault."

Even after all this time, it hurt. Jenny gave in to a little rancor. "I forgot. You weren't even in the neighborhood when either of them was conceived.'' Emma, who had his blue eyes. Kevin who had his heartbreaking smile.

"I gave in," he retorted. "You know that. You wanted them, I let you because it seemed to make you happy. But nothing really made you happy, did it, Jen? You just wanted more."

"I just wanted more from you," she answered, suddenly exhausted, suddenly tired of the recriminations, the endless, pointless bitterness. She just wanted to go home. Heaving herself to her feet, she picked up her purse.

Behind her, the secretary slipped into the door. "Mr. Wellerby is waiting for that report, Mr. Lake."

He whirled on her. "I know that, dammit! Why don't you explain to him that I couldn't finish it because *you* keep letting every passing pedestrian into the office!"

The secretary looked stricken. Jenny felt guilty, and then hated herself for it. For always feeling guilty when he was the one who was the jerk. She lifted a hand to the girl in silent apology and headed for the door.

"Jenny!"

Sighing, she turned. He was bent over his desk rifling through a drawer. "Here," he barked, pulling something out. "Take it. Just take it and go. I'll get a way home. And this is the last time."

Suddenly Jenny was catching a set of Porsche keys. She stared from them to the Jerk and back again. "I don't want your Porsche."

"No," he retorted, ignoring the secretary who still hovered in the door. "You want my butt. Don't dent the car, and for God's sake don't lose it. I want it back by Monday at the latest."

Which meant that he and Amber Jean had bought yet another car. It was a cinch he wasn't going to let the little woman drive him to work each day to appease his ex. When she followed the secretary out into the anteroom Jenny lifted the keys for her to see. "Just in case he tries to claim it's stolen."

She looked stunned. "He wouldn't."

Jenny grimaced. "He did. Twice."

She was going to enjoy the ride in that damned Porsche if it killed her.

And then she was going to deal with Nick Barnett.

Chapter 8

I'm not going out with him, and that's final."

Detective Richards didn't seem impressed. "It's your neighborhood, lady," he shrugged, draining yet another glass of Barb's tea in a gulp that sent a good proportion sliding down his chin.

Today, he was wearing food on his tie and enough oil in his hair to service the entire U.S. fast-food industry. Jenny wanted to throw him out. But before she let that decision reach her lips, she saw Barb frown.

The blonde didn't say anything. She knew it was Jenny's decision. She also knew what Jenny was risking in continuing with the venture, more than Detective Richards could ever understand or appreciate.

His way of looking at it was that Jenny was getting a free meal and maybe a quick cuddle. Barb had been there when Jenny had reached home from the Jerk's office two days earlier, sobbing with frustration and impotence. She'd cushioned the rage and given Jenny room to defuse before facing her children again. But she had also just heard the detective's update on Nick, and it worried her even more than Jenny's state of mind.

First, his car. Richards had traced it to Marco Manetti Food Industries, a number that seemed serviced by no more than an answering machine. The address given was a blind, a room with a set of connecting phone systems to reroute calls. Manetti, an immigrant who owned everything from food stalls down at Soulard Market to mushroom caves in southern Illinois, was harder to catch than the Pope on a quick trip.

Second, the school. Washington University still couldn't cough up any Nick Barnett.

And third, the point that seemed to satisfy the detective the most. Three days before, two fourteen-year-olds had been busted for possession of cocaine, both with home addresses not more than six blocks away. Both stolidly contesting that they got the stuff through a friend who bought from a third party, somebody they claimed had been working the neighborhood during the summer. So far the friend had been unavailable. The family had taken him to Europe for a week or so, therefore preventing the fingering of the third party.

But who was new to the neighborhood this summer, the detective had asked with a sly smile. And who had access, and mobility and opportunity?

"Listen," Richards said, wiping the tea away just before it sank into a once-white collar. "I'm not gonna wire you or nothin'. All I want is a phone number. An address. See if he'll take you home."

Immediately Jenny stiffened again.

Richards lifted a hand. "Okay, okay. See if he'll tell you more about this apartment of his. Anything. Find out how he affords that fancy school he says he goes to."

Jenny paced the room to work off her temper. She ended up by the front window where she had a great view of the red Porsche sitting in her driveway. It was a great car, shiny and fast and seductive, with seats that caressed you like a lover. And it was only going to be hers for another few days—until her own was repaired or until the Jerk demeaned himself by stopping by and picking it up.

Well, why not enjoy it as much as she could while she had it? She was sure going to resent having the old car back with its hot, worn seats and loose clutch. She'd miss the fun, the adventure. Probably resent never being able to afford something as beautiful as the Porsche as long as she lived.

But for three more days, it was still all hers.

Well, why the hell not?

This time there was a note on the front door. Taped at what must have been Jenny's eye level, it read that she had to run the kids to her sister's because of a baby-sitting crisis and to just go on in.

Nick took a quick look around, unable to believe that Jenny would leave an invitation like that on her front door. Surely she didn't mean that the house was open to anyone who walked through the neighborhood.

She did. When he tested the doorknob, it turned smoothly. Nick took another quick look. The last thing he needed when he had the opportunity of a lifetime was for that old bat across the street to call the cops on him.

He saw Todd's mother—Lauren, he thought her name was—pulling into their drive in a very shiny BMW. Then there was that Hobbs guy, the one with the diseases. He was out with a small, yapping dog that was decorating other people's lawns. Nick had been amazed when he'd seen the guy for the first time. He'd expected a retiree, one of those guys who delighted in regaling audiences with his surgery stories. This guy wasn't more than fifty, a skinny little thing with a melancholy look like he thought he was Lord Byron composing poetry or something. His wife looked just like him, except she had the shrill voice in the family. Probably handy for yelling at inattentive doctors.

Nick shook his head with a wry grin. Ah, humanity. Anybody in the damn neighborhood could be filching those checks. Come to think of it, anybody in the neighborhood could belong to that latest satanic cult they'd unearthed. Cultivated lawns and nice cars didn't necessarily spell civilization.

Well, at least the dragon across the street seemed to be sleeping. Her curtains didn't do so much as flutter when he tested the knob again, so he slipped into the house.

Cool. Comfortable. Nick took a deep, slow breath, savoring that elusive smell of summer and citrus groves, and looked around.

Nobody could accuse Jenny of repressing her kids for the sake of a clean house. Evidence of that lay scattered everywhere, from books to planes to sticks wrapped together in a form familiar to anyone with male hormones. Nick grinned. She probably didn't let the kid have guns, so Kevin just invented them. Nick remembered when he'd made his first tommy gun out of Legos. Now, he supposed kids made Uzis and lasers, but basics just didn't change.

Walking through, he picked up a scarf that lay draped over the oak banister. Silk, smooth, a dusty rose color that he'd seen on her the other day. It smelled like her. He thought it probably felt like her, too. Walking on into the house, Nick ran a thumb over the silk and anticipated.

Restaurants. It had been what had been missing on those charge slips. In reviewing Jenny's file, Nick had run a finger down every charge he could find, and not one of the listings had been for food. She'd charged gas and house supplies and school clothes for the kids. There had been a charge from a doctor's office and the vet. Nowhere on the four-month listing did Nick see anything that hinted that Jenny Lake took herself out for an evening away. From what showed up on her file, she worked, took care of her children and juggled finances.

The invitation to dinner had been a means to soften her up and to gather more of the information that McGrady seemed so sure would lead back to Jenny. In reality, Nick could have done it any number of ways, but it had just seemed too unfair that when Jenny's husband was on a first-name basis with the maître d' at Anthony's Jenny couldn't dress up for anything more impressive than McDonald's.

Besides, he wanted to spend an evening with her away from the prying eyes of neighbors.

Walking through to the living room, Nick caught his reflection in the hall mirror. He hoped he looked more appropriate for his mission tonight. After all, he'd pulled out his best yuppie camouflage, a gray-linen suit with pleated pants, white shirt and bright aqua tie with gold-bar tie clasp.

His hair was still too long for the image, but he'd tried to brush it back out of the way so that it wasn't so noticeable. Still a little too fast for this neighborhood, but closer than the Grateful Dead T-shirts, he was sure.

He just wished he could enjoy the evening without having to let work interfere. He wished he could sit in the quiet comfort of her house instead of taking advantage of the chance to search. Taking a moment to size up the sleek lines of the bright blue Danish modern furniture in the living room, he chose the window desk as his next target.

Nick was rifling through the bills when he saw the lights swing into the driveway. Scooting just out of visual range, he quickly reassembled the pile. That was when he saw the cards. With an eye to Jenny's approach, he flipped a few open.

Birthday cards. Obviously left after the party the other day. *We won't take it back, so have fun. Buy something for yourself with it. You can't spend gift certificates on the mortgage.*

Nick couldn't help but smile. So, the two-hundred-dollar deposit was explained. Her family had stuffed money into her hands for her birthday, and Jenny had let them. He could just imagine how hard it was for her to do that, but he also knew how much she'd needed to. His bet was that most of it had gone to the gas company, anyhow.

By the time Jenny opened the door, Nick was comfortably seated on the couch flipping through *Sesame Street* magazine.

"I'm sorry I'm late again," she called on the way in. The door slammed shut behind her and her shoes clacked against the parquet flooring.

Nick looked up with a smile. When he caught sight of Jenny, he froze.

Jenny came to her own shuddering stop.

Nick's magazine slid to his lap, forgotten. He couldn't take his eyes from where Jenny stood staring at him. She was in a dress, soft wrinkled silk the same color as his tie. It still floated in the aftermath of her rush, skimming her hips and swirling around her legs. It was a simple dress, a shirt-waist with an ecru belt and gold buckle pulling the billowy

silk in at the waist, so that the dress hinted rather than out-
lined, flirted rather than seduced. On Jenny, it took Nick's
breath away.

He got to his feet, Jenny's eyes following him up. Her
expression must have matched his, and it made him smile.

Holding his arms out in diffident display, he shrugged. "I
figured that I'd show you the other side of Nick Barnett."

Jenny's smile was hesitant, as if caught between attraction and flight. "I'm not sure any of the neighbors would
recognize you." Her voice was as breathy as her smile.

"You look . . . wonderful," he finally admitted, wishing
suddenly that he hadn't suggested this. Just the sight of her,
eyes wide and glistening, hair tumbled around her face like
a wind-ragged cloud, hand caught at her throat, sent his
objectivity toppling.

He wasn't going to get off this case intact. He finally,
certainly, inevitably admitted that he would do his best to
take this woman up to that soft, tumbled bed of hers and
make love to her.

And what was worse, he saw the realization flare in her
eyes, as well.

"It's Kate's dress," she demurred, hand straying over
material Nick desperately wanted to test. "She let me bor-
row it since she can't wear it for a while longer."

Nick had to think Jenny had more practice averting
temptation than he—or maybe she'd had more reason to.
The heat had no more than flashed in that emerald green
before she offered him a quirky smile and motioned to the
two objects he'd left behind him on the couch.

"Uh, is there something I should know about what you
play with while other adults aren't around?"

Startled, Nick looked around. He'd forgotten. Lying
alongside the magazine he'd just dropped was the silk scarf
from the banister. The silk that had run through his fingers
much as her dress would . . . as her skin would, with a soft
sibilance that beckoned, tempted, seduced.

Pulling away from the image with a start, Nick turned
back to her with a grin he hoped like hell looked sheepish.
"I was hoping I could find something to talk to Emma
about."

Jenny arched an eyebrow. "The magazine or the scarf?"

Nick shrugged, finally admitting the truth. "I could smell your scent on the scarf."

Jenny didn't seem to know what to do with that information. Ducking her head a little, she looked around as if seeking escape. "How about a drink before we go?" she asked, shoving her hands into her skirt pockets. "It'll give me a chance to settle down after the police."

Immediately Nick stiffened. "The police?"

With a shrug that was equal parts consternation and allowance, Jenny led the way into the kitchen, sure Nick would follow. "The reason I'm late was that I got stopped again. I guess the police have some fascination with red Porsches. I've been driving this one for two days and have been stopped three times. I haven't had a ticket, just warnings. For being...red."

Nick almost gulped. "A red Porsche?"

Flashing a wry grin over her shoulder, Jenny flipped on lights and opened the refrigerator. "The Jerk's. The compact died right in front of his office building Wednesday when I went to see my lawyer. I ended up having to drive his car home. Beer? Bourbon?"

"Beer. The compact? The compact died?"

Jenny handed him a beer. "You're forgiven. It seems that the fuel injectors were just the tip of the iceberg. Once those were fixed and the pressure increased all along the line, a lot of other little things went wrong. The car dealership was thrilled to see me."

Nick was feeling progressively worse. He had to get hold of Baker and call off the dogs. "How long are you going to be driving the...uh, Porsche?"

Taking a sip of a wine cooler, Jenny sighed. "Only until Monday. That's when the Jerk comes to pick it up." With a feral smile, she tilted her head a little. "I think he doesn't want us seen in his neighborhood."

Nick scowled. "His loss."

Jenny grinned back. She was leaning against the sink, bottle in hand. "That's what I keep saying. But then, I don't think I'd like his neighborhood, either. I don't think anybody up there'd recognize reality if it ran over them with a truck."

Taking a pull of his own beer, Nick settled a hip on the kitchen table, perfectly at ease with the unique seating arrangement. "You know, maybe I'd like to be here Monday when he shows up. I'd kind of like to see what kind of a man could give this up." He swept the bottle in an arc, encompassing the house in his statement. "This is just the kind of house I'd like when I get out. I think I could really bust my butt for it."

Nick didn't really think of just what in the house provoked the sentiment. Not the architecture. He wasn't the kind of person to notice architecture. He couldn't tell Doric from derrick.

It wasn't the neighborhood. He wasn't heavily into suburbia, especially after working the yuppie detail all these years. He just knew that this house felt like home. There was a peace that filled it that had nothing to do with noise, a comfort that couldn't be equated with furniture.

Looking around in the soft shadows, Nick nodded. He didn't examine his statement more than the feeling of satisfaction it gave him. When he turned for Jenny's reaction, though, he was brought up short. She was staring at him as if he'd slapped her.

"Jenny?" Nick pushed away from the table.

Before he could reach her, Jenny visibly shook herself. "The Jerk didn't give it up," she said with a faint smile that spoke volumes. "He fought tooth-and-nail for it."

Nick didn't know how to answer. He had the feeling that the two of them were referring to two completely different things. He just didn't know how to explain what he meant. He didn't know if he could explain even if he knew how. That was the kind of thing Nick didn't share.

Giving up, he finished off his beer and set it down. "Does Italian sound okay to you?" he asked, facing Jenny but avoiding her. "I made reservations, but I can change them."

Her eyes more troubled than she knew, Jenny nodded. "Italian's fine."

Italian could mean anything in St. Louis. For a city founded by the French and Spanish, it had a preponderance of restaurants specializing in Italian cuisine. Nick had picked Ruggeri's, a small, neighborhood restaurant located in the south end of the Hill, the mecca of Italian culture in town. Tucked into a basement, you entered the place by going down stone steps and passing beneath exposed brick and pipe.

Ruggeri's wasn't the fanciest place in town, by far. It wasn't the largest or smallest. But it packed a lot of flavor into its claustrophobic little rooms. Books and antiques lined the bare brick walls. Formica tables scraped uneven floors, patrons ducked low ceilings and the phone was wedged in between two supporting beams.

The Jerk would have never been caught dead in a place like this. The maître d' didn't ignore patrons and the waiters didn't sneer. The minute Jenny stepped through the door, she decided she liked Nick's taste a lot better.

Just that thought resurrected her anxiety.

"When do they bring out the chili?" she asked with a grin that belied the clammy fear that had suddenly bloomed.

Nick refused to rise to the bait. "One excuse is as good as another."

They were shown to a little table back in the Pipe Room. Nick held Jenny's chair and then slid in across from her. Jenny saw him unbutton his suit to get comfortable and found the panic taking over. The room was too close, Nick too handsome, the situation too suddenly threatening. Scraping her chair back as the waitress showed up, Jenny shot to her feet.

"Excuse me," she stammered, hoping Nick didn't hear the sudden crescendo of her heart. "I'll...uh, be back."

"That way," the waitress offered with a vague wave of the hand.

Jenny interpreted correctly.

It was so stupid. There wasn't a reason in the world she should be having an anxiety reaction. Just because this was the first time she'd been out on a date in about ten years. Just because she hadn't even had the luxury to go out to a restaurant since the divorce. She had no business having sweaty hands and a racing pulse. She shouldn't be trembling like a virgin on the verge of a swoon. Even so, when she looked in the little bathroom mirror what she saw was a woman a little too wild-eyed for her taste.

And she still had to go back out there and get Nick to cough up an identity.

What was it that had her so excited, so upset? Was it the duplicity or the adventure? Was she more afraid of him or more attracted to him? She certainly hadn't expected him to look quite so good in a suit. She guessed she hadn't expected more than the turtleneck he'd worn before. In that tailored gray linen, he looked like a powerbroker. It fit him better than the T-shirts and jeans, somehow. She could so easily see him treading the boardrooms of multinational corporations that the ice cream truck seemed the fantasy.

That made her realize her first impression had been right. He didn't belong on that ice cream truck. He wasn't the same kind of person as Marco Manetti. He had too much grace, too much power leashed behind those tawny eyes and quirked grin. Nick Barnett was a puzzle wrapped in an enigma, and if Detective Richards was right that all had to do with high-level drugs. If Jenny was right, it had to do with law school.

She didn't see that it was much of a choice. On the other hand, it had been a long time since she'd been alone to dinner with a handsome man. Taking a few deep breaths to settle the terror that still tasted too much like exhilaration, Jenny washed the stale perspiration from her hands and set her shoulders before opening the door again.

"Everything all right?" Nick asked, sincere concern in the honeyed depths of his eyes.

He stood to help Jenny back in her chair, and she had to keep from looking around for the gag. It had been a long time since a man had done that for her.

"Everything's fine," she admitted, looking down at the table and then forcing herself to have the courage to face him. "I just had a sudden case of cold feet. It's been a ... well, a long time since I've been out."

"On a date?" Nick finished for her, that damn smile tugging at his mouth.

Jenny wanted to sigh. She wanted to taste that smile. "On a date." She grimaced with the admission. "Sounds archaic, doesn't it?"

"Not at all. It sounds about right." Leaning closer, he took hold of her hand. "Is there anything I can do to make it easier for you? Sign a prenuptial agreement or something?"

Jenny fought the sudden suffocation just the touch of his hand incited. His fingers were so warm, so solid. So gentle as they wrapped unconsciously around hers. This was wrong. She had to keep her head. And she damn well couldn't do it when her heartbeat skipped every time she came in contact with the man.

"Give me your phone number," she blurted out.

Nick stiffened. Jenny faltered. Her heart slipped again, knocking against her ribs at the sudden caution in Nick's eyes. She'd had to ask the question. She just didn't want to have it answered.

"My phone number?" he asked, an eyebrow cocked.

She dipped her head, filling her eyes with the sight of empty table and chianti bottle. "I was going to call you when the car died. I mean, you fixed it . . . you know. But I didn't know your number. You'd never told me. And, well, then when I got home I checked." Jenny lifted her eyes and skirted his, her chest still too filled with dread to allow a good breath, her eyes wide. "Your number isn't in the phone book."

His nod was a slow one. His hand loosened around hers. "I know."

Finally drawing enough breath, Jenny tilted her head. "What is it about me you don't trust, Nick?"

"Lasagna?"

Both of them started. The waitress, a middle-aged motherly type was poised with pad and pencil, doing her best to intimate that this was the optimum time for them to order. Jenny shot Nick a look and pulled her hand away.

"Five-five-five, two-two-eight-nine," Nick said, his eyes still on Jenny.

She looked up in time to see the smile, that soft, little-boy look of satisfaction.

"Thanks, honey." The waitress grinned dryly. "I'll call tomorrow after work. But right now I'd prefer an order."

"Do you have chili?" Jenny asked, smiling back at Nick.

The waitress wasn't exactly sure how to take that. "Not even if he gave me his address and measurements," she assured them.

"I keep feeling like I've forgotten something," Jenny admitted later. They had long since finished dinner, and had progressed to drinks down in the Grand Hall at Union Station.

Seated in the wing chair alongside her, Nick balanced the balloon glass of cognac against his crossed leg and smiled. "You're just not used to going anywhere by yourself."

Jenny chuckled. "I'm not used to being wined and dined. This is wonderful, Nick. Thanks."

Across the floor, a tuxedoed man was playing Gershwin on the baby grand. Glasses clinked and conversation floated through the barrel-ceilinged art-nouveau room. Wrapped in the green wing chair and pleasantly warmed by alcohol and companionship, Jenny couldn't remember another evening as pleasant, or another date so solicitous and fun.

Nick had drawn her life from her, laughing at her family anecdotes and companionably discussing everything from literature to sports. It wasn't lost on Jenny that she hadn't learned anything about his past, or that his opinions didn't always mesh with the image he portrayed. Ambitious types didn't usually quote the romantic poets. Ponytailed rock fans didn't rattle off baseball stats like an announcer. Somehow she had to find out more than his phone number and taste in clothes. Somehow, the enticing pieces of Nick Barnett had to fit into a whole.

"Your entire neighborhood's going to be at your door when they find out you've gone out with the ice cream man," Nick warned with a wry smile.

More than you know, Jenny thought with a stifled scowl. "It would almost be worth it to stay out until dawn just to see Mrs. Warner lose sleep."

Nick's answering smile held more than conspiracy. "It could be arranged."

When Jenny met his gaze, she felt those whiskey eyes consume her. They dipped into her, breaching the chill around her heart, stealing into the depths of her resistance and sapping it. For long moments Jenny could do no more than face him, emerald eyes wide and wary, fingers wrapped tightly enough around her own wine glass to soak in the chill. Suddenly she couldn't remember what she'd originally come here for.

"Not unless you're talking about all-night bowling or breakfast at Uncle Bill's Pancake House," she countered, her voice unaccountably hushed.

Nick lifted an eyebrow in an elegant shrug, his own thumb stroking the smooth glass. "I'm just as happy sitting here talking."

No, you're not, she thought with sudden insight. There's too much heat in those eyes, too much tension in the muscles along your jaw. It should have stunned her, frightened her to know that Nick wanted her. Jenny tried her hardest to make it so.

In the end, all she could feel was the first stirring of anticipation, curling around in her belly like smoke, slipping out into her veins and infecting her limbs.

She wanted him, too. She wanted to find that hot, empty apartment of his and see how the sweat tasted on him as he took her on a hardwood floor. She wanted to watch those eyes take light and hear him gasp her name. She wanted to know that she really infected his dreams the way he did hers.

Desperate to push the mutinous yearning aside, Jenny turned her gaze to the pale gold liquid in her glass and the arsenal of questions she'd never gotten around to asking. Anything, anything but what she was contemplating, because it was the surest route to disaster.

Maybe it was a good thing she hadn't been away from the children in a long time. At least they kept her grounded. It became too easy somehow to ignore consequence and responsibility seated in an echoing room with whispering waitresses and standards drifting from the piano.

"You never mentioned, Nick," she said, trying to keep her voice even and unconcerned. "Are you originally from St. Louis?"

It took a moment for him to answer. When Jenny looked up, it was to find a wry smile on his face.

"I'm proud of you," he admitted. "It took you more than three hours to ask the obligatory question."

Suddenly he had Jenny grinning, too. "Yeah, I know. And where did you go to school?"

St. Louis was often called the biggest small town in the world. Everybody knew everybody, or somebody who knew somebody else. Social life often revolved around the questions "Where did you grow up?" and "Where did you go to school?" because just those two answers clearly defined life-styles and social circles. Jenny's mother had liked the Jerk's answer to school, not so much to neighborhood. The Jerk's family, on the other hand, hadn't liked either of the answers Jenny had given.

"Sorry to disappoint you," he offered with a salute from the cognac before he took another drink. "But I've lived all over the state. I'm originally from Springfield."

"Is your family still there?"

Nick still watched his liqueur, swirling it gently in the palm of his hand. Jenny thought she saw his eyes darken, his mouth tighten. For some reason it made her go still, as if bracing for pain.

"No family," he admitted, lifting his eyes to meet hers with surprising nonchalance. "When people call me a bastard, they mean it."

Something caught in Jenny's chest, a sharp regret that seemed to echo the faint tightness in his voice. She recognized more from his offhand words than he knew, heard the emptiness behind them, the defenses built over the years. She wondered what he had felt when he'd met the mad affection of her family.

She knew better than to ask. Instead, she nodded. "Where did you meet up with Marco?"

Nick smiled, the expression in his eyes lightening noticeably. "The Mad Manetti?" he asked. "He arrested me. Four times."

Jenny faltered. "Arrested you? He was a policeman?"

"Policeman and ex-Marine D.I. The perfect combination to scare the snot out of an obnoxious fourteen-year-old on his way to grand theft auto. It was the stuff of old B movies."

A policeman. How could Detective Richards have missed that particular bit of information? Jenny couldn't understand it. Suddenly, beyond anything else she felt about Nick or the dubious mission she carried out, she felt anger. Why should she be sitting here picking Nick's brain when the purported pros couldn't track down the basics?

"But you said he didn't speak English," she objected.

Nick's smile was lazy. "A barefaced lie to get inside your house. I wanted to get to talk to you."

Jenny wanted to hear that. But at the same time she didn't. Finding her courage seeping away, she went back to studying her wine. "So," she said, "Marco was your incentive to join the Corps."

His expression betraying his well-laid caution, as if still expecting attack, Nick gave a small nod of concession. "When I was seventeen. We'd run out of foster homes, and the courts had run out of patience."

Jenny nodded back. "Nam?"

He shrugged. "If you can make it there, you can make it anywhere."

"How did you get from the Marines to law school?"

When Nick smiled now, there was serious purpose in his eyes. "Career-planning."

Suddenly Jenny thought he wanted to say more. There was a softening in his eyes, almost a yearning as he looked at her, as if wishing he could share with her. She held her breath, wanting him to. Knowing she shouldn't.

In the end, without moving, without changing the inflection in his voice, he backed down. "I had a lot of time to plan my future. A lot of reason to succeed. I decided that my best route out would be law school. I still think so."

"And nothing's going to get in your way?"

Nick shook his head, never taking his eyes from Jenny's, making sure she saw the purpose there, the drive that had brought him from the Protestant Boys' Home to Washington University Law School. "Nothing," he said. "Living well is the best revenge, they say. Well, I'm due some."

Jenny did her best to summon up some anger. At least a feeling of betrayal. Here she sat with the first man she'd let take her out in two years, and he was telling her that he'd cloned himself from the Jerk. She should have hated him, if not herself for letting her want to trust him so much.

Somehow, she couldn't do it. All she could feel at his words was regret, a bittersweet frustration that all that life locked behind those whiskey-brown eyes would stay there. He wouldn't sleep on anyone else's couch again, because even as Jenny watched he pulled back a little from her. And—she thought with more than a little remorse as she drained the wine in her glass—he would continue to do so, even as he courted her.

He would sacrifice for goals rather than people. Status rather than love. And Jenny would spend her summers listening for the bell of an ice cream truck and longing for the sight of a vulnerable, little-boy smile.

She held his hand as they strolled back down the near-empty halls of the train station, their footsteps echoing up beyond the balcony and its closed shops, their voices hushed amid the fountains and foliage. She tasted that anticipation once again when he wrapped his arm around her shoulders, the unaccustomed hunger snaking through her like a hot current. She sat alongside him on the way home watching the heat lightning flicker against a dirty night sky and ached for more time alone, more time away from the relentless morning and the return of reality. And all the while, the regret built.

When they reached Jenny's house, she found herself wandering over to where the Porsche sat, the hot red an exclamation in the shadows and silence of the late-night street. She ran a hand over its sleek contours and thought of its smooth grace and power, the escape it promised and couldn't ever really deliver. She thought of how very much she wished it were hers.

"Jenny," Nick said, his voice bemused as he walked up alongside her. "What's wrong?"

Jenny couldn't quite face him. There were tears in her eyes, and she didn't want him to get the right idea. "Oh, nothing. I just hate to give it up."

"Maybe someday you'll have one of your own."

Finally braving a look, Jenny caught a glint in the depths of his eyes that made her wonder if he knew what she'd been thinking. "Oh, I don't think so," she smiled, the yearning stifling her. "I don't seem to have that kind of luck."

She turned so quickly that Nick didn't have the chance to answer. He'd seen it. Recognized the longing in her eyes as twin to his own. His conscience clamored to tell her, to set things right before it was too late—even as his common sense told him it had been too late right from the start.

He followed her across the walk to her porch and waited as she selected keys, her fragrance drifting like a soft vapor on the late-night breeze, the tang of orange sharpening the soft bouquet of summer foliage until it swam through him. He could smell it in her hair as it trembled on the night, could almost taste it on her skin. Frustration battled with sense. Hunger clamored more loudly than duty. Nick saw her walk into her house and followed her in.

Stepping onto parquet flooring, Jenny turned.

"Nick, I—"

"Jenny, I—"

Neither managed to finish. Suddenly the door was closed and Nick had Jenny in his arms. He hadn't meant to. He'd intended to explain, to make her understand why it was he had to gain some distance from her before they were both hurt. But when she'd turned her face to him, those forest-soft eyes liquid with pain and separation, her shoulders rigid with torment, he'd surrendered.

He never gave her a chance. Once he felt that silk beneath his fingers, Nick knew he couldn't stop without the taste of her. He bent to that upturned face, dipped into the cloud of orange blossoms. Her lips were open. He could feel the soft brush of her surprise, sensed the shudder of anticipation in her. Tangling his hands in the ebony silk of her hair, he finally took the kiss that had hovered between them since the moment they'd met.

Sweet. She tasted like nectar. She stirred beneath him as he skimmed and nipped at her tender lips. Nick felt her hesitate, soften, and just as surely come to life. Her arms came up to him; her small hands wound around the back of his neck. She straightened in his arms, folding into him, taking her own taste and igniting the fire that had smoldered for so long.

Nick pulled her to him, both hands in her hair, her head back before his need, her murmurs fueling his desire. She opened her mouth to him, invited him, and the need exploded in him.

He wanted her. He wanted to fill his hands with her and make her writhe with hunger. Her body was so soft, so strong and vibrant. He could hear her humming, deep in her throat as she curled her own fingers in his hair. She met his kisses and took his bottom lip between her teeth. Nick brought his hand down along her throat and she stretched for him, arching into his touch and lifting up on her toes to better fit into his hold.

He was melting. He was burning. He couldn't satisfy himself with the honeyed taste of her, the silken feel of her. Her breasts pressed against his chest, her nipples button-hard and tantalizing. Her thighs strained against his, hot and soft, promising, enticing. He ached. He groaned. He was seconds away from lifting her into his arms and carrying her upstairs.

He never knew how he heard it.

Suddenly both of them stiffened as if they'd been shot. The doorbell rang again.

"The kids..." Jenny gasped, pulling away, reaching for the doorknob before thinking.

There on the other side stood the blond cheerleader from next door and her male clone. Smiling.

For a moment there was stunned silence. The two of them managed to keep their smiles, but only barely as they gazed in on the rumpled evidence of interrupted passion.

"Oh, good," Barb finally said. "Your friend is still here. Maybe he'd like to join us in our coffee-tasting."

Nick stared. The man smiled diffidently and held up a full coffeepot.

"Our . . . coffee-tasting," Jenny echoed, her face a study in control.

"Of course, silly," Barb retorted with a bright smile, opening the door for her husband. "Isn't it one o'clock? We always do this on Friday nights."

Her husband followed her in. Nick still stared. Jenny still struggled to maintain a straight face. He could read the entire situation just in the fact that she couldn't manage to look at anybody.

"Of course," she damn near giggled with a hand to the forehead in a gesture of remembering. "Our coffee-tasting." Then, turning to Nick, she grinned much too brightly. "We do this every Friday."

"At one," Barb emphasized.

Jenny looked from Barb to Nick. "At one," she echoed.

Well, she did say that her neighbors took care of her. Finding no alternative other than hauling all three into the station for criminal improvisations, Nick shrugged. "Sure. Why not?"

And so it was that fifteen minutes later he found himself not in Jenny's bed, but in her kitchen trying to keep a straight face when he was introduced to Bill and Barby Bailey.

Sometimes there was just no justice.

Chapter 9

The next time Nick kissed Jenny goodbye, it was much less disturbing. It was also witnessed by Barby and Bill, who were doing their best to camouflage the fact that they weren't used to sitting up talking until three in the morning.

Jenny should have been relieved. Her friends had, after all, come to her rescue—more than they knew. But somehow the brush of Nick's lips against hers as he swung his jacket over his shoulder and headed out was far too tantalizing. It resurrected the fear, the anticipation, the shaky challenge of attraction and responsibility.

Watching him walk into the shadows, all Jenny could think was that she wished Barb and Bill had never interfered.

Distance, she thought the next morning as she plodded along the track at the YMCA paying for her sins. That's what I need right now. A little objectivity about the fact that he pulled and pushed at the same time. About his penchant for echoing some of the Jerk's finer sentiments while melting her like a hot chocolate bar with the quick uncertainty in his eyes.

At least she wouldn't be seeing him until Monday. Maybe she could regain a little of her balance in that time. Maybe she could start sleeping again.

She should have known better.

It was all Barb's fault. It had been Barb's idea to sign the kids up for swimming lessons, and Barb who had suggested utilizing the free time and air-conditioned building to exercise. Barb craved aerobics. Jenny had settled for earphones and walking on the elevated track. So while Jenny's kids went to class, Barb walked. When Buffy went from there to gymnastics, Barb bounced up and down with twenty other women who loved to sweat.

And it was Barb who almost caused the accident.

She'd been walking ahead of Jenny—*everyone* had been walking ahead of Jenny—when she happened to take a look down at the basketball game that was forming in the gym below. Occupied by the Eagles music in her earphones, Jenny wasn't paying attention. Within three steps, Barb came to a dead stop and people threatened to pile up over her like a freeway accident.

Jenny caught hold of the rail and glared at her friend.

"Oh, my God," Barb was mouthing, carefully made-up eyes wide.

Jenny pulled off her earphones to better chastise her friend. Her first reaction was that Barb had seen someone on the gym floor with a better Lycra outfit than hers. Her second was that it was much more serious than that. Barb was speechless, and it took a lot to put her in that condition. So of course Jenny made the mistake of following her gaze.

"O-o-o-h, my God."

It wasn't Lycra, at all. It wasn't even women. It was Nick. Somehow he'd walked right out of her anxieties and onto the court below in a shirts-and-skins basketball game. On the skins team, of course.

This wasn't fair. She shouldn't have to face this so soon after last night, when the taste of Nick's kiss still lingered, when the feel of his arms had invaded her sleep and set her to tossing and muttering with frustration. She had to regain her footing, restore her good sense. And she just couldn't do that with Nick sweating six feet below.

Jenny had always known he'd had a good physique. Fact only served to amplify that impression. He had a lean line to him, with strong shoulders and those third-baseman arms. His chest glistened, the soft brown hair that fanned out curling with the sweat. Clad only in dark blue gym shorts, his tush was everything she'd imagined.

But it wasn't just the way he looked. It was the way he moved, with a ferocious grace that ate up the floor and intimidated his opponents. When Nick went up for a basket, the ball whistled on its way down. When he attacked he did so with gusto, and when he defended he smiled like a wolf. Jenny saw an appetite there, a keen competitive drive that should have set off every warning bell in her common sense. All she could think to do was sweat right along with him.

"He kissed you last night," Barb said, deaf to the impatient urgings of other joggers as they parted around the two like a river around a logjam. "Didn't he?"

Jenny could only nod, the remembered heat intense enough to stain her cheeks.

Never bothering to look away from the game, Barb just nodded back. "I thought so."

In silent assent, Jenny and Barb began walking again. Barb never said another word. Barb wouldn't. But the two of them lost a lot of the aerobic benefit of their exercise when they couldn't keep their eyes from the game.

"I didn't know you came out here."

Jenny was drinking from the water fountain. She straightened and thought to scowl. There was such a wry humor in his eyes. For the first time, she really didn't believe him.

"The kids are in swimming lessons," she explained, automatically pushing damp ringlets out of her yes. She only wished she could do something about the sweat-stained shorts and Mickey Mouse T-shirt. "So I get in my weekly allotment of torture."

Taking her place at the fountain, Nick doused his neck with water and took long, thirsty gulps. Jenny couldn't take her eyes from his throat, from the gleaming line of his arm. She hadn't been able to breathe properly since she'd spotted him down on that court, and she had a feeling it wasn't about to get better soon. He even smelled great, like soap and exercise.

It was just too soon after last night. Then again, next year would have been too soon after last night.

"You play basketball much?" she found herself asking, unconsciously wiping her hands on her shorts.

Nick straightened alongside her and toweled the water from his head and neck with his discarded shirt. Somehow the action only further threatened Jenny's respiration rate.

"Not as much as I'd like to," he admitted. "It tends to defuse a lot of my aggressive tendencies."

"You?" Jenny echoed in mock surprise. "Aggressive? I can't imagine. Although I guess the arm-wrestling challenge that you threw off to Bill last night should have been a clue."

Nick chuckled, an easy sound, and Jenny ached. "Guys like that make me nervous. They're too...perfect."

Jenny nodded, only a vestige of guilt casting her eyes briefly upward to where Barb still walked. "Imagine living next to them. I feel like the 'before' in a before-and-after poster."

She began heading down toward the window where she could watch the rest of the swimming lesson. It only seemed natural that Nick follow. Jen cast a fleeting thought to Barb, still up there pounding down her tennies. Barb would never miss her. The endorphins were due to kick in any minute now. From that point, Barb could go on for hours.

"Tell me they instigated that little rescue raid last night on their own initiative," Nick asked.

Now it was Jenny's turn to chuckle as she pulled her attention back to the present. "The imported coffee had to be a dead giveaway. I can't afford it, much less suggest it."

Nick nodded. "I thought so. How come Mrs. Warner and old Miss Lucy didn't show up, too?"

Jenny couldn't help the self-satisfied smile. "They called this morning."

Nick just groaned.

The front room was crowded when they arrived. A cluster of parents gestured through the window and another was scattered on the couches waiting out lessons. Jenny squeezed her way in to get a look at the kids and was surprised when Nick followed right behind.

Of course, she wished he hadn't made such a concerted effort. He was still hot from the game, and the humid closeness seemed to surround her. She could hear him panting a little just beyond her ear and smelled the tang of sweat. Her tongue strayed again, licking her lips when that wasn't what she wanted to taste.

"She sure has a mind of her own."

Jenny started at the wry humor in Nick's voice. Deliberately, she turned her attention to the pool, where Emma was facing off with her teacher. Standing on the tile, shivering as if she had the ague, the little girl had her hands on her hips and was shaking her head emphatically. Not hysterically. There were no tears. She just wasn't going to do what the teacher wanted.

"I've wasted more money on these damn things," Jenny mourned. "Emma just can't come to grips with the fact that someone else knows something she doesn't. About anything."

"I just thought she didn't want to go in."

Jenny chuckled. "Oh, no. She thinks the teacher's doing it wrong."

"What are you going to do when she goes to school?"

"Suffer."

They watched a moment longer, oblivious to the fact that more than one well-clad young woman was casting second and third glances Nick's way. He'd draped his shirt around his neck and bent over to get a better view of the pool.

"You followed me this morning," Jenny accused without turning away from watching Kevin belly flop from the low board. There was a noticeable dearth of heat in her voice.

Nick looked down at her. "How did you know?"

Jenny grinned, trying her best to contain the sudden flight of butterflies in her chest. "Even the most fanatic exercise addict in the place doesn't travel fifteen miles to play basketball. Although I think a lot of them wait in the lot for the building to open in the morning."

"You're not one of the chosen?" Nick asked with a dry grin.

Jenny proffered a scowl and the tail of her T-shirt for closer inspection. "I'm wearing the wrong outfit. I'm also wearing the wrong figure. Most of those women won't even let me in the same exercise class with them. I guess they think full-figure is catching."

She wasn't in the least oblivious to the assessing look Nick passed over her. If his eyes had been radioactive, she would have glowed in the dark. Jenny wasn't sure she didn't anyway.

"Man doesn't want to gnaw on a chicken bone," he drawled. "Likes a little meat."

Jenny gave him another scowl as she gestured over to the sleek line of a jogger. "You mean you don't buy *Sports Illustrated* just to see somebody like that in a swimsuit?"

Nick turned to look. "She looks like Gumby in that outfit."

Casting one last envious look at the woman who probably didn't know what the word cellulite meant, Jenny sighed. "She's probably frigid, anyway."

Nick's surprised laugh turned a few more heads. "How 'bout if I take you away from all this?"

Now Jenny blinked, not sure what he had in mind. Not sure what she had in mind if he asked. "Where?"

"Fried chicken and coleslaw. Eleven herbs and spices. Blankets, grass, trees."

"A picnic?" she demanded. "It's almost a hundred degrees out there."

Nick proffered lifted arms. "I'm dressed for it. How 'bout you?"

Jenny tilted her head to the side, hearing fast car engines and gulls. "You're crazy."

When Nick nodded this time, Jenny wanted to know why he carried so much more than agreement in his expression. "You got that right, lady. Comin' along?"

"I'm crazy enough on my own, thanks." She almost found herself running to Barb, suddenly desperate for an excuse, for some support, for some sanity. Surely Barb in her pink exercise leotard and matching bandanna wouldn't let Jenny walk off to the park with a madman. Surely she'd remind Jenny why she shouldn't keep wanting more from Nick.

But Jenny knew even as she tried to excuse herself from Nick's impulse that she wasn't going to ask Barb for help.

Okay, so he'd given up trying to glean information out of her. So he'd thrown his objectivity right out the window. Sprawled out on the handmade quilt on the grass watching Jenny share a fuzzy caterpillar with her kids, Nick couldn't really pull together any regret.

McGrady wouldn't give a damn about gut reactions. McGrady's world was built on paper. But Nick's gut had rarely gotten him into trouble, and his gut just didn't come up with Jenny as a suspect.

Of course, McGrady would point out that Nick had never gotten involved with a suspect before. McGrady was like that. Nick didn't care. He had finally stepped across that tenuous line that divided suspicion from belief. Baker would have to show him a picture of Jenny at a bank cashing those checks for him to believe she was involved.

But in the meantime, it didn't hurt to keep tabs on her.

"You never told me," Jenny said, settling back onto the quilt.

Nick looked up, enchanted by the dew of perspiration on her cheeks. He wanted to curl the damp tendrils along her temples around his finger. "Tell you what?"

Dividing her time much as a race-goer, watching Nick and the action as the kids ran back over to the playground, Jenny offered a scowl. "How you knew I'd be at the Y today."

"Barb didn't mind your running off like that?"

"Heck, no. She probably never even knew I was gone. Barb *enjoys* that stuff."

Nick just shook his head. "I just can't understand the middle-class obsession with exercise."

"Then why did you travel across town to play pickup basketball?"

Nick looked down at the sunlight in her eyes, the line of her neck and arms as she leaned back on her elbows and thought of how she'd look in a bed, waiting to be kissed. Waiting to be loved. It took him a minute to pull himself back.

"To see you. Barb said something about your schedule last night. I thought I'd give it a shot."

Pulling herself into sitting position, Jenny grabbed another piece of chicken. Her expression wasn't exactly trusting. "Barb was talking about college-prep preschools last night. I don't think I remember the YMCA fitting into that conversation."

Nick knew that she wasn't fooled. Wondered how he was going to keep tap-dancing around this acute lady. He was seriously beginning to ponder the merit of keeping up this charade.

"Mom, look at me!"

Nick looked up to see Kevin hanging upside down from the top of the jungle gym. One leg slipped and Kevin shrieked. Nick jumped. Jenny munched on her chicken leg without moving.

"Nice, Kev, but try and keep both feet up."

Nick shot her a surprised look. "He almost fell on his head."

The smile Jenny bestowed betrayed that same smug superiority mothers had for the uninitiated. "Nah. He's been doing that since he was three."

Nick shot the boy another look to see him teetering along the top of the domelike structure as if he were walking a tightrope. Suddenly Nick was entertaining visions of broken arms and emergency rooms.

Jenny grinned. "He has the balance of a cat. Besides, aghast is just the reaction he's looking for."

It took some effort, but Nick settled back and took a swig of beer. "Why do you do this?" he demanded.

"The picnic was your idea," she reminded him equably.

Nick shook his head, an eye still to where Kevin was doing daredevil acrobatics on the equipment and Emma was doing her best to imitate him. "This mother stuff. How do you survive?"

Jenny just shrugged. "Lots of practice. I had most of the responsibility for that circus that was over at the house the other day."

Nick couldn't understand. He'd had responsibility, too. It just made him want to shy away. He'd never had a childhood, he'd always said. It was always much easier to foist one foster kid off on another. So, why should he spend the rest of his life wiping runny noses and cleaning up dirty diapers? But when Jenny talked about it, she got that faraway look that had taken her when she'd had the baby in her arms. The one that made him ache in a way he'd never known a person could.

"Didn't you get your fill?" he demanded without thinking.

When Jenny looked up, Nick realized that more had escaped in his tone of voice than he'd intended. For a moment she flirted with disquiet, uncertainty. Then she simply shook her head.

"It's different when they're your own."

Nick snorted. "Yeah, I've heard that before."

He wanted nothing of this hearts-and-flowers garbage. Nick had lived reality. He knew what a load kids were. After all, he'd been such a load that Dora had dumped him on the foster-care system rather than raise him herself. Where did it say that Jenny was different?

But she was. And that crowded Nick, taking his room, stifling his breath.

"I know," Jenny agreed. "Dumb cliché. But true. As much as I wanted children, I wasn't really sure I meant it until I had Kevin. I spent my entire pregnancy wondering how the heck I could actually love a baby enough to put up with midnight feedings and toilet training. I spent my pregnancy with Emma wondering how I could possibly love a second baby as much as I had the first.''

But Nick was shaking his head. "I'm sorry. I don't think I could do that."

"Be pregnant?" Jenny asked, her voice soft for the teasing light in her eyes. "I hope not."

Nick couldn't name the sudden tightness in his chest. It had to do with the fact that Jenny refused to challenge him, that she was so calm and practical, ignoring her son's more outrageous stunts even as she spouted off about love and babies.

Suddenly the humidity was too close. The sun too hot. Nick climbed to his feet, intent on movement. He didn't see the sorrow in Jenny's eyes as he tossed his empty beer can into the trash.

"Mr. Nick?"

Looking down, he came upon the upturned face of Emma, her expression intent.

"Yeah, peewee. Whatchya want?"

"Swing me, please. My mommy hasn't learned me to kick my feet."

She held up a hand. Nick looked at it as if it were a trap. As if in accepting it, enclosing its tiny warmth within his, he would be caught. You couldn't deny the certain consideration in those blue eyes, though. In the end, Emma won.

"Mr. Nick?" she asked when her hand was safely in his.

"Yeah?" He looked down again, amazed at the amount of presence in that tiny face. Her hair was in braids and she wore a jumper, with an old watch hanging from her wrist. Why should that make him hurt?

"Do you have peanuts?"

"Huh?" He dragged himself back and instinctively began to check pockets. "No, I don't think I do."

That was when he heard the rumble of Jenny's stifled chuckle. But by then it was too late. He'd walked right into it.

"Oh." Emma nodded, brows pursed. "I don't have peanuts," she announced up to him. "I'm a girl. Kevin has peanuts. He's a boy."

And with that, she led him off. And Nick had thought Jenny had had trouble controlling her laughter.

It was getting worse. The very moment Jenny should have been calling a halt to this fantasy, she was seated cross-legged on her grandmother's quilt watching her children tumbling around Nick like puppies. And she couldn't bring herself to stop it.

This was what she wanted from life: an afternoon in the park listening to the shrill laughter of her children, smiling at the bemused humor in Nick's eyes, content with the sun and the languorous hypnotism of the heat, the creak of swings and the gurgle of the fountain down in the pond where the ducks swam.

But today instead of settling her, the idyllic setting churned her up even more. She saw here a man who needed her, needed the spontaneous affection of children—a man who only grudgingly allowed his own emotions. She saw a man who could share beautiful children with her and collect a noisy, wild brood to keep their dinner table in chaos and their old age warm.

She saw a man who didn't want children. And Jenny wanted more children. She could hear the echoes of their absence as clearly as the shrill glee of the children she had, and she missed them unspeakably. Tiny babies with wide, guileless eyes, toddlers with tumbling, stumbling gaits. Children with endless questions, endless surprises and pleasures. Past and future wrapped up in the silent, sweet face of a sleeping daughter or son, cocooned in the peace of night.

Jenny couldn't bear the idea that she would spend no more early mornings with a baby in her arms, exchanging their most private secrets in the quiet hours when the world slept around them.

And the man she was falling in love with couldn't understand that.

She'd begun to suspect the night before when he'd kissed her. When she'd wanted nothing more than to be lifted to her bed and thoroughly made love to. The realization had crystallized the minute she'd seen him walk away with Emma. Jenny had walked into this situation on a whim. She was going to walk away with a broken heart.

She still didn't know who he was. Nick Barnett didn't exist, and she didn't know why. She had his phone number. She should call Detective Richards and have it traced. She should find out once and for all just what it was that Nick— or whoever he was—was hiding from her.

It wasn't drugs. Her instincts rebelled against that idea. She wouldn't allow a drug dealer to enchant her daughter. Heck, her daughter, without even knowing what a drug dealer was, wouldn't allow it.

But it was something, and Jenny should find out. Still, every time she'd walked to the phone that morning she'd faltered. Because if Nick wasn't the one who told her why he was living a dual life it didn't matter.

Jenny wanted to laugh at that thought. It didn't matter even if he did tell her. No matter how important he was becoming to her, no matter how much sleep she lost, how much she ached to see him open those very private doors to her, she already knew his stand on the two most important issues in her life. He didn't like kids and he saw success in terms of achievement.

It wouldn't be enough for Nick Barnett to sit in a park and watch his children, and it would have to be for Jenny's husband.

"You didn't warn me about her."

Looking up, Jenny tried to force the knot of tears back in her throat. Nick plopped alongside her and reached over for another beer. He was grinning, that wide, easy smile that she'd seen him save for Marco. He looked so relaxed, so much more at peace than usual. How did Jenny tell him that her children were the therapy he'd needed all along? How did she ask him to stay?

"I tried to warn you about Emma a long time ago," she reminded him, looking down at her hands. They were still shiny with leftover chicken grease. "But there's only so much people will believe." Jenny tried her best to keep her attention away from the way Nick felt next to her. A fresh breeze picked at the damp hair at her neck, but it didn't serve to cool her.

Absently tossing her chicken bone back into the box, Jenny licked the taste from her fingers, one of the decadent pleasures her mother would never have allowed. She looked up just in time to see that Nick watched.

His face grew still. His eyes darkened. Jenny pulled her wet fingers from her mouth, the air tingling against them. She could almost feel his lips around them, sucking, licking. Tantalizing.

Pulling in enough air to cool her furnace, Jenny turned her eyes away. "Would you mind my asking you a question?"

"No." His voice was husky, tight. Jenny could hear the effort of control, and it fanned the embers in her belly. Still focusing on the blue-and-white double-wedding-ring pattern of the quilt beneath her rather than the clouds that gathered overhead, Jenny shook her head.

"What was it like being a foster child?"

It evidently wasn't what Nick had expected. When Jenny lifted her gaze it was to see the pain quickly surface, the chill of alienation and instinctive distrust. She hurt for him all over again.

Finishing his beer in a long gulp, Nick made another toss. The can hit home with a clang and sank into the trash. For a long moment he watched the pond where the ducks glided in silence and a little boy fished. Jenny held her breath, uncertain why she'd asked the question, afraid of the answer.

"There are a lot of good foster homes out there," Nick offered by way of disclaimer.

An expert in patience, Jenny waited.

Nick finally shrugged, still not facing her. "I kept waiting for my mother to come take me home."

Jenny heard the weight of his childhood in those words. She ached for him, for that little boy standing so expectantly by a window—for the man who had never gotten over it. "And she never did?"

Now he shook his head. "Not Dora. She wasn't much more than a kid herself. She couldn't bear to give me up, but she couldn't stand the responsibility. I guess she thought this was the best compromise.'' Again, a shrug. A stiff distancing from the endless wait. The hope and disappointment. The cycle of rejection. "I stayed in about ten places, I guess. Some houses better than others. Some people really tried, but by the time I was fourteen, I guess they'd pretty much given up on me."

Jenny could almost read it in his eyes. *How much could I be worth if my own mother wouldn't even come for me?* She saw it in Kevin at times, when the Jerk forgot him, that brutal pain of disappointment. The defenses already being constructed in a six-year-old boy. What must it have been like to have nothing but that conviction?

"And then, Marco," she offered.

Nick grinned. "And then, Marco. Caught me in an alley in south St. Louis ripping off hubcaps. Manetti decided that I made a lousy crook."

A wind lifted the edge of the blanket and ruffled the lake. Jenny didn't feel it. She didn't notice the pall cast over the sun. Her attention was on Nick, on the war he waged within himself.

"Marco's still one of the only people who can put up with me," Nick said, his good humor faltering, his eyes straying, softening.

Jenny felt a cool sigh against her cheek. The trees were beginning to whisper. "Yeah," she retorted, her eyes locked uncomfortably with his. "You're such an ogre to be around."

"I've been on good behavior."

She wanted to nod. Wanted to move or speak, anything to break the sudden tension. She could feel him struggle toward a decision. His muscles quivered with tension. The dimples alongside his mouth deepened, drawn downward with the weight of his struggle.

Jenny wished she knew what it was. She wished with all her heart she knew the outcome.

"I don't suppose the kids would like it if I kissed you," he said softly, just the tone of his voice more intimate than touch.

Jenny licked her lips. "They might not even notice."

He leaned closer, his gaze straying to her lips, to the moist trail left by her tongue.

"Jenny..."

No more than a mile away, lightning split the lowering sky. Jenny jumped back. The crack of thunder thudded into her chest. Right on its heels came the shriek, and she was on her feet.

Nick followed, trembling with the effort of control. Emma was running toward them, arms out, face already tearstained, sobs racking her small body. Storms were Emma's Achilles tendon, the unexpected chaos a frightening threat to her well-ordered little world.

"Don't let them take me," the little girl begged, arms like vises around Jenny's neck.

"Did you arrange this?" Nick demanded, only half joking.

Jenny swept Emma up into her arms. "Only if you believe in divine intervention," she answered with a faltering smile. When Nick cast an uncertain look to Emma, she made a shrug. "Post-*Wizard of Oz* syndrome," she allowed. "Emma's afraid a tornado is going to take her someplace where she can't get home to me."

"Don't...let them...Mommy!"

"I won't, baby," she crooned, eyes still on the tight discomfort in Nick's expression. "I won't."

The wind erupted then, smelling of rain. More lightning shuddered. Kevin showed up on the run. Still Nick watched her with those hesitant, hungry eyes. And Jenny thought she knew exactly how he felt.

"Would you care to continue our conversation later?" she asked.

For a moment, even as the storm descended on them at record speed and Kevin bent to retrieve the remnants of their meal, Nick stood stock-still. "Yes," he said. "I would."

And then they ran.

Chapter 10

Jenny, it's only the Jerk. Why do you want to make a good impression on him?"

Jenny never bothered to look up from where she was digging for buried treasure among the sofa cushions. "Shut up and clean, Kate," she said to her sister.

The last forty-eight hours had been among the worst of her life. From the moment she'd scrambled in out of the rain on Saturday, Jenny had lost the rest of her objectivity. The remainder of that afternoon had been spent in the house, where Nick and Kevin compared cartoons and Jenny soothed a terrified Emma. There hadn't been a chance for privacy, since the surprise thunderstorm lasted the afternoon, intensifying Emma's fear. Jenny hadn't even managed to unpeel the little girl's arms from around her neck. Of all the times for Emma to misplace her legendary self-sufficiency, it had to be the moment Jenny and Nick most needed to be alone.

Nick had had to settle for nonverbal communication, and in the eerie, flickering green light of the summer storm, it had crawled over Jenny like electricity.

He had kissed her goodbye again. This time the kids had been watching, so the two of them had kept hands to themselves and communicated every desire, every half-wished yearning through eyes and intuition. Jenny hadn't been able to sleep since.

She ached for him. She paced and fidgeted and lost track of time wondering what he was doing as she pulled the sheets back in her bed. He had no air-conditioning. Did he sleep in the nude or in shorts, the heat raising a sheen of sweat on his body? Did he put a fan in the window so that it winnowed his hair? Did he wrap himself in crisp white sheets or sleep haphazardly over the bed on his stomach, the pillow bunched up under his head?

Lying there in the dark with only the hum of appliances to keep her company and the cool wash of air-conditioning tempting her, Jenny could imagine all too painfully just how the stubble of his beard would feel against her lips. How the night-warm skin of his back would feel beneath her fingers.

If was ridiculous. She hadn't fantasized since she'd reached puberty. She hadn't awakened with the taste of frustration on her tongue and gone to bed with the ache of longing in her belly. But within a matter of weeks, Nick Barnett had planted that dreadful anticipation in her. His eyes, his cocky grin, the loose grace of his gait. The lost child in his eyes . . .

Suddenly, within the period of two, very abrupt kisses, he'd unleashed a yearning she'd never before known, a passion that frightened her. He'd made her grieve his loss before he'd even gone.

"Jenny!"

Startled, Jenny finally straightened to consider her red-faced sister. "Kate, they'll be here in a few minutes. I'm not having them think I need help."

Kate looked stunned. "But you went to your lawyer to get more money. You sat in that man's office and told him so yourself."

Pulling herself straight, Jenny gathered her frayed poise. "Yes," she admitted. "But Amber Jean wasn't with him."

And I didn't feel so lost, so set adrift and torn. I wasn't questioning my instincts.

Kate just sighed. "Of course. It makes perfect sense."

"Why would she come here?" Jenny demanded, tossing the small stuffed dog she'd unearthed into a clothes basket full of retrieved toys. "She's never set foot in this house."

"Well, they do have to drive two cars home."

"He could have paid someone to do it. He could have paid all of south county to do it."

Without warning Kate intercepted Jenny in mid-search and grabbed her by the arms. "Jen," her sister said, eyes sincere. "I've never even seen Amber Jean provoke this kind of tantrum. What's wrong?"

"Wrong?" Jenny took a quick look around for something else to straighten, but she'd already finished it. She even had a pitcher of sun tea steeping on the windowsill in the kitchen. "Nothing's wrong."

"And I'm just a little pregnant," Kate retorted dryly. "Is it Nick? Did he hurt you?"

"Nick?" That brought Kate's eyes home, but the rest there was too uncomfortable. Her sister read her better than most. "No, Nick didn't hurt me. He's a nice guy."

Kate groaned. "Bill Bailey is a nice guy. Nick is a major fantasy."

"Nick is a guy with hang-ups just like every other man in the world."

Kate lifted an eyebrow. "Besides wanting to be a lawyer? The American Psychiatric Association still hasn't classified that a mental illness yet, you know."

"Kate," Jenny insisted, her own message intent. "The Jerk and Amber Jean are going to show up any minute now. I'd rather take care of one unpleasant conversation at a time. We can talk about Nick later."

"As long as you're still coherent."

Jenny shot her a grimace. "Nothing like a sister for undying support."

"It looks fine in here," Kate assured her, eyes sparkling. "Just keep the door to the kitchen closed so that nothing escapes."

That brought Kate an answering grin. "Snot."

Kate gave her a hug. "I do my best. I'm taking Brooke to tea. Would Emma like to come?"

Picking up the basket and following her sister out to the foyer, Jenny shook her head. "She won't leave the house yet."

"She still sees Munchkins under the rocks?"

Jenny shook her head again, long past understanding the convoluted workings of Emma's mind. "Emma's just my baby who needs her stability. And she hasn't really had much. I can hardly hold the fear of losing me against her."

Funny, it had been Nick who'd best understood. He had taken his turn with Emma, unbelievably patient when she'd insisted Jenny stay within arm's distance during the storm, spinning stories for the little girl's wide-eyed enjoyment during the lulls. Jenny was sure it was only her imagination that his fairy tales bore a striking resemblance to reworked Fitzgerald and Hemingway.

"Well, then," Kate decided, hand on the door. "We'll all four go next week. Tell the Queen to wear her best gown."

Jenny nodded. Sharing one last quick hug, Kate opened the door.

"Oh. Hello."

Jenny almost dropped the basket. She hadn't gotten the chance to change yet, and there they were, standing on her front porch, acting as if they'd just been caught necking. The new Mr. and Mrs. Lake.

Kate faltered and then smiled, all of the family's censure in her chilly green eyes. "Well, *I'll* be going."

She never even gave the two of them the chance to respond. Left behind, Jenny overcame the absurd impulse to thrust the basket of toys into Kate's hands and announce she'd been donating it to charity. She hated being caught off guard like this. Especially when Amber Jean looked as if she'd dressed for an afternoon of bridge at the country club.

"Come on in," Jenny invited. There was a new Mercedes in her driveway and enough diamonds on Amber Jean's manicured fingers to warn ships off rocks. Jenny thought she was going to be sick.

Out on the lawn, Kate was turning around, motioning down the street for Jenny's benefit. Jenny dropped the basket on the stairs so she could hold the door for her guests, and then followed Kate's attention.

The ice cream truck. It was a little late for Nick to still be around. Even so, there he was parked at the top of the street. Offering support or spying? She wished she knew, because the sight of it only served to increase the weight of the knot in her stomach. When Kate got into her car, Jenny damn near followed.

"Oh, Danish furniture," Amber was gushing in that little singsong voice of hers. "You're so brave. I wouldn't have the nerve to put it in my house."

Biting back a dozen retorts, Jenny shut the door. "Thank you."

They had both taken a seat on the couch. Suddenly Jenny wished she would have left at least one toy in the cushions. Preferably one with sharp edges. "Tea?"

"Lemon and sugar," Amber smiled brightly.

When she walked back into the living room, Jenny brought the Porsche keys with her. "I think you have a bull's-eye painted on the back of that thing," she admitted, handing them over with the Jerk's iced tea. "The police have been following me like bird dogs."

He snorted and shook his head. "They must have a quota to keep. They stopped me five times in a week."

Jenny lifted an eyebrow. "Five times. Imagine." She knew better than to think his only offense had been red paint.

For a moment there was a silence in the room. Amber Jean concentrated on her drink, her gold bracelets clinking. The Jerk concentrated on Amber Jean. Something was brewing here, and it was churning all the way to Jenny's stomach.

"Look, Jen," the Jerk finally spoke up, his tone conciliatory, his eyes straying to his new wife. "I'm sorry about how I acted the other day. It's just...well, I was on edge. We were waiting for Amber Jean's test to come back, after all."

Suddenly Jenny felt uncertain. No matter what she thought of her husband's new wife, she didn't wish her real harm. "Test?" she asked, turning concerned eyes on the blonde. "Are you all right?"

Amber Jean burst into bright giggles. "Oh, I'm just fine," she cooed, finding her husband's hand and squeezing it. "I'm going to have a baby."

Jenny did her best to hold on to her glass. She stared. Somewhere deep inside her, something precious shattered. "A baby?"

Suddenly the Jerk was smiling as if he'd invented the idea. He put his arm around his little blonde, looking proprietary as hell. "It's time I was a real father," he said. "Amber Jean convinced me. We have so much to offer a baby."

What about the ones you have? Jenny wanted to demand. She wanted to scream, to shriek, to rip something apart. She never got the chance.

"Mommy?"

Saved by Emma, Jenny couldn't help but think, her eyes leveled on the silly smile on Amber Jean's vapid face. Jenny wanted to get to her feet. She settled for turning to greet her child. "Amber Jean, I don't think you've ever met my daughter Emma, have you?"

Amber Jean didn't seem to appreciate the inference. She only smiled more brightly. Emma reached the doorway and Jenny prepared for introductions. Emma never gave her the chance.

"Mommy!" she shrieked suddenly, whirling to grab Jenny's pant leg. "No! Don't make me!"

Even Jenny was confused. "Emma?"

The little girl's head was buried in Jenny's lap, her body convulsed with fear. "It's her! It's her! The witch! They're going to carry me to her castle and never let me out!"

Emma did everything but climb straight up Jenny's chest. The Jerk got to his feet, furious. Jenny did her best not to laugh. Not at Emma—the little girl was sincerely terrified—but at her accusation. Jenny couldn't have put it better herself.

"Excuse me," she announced to her stunned guests. "I'll be right back."

By the time she got Emma safely settled in her room with Kevin to watch guard against invasion, Jenny returned to find her two guests growing restless.

"Look, Jen," the Jerk announced, getting to his feet. "We came here to share this with you. Amber Jean felt it was important." Amber Jean was rock-still, a brittle shock still on her features. "Because she also thought it was time we talked to you about custody of Kevin and Emma. We could—you know—take them off your hands."

Jenny had reached her chair. Halfway to sitting, she bolted upright. The other shoe had just fallen. She stiffened with outrage. She knew she'd never strike another person, because at that moment she didn't belt the Jerk right where he deserved it.

"After all," he was saying, his eyes straying after Emma. "We have a stable home. And we're moving soon, so we'll have more room. It'll be a good place for them."

"I don't think so."

He gave glare for glare. "I'm their father, Jen."

Jenny laughed. "According to Emma, you're a flying monkey."

"Jen," he retorted, straightening into his best intimidating posture, which negated his next words. "We're trying to bridge the gap here."

Jenny nodded, a stiff, jerky movement that betrayed the cost of her control. "Fine. Start by remembering your children's birthdays. Show up for a few soccer games. Then we'll see."

Amber Jean made the mistake of sighing. "But we don't have time," she objected, still trying to smile her way through with a flutter of her hand. "I thought it would be really nice to get to know Emma and Kevin, ya know? Kinda be like practice before our own little Junior came along."

That did it. The frail remnants of Jen's patience evaporated. "Buy a doll that wets. My children aren't educational toys."

Turning away from temptation, she walked to the door. By the time she held it open, her guests had gathered themselves enough to follow.

"Congratulations," she said to the blonde, her voice trembling with the effort of sincerity. "Babies are wonderful. I hope you're happy." Then she turned to her ex-husband and the shock turned to acid. "Maybe it will teach you enough responsibility to take care of your other children.''

"Don't be a bitch," he snapped.

She smiled frostily. "The car is in perfect condition. Don't try and pin any dents on me. Goodbye."

For a long time after she shut the door, Jenny stood staring after it.

A baby. Amber Jean was going to have a baby. Jenny heard those echoes again, the laughter that had never reached her rooms. The children she wanted. The children she should have had. The children she never would now.

The tears formed in her chest, great greasy lumps that weighed down her heart and blocked her lungs. Hot coals that ate away at her, stealing all the fortitude she'd worked so very hard to build over the years.

A baby. Oh dear God, it wasn't fair. It just wasn't fair!

And then, bubbling out of the depths of two years of frustration, two years of loneliness and heartache and disappointment, stripping away the last of her facade, the sobs took her.

He'd watched them pull up. Field glasses did come in handy, after all. The guy had miserable taste. That blond bimbo looked like she had all the brains of a chocolate-chip cookie. Nick found himself sneering at the fact that this upscale yuppie didn't have the sense to spot class if it hit him in the face. After all, he'd tossed Jenny aside and taken up with Miss Congeniality here.

Evidently the visit didn't go well. Before Nick had even gotten a chapter of his book read the two of them shot back out the door like scalded cats, the guy scowling at his wife as if she'd personally hiked his shorts. When they spun past the ice cream truck, she looked confused and he looked mad as hell. Nick smiled. Jenny must have sent him out with his tail between his legs.

Served him right.

Nick decided to give Jenny another few minutes before he showed up. After all, he'd seen her sister point him out. He'd waved as she'd pulled past him. So Jenny knew he was here. It was just a matter of giving her some room to cool off. Lighting up a fresh cigarette, he turned back to his book.

"Mr... Nick! Mr. Nick!"

No mistaking that voice. Grinding the new cigarette back out, Nick prepared to intercept the human missile headed his way. Emma was a good half block away when he saw the distress on her tiny features.

She'd looked that way at the picnic the other day, when she thought she was going to be blown to Oz. Only there wasn't a cloud in the sky. The book slapped onto vinyl and Nick swung out of his truck on the run.

"My mommy," she sobbed, lifting easily into his arms. "The wicked witch came, and now my mommy's crying. Come help her, please, Mr. Nick. She hurted herself..."

He was sure the rest made sense, but Nick couldn't quite pay attention. Jenny hurt? Did that bastard do something to her? By God, he'd have the entire force down on his butt in ten minutes flat. He'd personally rearrange that smarmy, upscale face. He was running without knowing it.

Nick shouldn't have been surprised that somebody noticed him enter Jen's house. He slammed in, the door bouncing off the wall and back again. Kevin stood in the hallway, eyes focused into the living room, hands in pockets.

"I think she's mad," he said without turning away.

Nick reached his side and set Emma down. She clung to him, terrified.

"Jenny?"

She sat dead-center on her living room floor, a laundry basket next to her, the room strewn with toys. As Nick watched, she heaved yet another, a metal truck that clanged with effect against the wall. She seemed to be aiming for a little crystal object on a shelf by the fireplace, but the sobs that racked her ruined her aim.

"I can't... hit it!" she cried, picking up a small, stuffed dog. "I can't even break the damn thing."

"Jenny?" Carefully Nick stepped into the living room, Emma still clinging like a limpet. "You're scaring Emma."

You're scaring me.

Abruptly Jenny looked up. Her eyes were swollen and red. She fought to control the tears that still splashed on her bare arms, but it was a losing battle. Holding out her hands, she took her little girl into her hold, her grip so tight Nick wasn't sure how Emma was breathing.

"I'm . . . sorry," she apologized on a hiccough, still shuddering. "I'm . . . sorry, baby. Mommy's just having a . . . tantrum, okay?"

Quizzically Emma backed up. "Like Kevin?"

Jenny proffered a watery smile, her control slipping a little. "Like Kevin."

That was when Barb made it through the front door on the run.

"I'll explain later," Jenny said without looking away from the face she stroked, "but would you mind if the kids came over for a while?"

Barb looked aghast, so Nick figured this was unusual behavior for Jenny. "Of course not."

"No!" Emma protested, holding more tightly. "*She'll* come back!"

Nick was surprised by Jenny's bubbling laugh. "No she won't, Emma. I promise. Mommy will be right here. I just think tantrums should be private, okay?"

Emma edged back again. "Promise?"

Jenny nodded and hugged her daughter again. Kevin never questioned the actions, and followed Barb and Emma back out the door. He did, however, close it behind him. Nick thought he was a brighter kid than he'd given him credit for.

"Damn him," Jenny was chanting, the tears building again, her hands up to her eyes. "Damn him."

Uncertain, untried, Nick eased closer. He didn't know what to do with Jenny. The only crying women he'd ever dealt with were suspects. And they sure as hell hadn't made him feel like he had a knife in his chest. "Come on, Jen. Come sit on the couch."

"Sit?" she countered, not seeming to notice that he was the only one left with her. "I can't . . . sit. I can't even hit that damn shoe!"

Pulling out of her crouch, she grabbed for a block and sailed it straight to the wall, scoring a perfect hit. The little glass object shattered with a sharp tinkle and rained down on the carpet.

"Why that?" he asked when Jenny met her victory with a gulping sob.

"Because," she said, hauling herself to her feet to face him, "that was my gift for having Emma. A crystal shoe from Neiman-Marcus. The Jerk's secretary took her lunch hour to get it for me, and then signed the card."

She was pacing now, pulling her hands through her hair, distraught beyond Nick's comprehension. "What did he say to you?" he asked, following as she pushed the French doors open into the kitchen.

Jenny reached her refrigerator, where Kevin had hung a huge sign proclaiming his love for his mother, and stopped. And sobbed. "He says he's going to ask for custody. That bastard hasn't paid attention to those kids since he filed them as a tax deduction, and now he wants custody."

She was so still, so rigid. Nick kept his distance, aching to hold her. Suffering more with each of her sobs than he had in years of silence. "Why now?"

"Why?" she asked, turning, her face crumpling a little. "Because Amber Jean's pregnant, that's why. He finds religion, and now *she's* having my babies."

"You don't really want his kids, do you?"

She brushed aside the question with angry hands. "Of course not. But, dammit, I don't want her to have them either!" There was lightning in those green eyes, a fury that paled the tears, a wild frustration that was born of places Nick had never gone. "*I'm* the one who wants babies. I'm the one who was told by him that more than one was obscene. And *he's* the one having more children."

Nick didn't know what to say. He felt the whirlpool of her emotions suck him in, felt the pull of that deadly, dangerous current. He understood in ways he didn't name and yet couldn't bring himself to address them. "Jenny, don't you think this is pretty intense?"

Jenny considered him with tear-swollen eyes, quieter for her tirade, no less devastated. Nick saw the weight of years in those tears.

"I've been saving this one up," she said on a soft, sad little sigh, the energy draining away. "I've kept my cool through every court contest, through every session begging for money and excusing indifference. I've broken my damned back so my children didn't know what a selfish bastard their father was." Lifting her hand in a futile little gesture, Jenny shook her head. "I've fought every damn day to survive. To somehow win *something* from all this. And one toothy grin from Amber Jean tells me I've lost. I've lost everything." She framed her words with shaking hands. "Young tartlet gets babies. Responsible mother gets twenty more years of frustration."

Nick watched her fold, watched the rage collapse into grief, the dark, endless minutes of the night betray themselves in heart-wrenching words. "And I never hold another baby in my arms."

He couldn't stay away. Crossing the space between them, he gathered her into his arms, tilting her head back, wanting only to give something back, to fill those suddenly empty places in her beautiful eyes. "Jenny, you're only thirty. Who says you can't have more children?"

Jenny's tears slid down his hands now. Her eyes challenged him, their light dying, the darkness all that was left of that teeming green. "Because I won't have them alone. I'm funny that way, Nick." She pulled away, intent on her message. "Look around you," she said, swinging an arm to take in the usual state of her kitchen, including in her gesture everything Nick had been witness to. "What man is going to jump at a chance to inherit this?"

Nick had never anticipated being asked a question like this. He'd never in his life considered answering. But answer he did, even as he looked around at the half-washed dishes, the crayon-strewn table and mud-speckled floor. Even considering the extras he didn't now see. Before he realized it, he looked Jenny in the face and admitted the truth.

"Me."

Chapter 11

Silence. Jenny heard it, full and pulsing like a tide, rushing along like seconds. She tasted the weight of it, the tension like copper, brackish on the tongue. She saw the cost of it in the astonishment that bloomed in Nick's eyes.

He wouldn't repeat it. She knew he wouldn't. Something about the startled edge to his eyes, the brittle hesitation from flight in his posture, warned her. Nick had made one admission too many and all the pounding in Jenny's chest, all the sudden hope that stretched across her like taut wire wouldn't provoke him to make a promise out of his words.

"Well, why not?" he demanded suddenly. He took her by the arms and pulled her back to him, fitting her tight against the solid length of his body. "Why wouldn't I want a life with you?"

Jenny couldn't help it. She had to break this bubble before it engulfed her. "Because you don't love me?"

When he turned his eyes on her this time, they pierced her. Honey and sunlight, sweet warmth and promise. Anticipation, hunger, trepidation. What was in her eyes, too? "But I do love you. I've been falling in love with you since the minute I first sat on your porch swing."

No.

"You don't like kids."

"You call Emma a kid?" He was smiling, a silly, crooked cant to his face that hurt her, that taunted her.

He couldn't mean it.

"Don't do this, Nick," she pleaded, struggling to get away, to find air, room, sense. She smelled him, dark and rich, like the earth. Like the fertile, fecund earth, and she wanted to lie down in it and rest. She wanted to till it, to watch it bloom in the spring and run her fingers through its cool, soft furrows.

She wanted children and he didn't.

"I mean it, Jenny."

Jenny tried to drag in a breath only to feel the solid plane of his chest against her breasts. Only to mold more closely to him, sharpening the ache to belong, to share.

"And I should just believe you," she challenged with brittle eyes, knowing he could see the war waging in her, unsure how to shield him from it—unsure how to protect herself from his sharp eyes and gentle hands. He'd made it worse, after all. He'd crystallized her ache for children when she saw his eyes, knowing how beautiful they would be on a son, knowing how she would sate herself on his smile if it appeared the first time their daughter smiled.

It was part of loving a man, wanting to see him reborn in a baby's chuckle. Wanting to see the special wonder in his eyes when he first held his child. Sharing and commitment. Two things Jenny couldn't live without in a man. Two things Nick couldn't afford in a relationship.

Instead of answering right away, he lowered his head. Gently, swiftly, like the skim of clouds over the sun, he brushed against her lips in a promise more potent than words. The ache flared in Jenny like a struck match. Pungent, searing.

"Yes," he said. "You should believe me. You know more about me than anyone. I've opened up to you, Jenny. I've never done that before. I've never told stories to little girls or had impromptu picnics in the park." Lifting his head, he captured her gaze again, the yearning melting his golden eyes. "I want to be your family."

A sob bubbled up in her, disbelief and longing. Shattered defenses struggling to hold.

"I know more about you than anyone, huh?" Jenny gathered her outrage anew, forcing it down deep where it could take root. It helped her push away from the sapping comfort of his arms. "How about your name, Nick? Do I know your name?"

For a moment Nick looked bemused. "My name," he echoed uncertainly. "What—"

"What do you think a man could be up to that he'd need an alias, Nick? Or is it really Nick? What *do* I call you?"

The light dawned. Surprise, chagrin, understanding. The sight of it brought the tears back to her eyes. Nick knew exactly what she was talking about.

"Oh, God," she moaned, absolutely still with the weight of her words. "You *do* sell drugs."

If she'd wanted a reaction, she couldn't have led with a better accusation.

Nick looked like he'd been shot. "I *what*?"

Jenny wasn't really listening. "All this time I've been defending you. I kept telling them that Emma couldn't like you if you were a drug dealer...that I couldn't like you..."

His expression had grown comical. "A drug dealer? You think I'm a drug dealer?"

"Well, why else would you wear your hair in a ponytail and ride in an ice cream truck and carry a beeper?" Jenny demanded, completely at the end of her wits.

Then Nick laughed, and she stared. "Because I'm a cop," he told her, laughing again.

Then he was pacing, walking off her kitchen with the same kind of steps that had eaten up that basketball court, his eyes darting back to Jenny again and again as she stood like stone before him.

"You are not," she accused, turning on him. "The detective would have known."

"Detective?" He came to a stop, the laughter still bright in his eyes. "What detective?"

"From St. Anthony. He's been watching you ... well, *we've* been watching you. He thought it was easier."

Nick bent close, his face inches from Jenny's. "You've been watching me?"

Jenny's first instinct was to shy away. With an effort she held her ground, chin up. "You had a ponytail..."

"And a beeper." He nodded. "I know. So this clown from St. Anthony's figures you can find out about me if you invite me over. Like, maybe, to fix your car."

Still Jenny didn't flinch, even though she desperately wanted to. "Something like that."

Why should she be defending herself? He was the one who hadn't been honest, who had only opened selected doors to her. He was professing love and still Jenny only knew fragments of him, like a scattered fall of jigsaw-puzzle pieces.

She wanted to turn away. She wanted to run before he made it all worse. Wasn't her day shaping up to be bad enough without finding out things she didn't want to know?

"But what about that black man? In the Cadillac."

For a moment Nick stared, lost. Then he shook his head, grinning. "Al Washington," he said. "From Narcotics. He bought some baseball tickets from me. It was the only chance we had to meet."

"A cop?" she asked, suddenly connecting the inference. "On an ice cream wagon? What were you doing?"

His grin was knowing, anticipating. "Undercover."

He wasn't making Jenny any happier. "What are you doing in our neighborhood?"

She really should have been insulted when he kept laughing. This time he pointed a finger. "Keeping an eye on you."

Jenny jerked back. *"What?"*

"You've been making unscheduled stops at mailboxes, young lady. Suspicious ones."

Overcome with the desperate feeling that she was sinking fast, Jenny slowly nodded her head. "And checks have been disappearing from the neighborhood." The silence closed in again as she met those laughing eyes with stunned ones. "You've been watching *me*?"

"It seems," he informed her with a grin, "that we have been watching each other."

Nick came to a halt before her, careful to keep his distance, his head bent forward as if listening to her, his eyes more alive than she'd ever seen them.

Jenny couldn't deal with it. She just couldn't manage. Too much had been tossed on her plate in too short a time. Her stomach churned and her chest hurt. There were still tears on her cheeks and a strange effervescence along her skin where Nick had taken hold of her.

She still felt the acid of Amber Jean's announcement eating away at her tenuous composure, and suddenly she was having to deal with Nick. Nick who said he loved her. Who said he'd been following her to make sure she hadn't been stealing checks from mailboxes. Nick who was everything she could want in a man and nothing she could tolerate.

Tears threatened again, hot, frustrated tears that didn't know whether to escape through sobs or laughter. Jenny shook her head, not even noticing anymore that the sun had sunk and taken much of the light with it. The lights weren't even on in the kitchen, so that Nick looked like an apparition—a savory temptation sent to taunt her, a delicious seduction meant only to remind her of what she couldn't have.

Knowing no other way to deal with the unimaginable, Jenny faced it with her embattled humor.

"So, you mean to tell me," she said, hands on hips, "that all the time I've been sneaking around behind your back, you've been sneaking around behind mine?"

Nick saw something in Jenny's eyes she hadn't anticipated. Instead of laughing, he shrugged. Smiled. Walked right up and gathered her back into his arms.

"Pretty despicable, if you ask me," he said in a gentle voice.

Almost without realizing it, Jenny wrapped her own arms around his back. There was so much support there, so much more strength than she could muster right now. Giving in to temptation, she closed her eyes and nestled against his chest.

"Reprehensible."

Jenny lost sight of her troubles. For just those few moments, she sought sanctuary. The tears escaped, after all, hot and bitter, sliding down her cheeks and soaking into his shirt. He stroked her hair. She refused to look at him, to move or return his touches. He just murmured to her, crooning her name like a litany, his voice soft and soothing. He held her against the world, against selfish ex-husbands and escalating bills. He held her against the growing night, and Jenny knew finally what she had been looking for when she'd once asked the Jerk to take her into his arms.

"I'm going to have to deal with some of this soon," she sniffed, not moving.

She could hear Nick's smile in his voice. "One thing at a time, Jen."

Jenny laughed, a harsh bark. "Where do you suggest we start?"

Nick went on stroking, his hand clumsy against her hair, as if he weren't really used to the action. It made Jenny hurt even more. "My name is Nick Barnes," he said. "Everything else is the same."

She lifted her head at that, eyes still full, expression battling against the absurd exhilaration the admission gave her.

"Even your phone number?"

He smiled. "Even my phone number. Why didn't you run over to the detective and have it checked? I gave it to you three days ago."

Jenny couldn't quite face him. "I don't know," she admitted on a half sniff, her eyes on the tearstains on his best white T-shirt. "I guess I didn't want him to be right. I didn't want you to be a drug dealer like everybody thought."

"Why didn't you just ask me?"

She shrugged. "I wanted you to be the one to tell me who you really were. Something about trust." A smile wavered along her mouth then, a tenuous return to sanity. "Seems we were both having that problem, huh?"

"Believe it or not," he told her, the shadows turning his eyes to sienna, the color of hills in early spring, the texture of honey. "I wasn't the one who didn't trust you. It was my boss. He got a tip."

"From whom?"

Nick shrugged, stroking her cheek with a calloused thumb.

Jenny wanted to lean into it, give in to the tender-rough sensation of his affection. She couldn't.

She did grin, though, a hesitant offering. "I'd put my money on Mrs. Warner. She thinks *you* get off a plane from Colombia every Monday morning."

Nick lifted an eyebrow. "She'd report you? I thought she liked you."

"Duty before all," she intoned. "Her nephew would be proud of her."

Nick grimaced, not so sure.

"But if you don't like kids," Jenny persisted, "how did you end up on the ice cream truck?"

For a moment Nick did nothing but watch her, a curious smile playing about his eyes. Surprised, troubled, intrigued. Then he just shook his head. "How about if we get ourselves some drinks and sit for this? I have a feeling it's going to get complicated."

"How 'bout if we get drinks and curl into the fetal position on the floor?" Jenny countered dryly. "I won't have to move so far to start my breakdown."

She didn't have to move far. She had to wait. Jenny should have known it wouldn't have been as easy as just pouring her troubles out to Nick. She still had neighbors who had an uncanny sixth sense and Barb for impetus. She had a family with Barb's phone number and two children whom she'd terrified. And Nick, even though he protested, had a truck he had to get back to the ex-Sergeant Manetti.

And so within the period of two phone calls and a tapping on the back door from an escapee with blond hair and very worried, three-year-old eyes, Jenny did what she'd been doing for two years. She shelved the turmoil in her for later. She wiped her eyes and assured Nick she was all right. She swept Emma into her arms and agreed, for a change, to let Barb send over dinner. And when Nick left, he promised her the end of the conversation if she promised to keep his secret.

Jenny wasn't sure what she expected, either of Nick or herself. She walked through the evening as if she were underwater, instinctively doling out food, chores and kisses as she did every other day, reassuring Barb even more than her children, especially when Barb found out about the Jerk's latest calumny. And all the while Jenny waited.

She couldn't eat. There wasn't enough room in her along with all the trauma residue. Betrayal battled with astonishment, curiosity with trepidation. Hope and dejection, anger, fear, all filled her like a roiling pot of corrosive.

And to top it, like frothy icing that was much too decadent to partake of, came the escalating hum of desire. Distracting her, preoccupying her, dancing around the edges of her perception like lightning and surprising her with its sudden shock.

She'd known it all along, from the moment she'd first walked out to see that Marine Corps tattoo where usually she just saw pimples. If Jenny Lake were another person, a less responsible person, she would have done anything to bring Nick Barnett to her bed.

Barnes. Nick *Barnes*: she had to remember that.

His other name, his other identity, a mystery man with a knowing smile and an ice cream truck. A policeman who might just be in love with her.

That revelation was what had finally unleashed the desire, setting it free from the constraints she'd imposed. It had swept out from the impulses of late-night hours to daylight, to the admission that the chemistry between Jenny and Nick was all the more potent for his proclamation. If he did mean it—if he did love her—Jenny had the disturbing suspicion that he might well consume her. What unnerved her was the fact that after almost thirty years of being the responsible one, it was what she wanted.

By the time the kids were in bed, Jenny didn't have any energy left. She'd waited for Nick to come back, to explain, to elaborate. He hadn't come. She'd even gone so far as to call him, needing to at least hear him reaffirm his promise. He hadn't been home.

She'd heard nothing. And now, as the clock snuck around to ten, she found herself in her cotton nightgown sitting on the living-room couch, where the Jerk had sat that afternoon to betray her. In the living room, where Nick had found her and asked her to be his family.

Jenny stared into the shadows of the room, seeing the nicks along the wall where her frustrated throws had landed short of the crystal shoe, seeing the modern Danish furniture Amber Jean wouldn't have had the nerve to put in her house. Seeing the mess, the evidence of active, challenging children—seeing the sum of her life.

Well, the hell with Amber Jean. No matter what she did, she was still the one who had to live with the Jerk. She had to hold up his mirrors and coo at his intelligence. No matter what she had, she didn't have Emma and Kevin. And she wasn't about to get them, no matter what Jenny had to do.

I am the lucky one, Jenny thought again, the assertion long since her litany of endurance. I'm the one with the love, with the friends and family. Even if I never have Nick, I'll survive just fine.

It should have been easier to hold back the tears.

Nick had meant to knock on the door. A bell ringing that late at night could permanently traumatize Emma, especially after the last few days that kid had spent. He wasn't even sure Jenny had waited up for him. He'd tried her number a couple of times, only to find it busy. Nosy neighbors, supportive sisters, probably. The stuff of family. The furtive dreams of a lonely child.

The street was silent tonight, the air cooler for the storm the other day, the night sky clear with a few stars braving the moonlight. Reaching the porch, Nick thought to check in the window for signs of life before knocking. There were a few lights on. Maybe Jenny would be sitting up over a cup of coffee, or munching popcorn in front of the TV.

She wasn't. Nick saw her right away, curled up on the living-room couch like a small child left behind at a party. Her eyes were closed, and her bent knees peeked out from beneath a soft yellow robe.

Waiting.

He recognized the position, the fight to hold out for the promised visit, the struggle to stay awake, to keep watch. The inexorable pull of sleep. Still she wouldn't quite give up, just in case. If he hadn't shown up, she would have awakened stiff and sore in the morning just where she was.

For a moment he vacillated. She probably needed the sleep. It had been a hell of a day for her. Should he stir everything up again or just let her sleep? Would it be better to work the rest of that poison free right now or give her a chance to get a second wind? He wished Manetti and Baker had given advice instead of sage smiles. He wished he had enough experience to know without having to ask them.

He could have stood on that porch for hours watching her sleep, sating himself on the sight of her translucent skin and parted, full lips. But he had a responsibility to her. Knowing this neighborhood, he realized, taking a quick look around, he stood out on that porch for ten more minutes and there would be police strobes waking the Baileys.

The door was unlocked. Nick shook his head. He was going to have to talk to Jenny about that. She had too much trust in her fellow man. On the other hand, he decided as he eased the door open and slipped inside, this would give him the chance to wake her the way he wanted.

Another dream. A fantasy that had been recurring ever since he'd seen that big, homey four-poster of hers upstairs. Turning in the morning sun to find that face next to him, waiting to be awakened. Waiting to smile. And he'd be the one to create it.

He could be very silent when he wanted. Jenny never twitched as he crossed the living-room rug and crouched alongside her. She never heard his soft intake of breath when he saw what he'd missed from the window.

Tears. Almost dried, enough to still make her eyes a little puffy, streaking just a little along her porcelain cheeks. She'd taken a bath. Her hair was still damp, its curls softer. Nick could smell the lemon soap and shampoo on her. It made him want to dip his face into her neck and rest in the sweet grove of her fragrance.

Nick knew better. He was beginning to know Jenny, and what she didn't need right now was to be rushed. She'd had a lot of surprises today, not many of them welcome.

Hell, *he'd* had a lot of surprises today. If he were honest about it, he'd admit he was still moving on momentum, refusing to question his statement to her. Manetti had just smiled when Nick had admitted the problem. But then, Marco always smiled. Nick hadn't found any help or hindrance. He was all alone on this one. And to be perfectly frank, he'd put off dealing with it until he'd talked to Jenny again.

Only now he wasn't so sure seeing her again was going to help. His gut was already churning. His chest tightened with that unaccustomed ache, the one that fed on her smiles and dreams that always seemed to appear around Jenny.

"Jenny?" He reached out to stroke her cheek, brushing away the tears with his thumb.

Oh, yeah, he was going to be able to make an adult decision around her. Just the feel of that velvet skin against his thumb sent shock waves through him. She was going to break his heart, and there wasn't a damn thing he could do about it.

Jenny could smell the rain. The wind. She heard her name called and smiled, because it sounded soft, like a distant gull's cry.

Then she heard it again.

She opened her eyes. Nick was there, just as she'd wanted. He'd changed, wearing jeans and T-shirt and jacket, letting his hair loose. Funny, he really looked like a drug dealer now. Unsavory and sexy as hell. Jenny thought in that half-asleep state when all emotions floated together, that she'd do something illegal for him. She'd run away with him and disgrace herself and outrage the townsfolk.

"About time you found your way back," she whispered, not moving. He was circling her cheek with his thumb, and his eyes devoured her. He was crouched down to her level so that his face was that close. Jenny saw the stubble and knew he hadn't had a better time of it than she. Absurdly, it made her feel better.

"Well," he admitted, easing into that crooked grin of his, "I figured if there was going to be any yelling and screaming, it should go on after the kids are asleep."

Jenny lifted an eyebrow. "Yelling and screaming?" she echoed. "Now, why should that happen? Are you going to

tell me you lied again? Your name is really Nick Bronkowski and you have a wife and seven kids.''

She shouldn't have said it. Just the words brought her
abruptly upright, almost sending Nick over backwards.
Jenny's breath caught in her throat, preventing her from
asking the unbearable. God, that's just what she'd need.
Not just a lawyer who didn't like kids, but a married lawyer who didn't like kids. What surprised her the most was
that she hadn't wondered before.

Nick was grinning at her now. ''I can see you still haven't
called Detective Richards. Thanks.''

Sitting four-square on the couch, Jenny narrowed her eyes
at him. ''How do you know?''

''Because he would have pulled my records and assured
you that I'm not married. Never have been—although
sometimes my partner gets just about as demanding as a
wife.''

Her eyes were narrowing again. ''Watch the slurs, Nick.''

He was still on his heels, elbows on his knees, watching
her with amused, contented eyes. ''Why the tears, Jen? Did
I scare you?''

''Tears?'' she countered, getting to her feet and over-
coming the urge to knock him over on his butt. ''No tears.
I don't cry for anybody anymore. I gave that up a long time
ago.''

Nick followed to his feet and grinned down at her.
''Yeah,'' he agreed with a nod and a quick swipe at some of
the remaining moisture on Jenny's cheek. ''About six
o'clock this evening.''

''Believe me,'' she countered, trying to keep the hope
from her eyes and voice, ''that *was* a long time ago.''

Nick took her by the shoulders. ''I know. I'm sorry. I
tried to get back sooner, but there were a few details to take
care of.''

Jenny tilted her head to the side, her hair brushing the
yellow cotton on her shoulder. ''Is it time to have that
drink?''

Nick nodded and followed when she turned for the
kitchen.

''What details?'' she asked.

She didn't see the wolf's smile on Nick's face. "Reinstating the watch on a certain red Porsche, for one."

Jenny whirled on him, almost slamming right into Nick's chest. "Watch?" she demanded. "As in police?"

He nodded.

She was surprised to find herself laughing. "*You* were behind all those tickets he got?" With his smile, she shook her head. "But why?"

"Principle."

Still Jenny didn't move. She didn't realize she'd tilted her head a little again, as if to better assess Nick and his motives. "What does principle have to do with it?"

Nick was still grinning. "You'll probably understand better when I tell you how I got stuck on the ice cream truck."

Somehow, they didn't quite get to the ice cream truck. They didn't even get to the drinks.

Jenny poured them, splashing a healthy amount of gin into each glass and sacrificing a real lime, but she never got her first taste. Something else got in the way.

Nick.

He stood right behind her as she poured, sending some of the gin dripping from the countertop and into the cat's dish. Silent, watching, waiting. And Jenny, her body suddenly much too acutely aware of what it had missed for more than two years, knew him there like a starving animal smells water.

"Maybe this isn't such a good idea," he murmured close to her neck, his breath fanning her.

Then he'd been struck by that same mysterious bolt of lightning. Jenny should have been upset. She couldn't quite admit that instead she was glad.

"What is a good idea, Nick?" she asked without turning around. The gin was oily on her fingers and she wanted to lick it like the chicken grease. She wanted Nick to lick it.

"A good idea," he answered very quietly, "is for me to get the hell out of here before I take you right here on the kitchen floor."

He surprised a little gasp from her. Jenny held on to the chilled glass, wondering how desire could so quickly explode, like a forest fire crowning with only a few words. Her hands were shaking. Her heart slid and skipped, threatening to tumble right out of her chest where her lungs suddenly weren't working. Her trembling hands began to sweat.

"Did I tell you," she said, eyes closed, "that imagination is something I value in a man?"

For a moment there was no answer. The light over the sink kept the shadows at bay. It also seemed to throw off an inordinate amount of heat. Jenny's skin was flushed, and the brush of Nick's breath against her neck raised goose bumps.

He tried one last time, his voice tight and unhappy. "My name is Nick Bronkowski and I have a wife and seven kids."

When Jenny smiled, she opened her eyes. Nick was reflected in the window, his dark head almost lost in the shadows above her. Like a dream, following her, shadowing her even in waking moments. Always there, always tempting, tormenting. Close enough to touch, never real enough to hold.

Except Nick was real. And he wanted her.

Jenny turned on him, finally allowing the tentative banners of anticipation to reach her eyes. One look at Nick very nearly took her resolve. His eyes were hot. They swept her as if unable to remain still, soaking in the sight of her, stirring the fire that glowed at their depths. Nick stood so rigidly Jenny thought a touch would break him. His mouth was set. His brow was creased. He was fighting for distance and losing.

"Did I scare *you*?" Jenny asked in a very small voice.

He never moved, either to close the distance between them or increase it. His breath was coming more quickly; his chest rose erratically. "Yes," he finally said, his voice as tortured as his eyes. "You scare the hell out of me."

She had on nothing beneath her gown. The cotton suddenly chafed her, too cool and crisp against her aching breasts, too heavy along fiery skin. Jenny thought she could feel the heat emanate from Nick like the waves from a summer street. It brought color into her cheeks and made her hands restless. It beckoned to her tongue. Jenny wanted to taste that heat, to bask in it and stoke it with flames of her own. She wanted to raise a sheen of sweat on him and lick it off.

"Jenny?"

Her own chest was rising as erratically now as the fire from Nick's eyes stole the oxygen. "Yes."

"I didn't lie. I do love you."

Jenny could hardly move her head to nod. She could hardly bring herself to speak without begging. Nick still hadn't moved, his hands rock-still by his sides, his tongue safely behind closed lips.

"I know," she finally managed. "I love you, too, Nick."

Still they stood apart, held by the ambivalences warring within them. Neither knew how to trust, neither could afford a mistake. Both knew what hunger was, how to bank it. How to control it.

But tonight, there was no control. Even Jenny who had marked every hour of the past two years with the constraint she maintained, could summon none now when she most needed it. All she could think of was that for once, for once in her responsible life, she wanted to be irresponsible. She wanted to take a chance that might not pay off. She wanted to test Nick's limits. She wanted to awaken and see him sleep alongside of her.

She wanted to be taken on her kitchen floor.

"Nick?"

"Yes?"

"Do you like your martinis dry?"

Nick frowned, never taking his eyes from hers, never breaking that precious contact. "Yes."

Now Jenny smiled, her gaze never wavering, offering delight with her desire, honesty with her decision. "Good," she nodded, lifting her hand for him to see the moisture still on her fingers. "I was wondering if you'd take care of this gin for me."

That quickly, Nick's control shattered.

Chapter 12

The tile would be cool against her back. The air-conditioning would wash her, chilling the moist skin Nick kissed. Jenny knew she would never again allow such abandon. She knew the price of it, and she wasn't prepared to pay it.

But now, now she would sing with it.

It began the minute she felt Nick's mouth close around her fingers. He took them one at a time, his eyes locked on hers, his hands wrapped around hers as if afraid she'd pull away. Jenny saw nothing but his eyes, the deliberate invitation offered there. She felt nothing but her finger, cool in the kitchen air, sliding in to meet the rasp of his tongue as he lavished over the liquor on her finger.

The sparks flared there and raced onward, anticipating his conquest, craving it. Skittering up her arm, shattering in her chest where they lodged in her breasts, tautening them impossibly, making her want to cry out with longing. Settling in her belly where they grew, crouching in her like a hot coil, glowing hotter and hotter just with the slick pressure of his lips along her finger. Just with the hold of his hands around hers.

Jenny stood with her back against the counter, her bare feet cold against the floor, her face flushed. She knew her lips had parted. Her eyes had widened, dilated. She was breathing faster to keep up with her heart. But her heart couldn't seem to keep up with Nick's eyes. He was taking her without even touching her, and Jenny groaned with it.

"Imagination, huh?" he asked, his voice no more than a harsh rasp as he ran her sensitized fingers against the bristle of his chin.

Jenny almost jumped with the fresh lightning. She couldn't seem to hold still anymore, as if movement would dispel the pressure building in her. She couldn't even answer. The uncertain wonder in her eyes must have been answer enough.

Nick smiled, a hunter's smile. A lover's smile when he suddenly knew how to best please. Without waiting for an answer, he turned away from Jenny and with one hand swept the contents of the kitchen counter onto the floor.

Jenny stared. She barely had time to react. Nick stole her momentum. He turned back to her and took her hand. "I think it's about time you got more from this kitchen than headaches," he whispered and eased her along to the empty section of counter, where it met the wall without interference from window or cabinet. Jenny wasn't sure she really wanted to test his imagination, after all. She'd never strayed this far. She never really had made love anywhere but on a bed. In the most traditional of terms.

But then Nick slipped out of his jacket and she forgot her objections. "I thought I got to do that," she objected, her voice breathy.

"Next time," he promised. "This time I want you to follow my lead."

Next time? Shouldn't she protest? Shouldn't she stop it before there was a *this* time?

His eyes still on her, Nick lifted his hands to her shoulders. "I've been waiting so long for this," he said, his hands moving to the white buttons that held her robe closed.

"You've only known me a couple of weeks."

He smiled down at her, dropping a kiss that promised so much it took Jenny's breath all over again. "But I've waited my life to meet you."

That very nearly did in Jenny's knees. Nick's fingers brushed against her, tantalizing, anticipating. She could almost feel her skin thrumming beneath them, and it unnerved her. When he reached the last button and reached back up to slip the robe from her shoulders, though, she helped him.

He mesmerized her with his eyes. He paralyzed her with his hands. Before she knew it, she was lifted onto the counter, sitting against him so that her legs wrapped him and her short cotton gown skimmed her hips.

"Nick, this is . . ."

"Fun," he assured her, a finger to her lips.

There was a ribbon at the bodice, a white ribbon that had seemed so safe and comfortable when she'd bought it. Nick reached up to pull it apart, and Jenny bit her lip. The gown fell open a little, and she knew that he could see her breasts. He still didn't take his eyes from hers. His hands strayed to her bare arm and set up fierce goose bumps. He leaned against her so that he fit neatly into the bared vee of her thighs, so she could discover his arousal. Jenny found herself wanting to wrap more closely to him, to get through the course brush of those jeans and share the heat she felt.

She found herself wanting to move again.

Nick lifted his hand and tangled his fingers into Jenny's hair. It tingled all the way to her toes. Standing so that his mouth was the same height as hers, Nick pulled her to him. His lips found hers and set to conquering. Soft, sweet, insistent, nipping and tugging at her until she brought her hands up around his shoulders. Until she tangled her own hands in his hair and kept him against her.

She felt his other hand stray, along her arm, back up her waist, at her collarbone, skimming her like a bird across bright waves. Setting up a chorus of reactions that all seemed to finally sink into her belly. Heating her until she ached for more.

He gave it. Even as he deepened his kiss, his tongue dancing along the edges of hers, even as he mingled sighs of pleasure, he slid his other hand around to ease her gown free. His hand roamed her thighs, her bottom and the tenderest skin right at the base of her spine. He groaned when she arched against him. When she let her own hand drop, he pulled free.

"Not yet," he repeated, the heat of him reflected in the languorous smoke in those whiskey-colored eyes of his. Pulling her hand to his mouth to kiss it, he brought his other hand up.

"You are so beautiful," he murmured, his eyes finally straying, finally seeing that her breasts strained against the cotton, the nipples button-hard against him. It made him smile. "So beautiful."

He watched as he brought his hand to her breast, skimming down the yellow cotton, so lightly Jenny ached to move closer. He stroked her back and cupped a breast in his hand, savoring the weight, the fullness, the delicious texture. Jenny watched him with wonder, her trepidation evaporated with just the delight in his eyes. She'd never known a moment like this, never a pride in herself like this man inspired. Never a crescendo of sensation like he provoked.

Taking her hands in his, Nick raised her arms over her head and lifted her gown away. And then, sliding his hands slowly back down her arms, caressing the underside and sliding lower, he brought them back to her breasts.

Jenny gasped. She arched in his hands, the rasp of his thumbs torture against her sensitive nipples, torment to the ache that now throbbed throughout her. She brought her hands back to his neck, to wind into his thick hair. She tested the hard line of his jaw and the taut tendons of his throat. She could smell him, dark and potent. She could hear him, the ragged catch of his breath, the brush of his hands against her skin. She could feel him, the lightning he sparked, the hunger he incited. It was becoming so hard to wait.

Nick bent to her, so that Jenny could see the top of his head, the glossy hair against her pale skin. He took her nipple in his mouth. Jenny groaned. She let her head fall back. His hand was there. His hand was everywhere. Even as he stirred the fires even higher with his mouth, nipping, laving, suckling until Jenny curled her toes against his denim-clad legs, he brought his other hand back to her thighs. Back to sate the hunger. To open her and please her and entice her.

Jenny instinctively moved against him, seeking his plunder, anxious for his company. She wanted him in her, deep where he would be safe, where she would hold him even when he was far gone from her. She felt his finger slip in to where she waited, swollen and slick for him, and shuddered.

Nick lifted his head, his hands suddenly still. "Jenny?"

Jenny answered by tugging his shirt free of his jeans. "You'd better hurry, bud," she warned breathlessly, "or I'm going to explode into a million pieces."

He took a second to make sure, his eyes dark and turbulent.

"Please, Nick," she begged, hands clutching the material at his shoulders. "Before I throw *you* on the floor."

When he smiled this time, Nick looked years younger, eons older. Jenny laughed, a tinkling sound, like a river in sunlight. Freedom. Exhilaration. Exultation.

"Then I think it's time for that bed," he whispered.

Nick couldn't believe Jenny's reaction. Straightening like he'd insulted her—or frightened her—she shook her head.

"No," she said, her eyes level, her hands against his chest. "Here. Please, Nick."

Nick could hardly argue with releasing the tension that was threatening to explode the denim stitching on his jeans. He'd known hunger in his life, but he'd never known obsession. His obsession had been born the minute he had taken Jenny into his arms.

"Why?" he asked, not wanting to hurt her in any way, unsure she really wanted what she was asking.

But when Jenny smiled, she was every siren, every seductress who had changed the course of history. "You promised imagination, remember?"

Slipping close enough to once again fill his hands with her, Nick nodded. "Yeah. Problem is that Barb and Bill

Bailey'd probably catch us when I carried you out to the sandbox.''

Somehow Jenny's answering smile only served to stoke the heat higher. Nick could hardly pay attention to what he was saying as it was. Leaning forward a little to brush her lips gently across his, she reached up and pulled the light chain. Instantly the kitchen fell into shadow and moonlight.

''We'll pretend,'' she whispered.

Nick groaned. ''Come here, you,'' he grated and pulled her into his arms. Just as quickly he felt her stiffen and gasp.

''Cold belt buckle.''

Nick silenced her chuckle with his mouth. He wrapped around her and wrapped her around him. And that way he carried her into the playroom where the moonlight streamed in the endless windows, dust motes dancing in the silence, the floor as dark as earth and as cool as water. And it was there he laid her, his nymph, amid the forest that was her imagination.

Nick straightened from her to unbuckle his jeans. He couldn't take his eyes from her, dark-eyed, her hair like smoke, her skin alabaster white in the moonlight, her nipples a tight dusky rose. God, he had never known such power. Such a delicious hurt. He wanted so much to drive her to a frenzy, to see those eyes go liquid, to see that head thrown back and that body rocking beneath him. He wanted her to cry out to him.

The floor was so cool against Jenny's back, just like she'd thought. The air swam over her like a lazy river, and Nick kept her warm with his eyes.

Jenny watched as he discarded his jeans. She did her best to wait, her body singing in clearer and clearer tones, the pleasure soaring with just the sight of Nick's lean, hardened body. She wanted this—needed it. She needed him. Holding out her arms, she welcomed him home.

She wanted him then. Nick made her wait longer. He rekindled the banked fires, his skin hot and cold at once against hers, the hair-roughened texture of his thighs agony against hers, his tongue greedy and his hands clever. He murmured to her, sighed with her own feverish exploration, nurtured her untapped passion until she danced beneath the play of his hands.

Jenny fought the precipice, waiting for him, wanting him with her. When Nick slid his hand down to test the way, she parted her thighs for him. When he stroked and tantalized, his fingers like lightning against her, she arched, whimpered, clutched at him. When he still stayed away, she took him in her own hands and guided the way.

Nick rode the crest close to the edge, sweeping along unheeded, racing, rocking with Jenny. Just the sweet dance of her hands over his skin threatened to shatter him. When she took him into her, he knew he was lost.

Nick dropped his face into Jenny's throat, soaking in her scent, the song of her cries, the delight of her soft breasts and velvet skin. He felt her shudders grow, felt her close around him and invite him along. The moonlight spiraled in him, swirling and dancing, swimming into music and shattering into day. He heard his name whispered, sung, chanted and answered with hers. And there, finally, spent, he pulled her into his arms and bid her sleep.

At some point the floor became too cool. Jenny was feeling goose bumps that hadn't been there before. She didn't feel regret for what she'd done. It was just that once the hormones had been sated, common sense tended to creep back. She was lying naked on her playroom floor with a man, and she had two children who could easily walk in. Not that either of them had ever wandered in the middle of the night, but Murphy lived for eventualities like this.

"You're shivering," Nick observed, running a languid hand over her arm.

"The air-conditioning has made its presence known," Jenny allowed, trying to work up the initiative to move. She didn't want to. She'd never felt so content in her life. There was something about this particular set of shoulders that seemed to carry the weight of the world, something about this chest that begged nestling. For the first time in her adult life, Jenny gave fleeting thought to resenting the intrusion of her children.

If it weren't for them, she could easily not move for days. And right now—except for the chilly Italian quarry tile—she thought she could manage that quite easily.

"Feel like a shower?" Nick asked.

Jenny shook her head against his shoulder. "Not with Emma and Kevin upstairs. No offense, but I think they'd take it wrong if they saw Mom step out of the bathroom naked along with a man."

Nick didn't seem too perturbed by her answer. "Okay, then we'll just stay down here."

Jenny thought to ask what that entailed, but before she could gather the energy Nick pulled them both up and made the move to the couch where one of Barby's trademark afghans resided. Nick pulled it up, slid in beneath so that they stretched out lengthwise, Jenny rested against his back, and laid the afghan over them both.

Jenny couldn't argue with the effect. Toasty warm on both sides, decadently comfortable. Unquestionably content.

"I'm not sure we should," she demurred anyway. "The kids..."

"Can you hear them get up from here?"

"I can hear them turn over from anywhere in the house."

Nick nodded against the back of her head and tightened his arms around her. "Gives you plenty of time to slip back into your nightgown."

"And your jeans?"

"No, I think your nightgown's enough."

Jenny elbowed and met with some satisfying ribs.

Nick just chuckled. "Ease up, Jen. You were the one who wanted imagination. When was the last time you hung out with a naked guy on the couch?"

"And how do I explain the naked guy to my kids?"

"If they show up, I promise I'll make it to the sandbox before they get this far. Then we only have to worry about traumatizing Barb Bailey."

For a moment Jenny considered what Barb's reaction would be to finding a naked Nick in the backyard. Then she found herself chuckling right along with him. "Might be worth it."

He must have been a magician. Just with the contact of his hands across her belly, Nick kept her on that couch. Jenny molded into him, savoring the alien feel of his male body against her, basking in the dying embers of lovemaking.

"Where do we start?" she asked a while later, the answers now even more important.

"I think we just did," Nick said, shifting a little so he could rest his cheek against her hair.

Jenny found herself sighing with the pleasure of it. She wrapped her arms around his and rested. "That doesn't solve all problems."

"Solved mine."

Jenny's eyes were closed. She smiled anyway. "What problems do you have?" she asked.

"Well," he murmured, "I can report back to my boss that I personally searched you and found you clean."

Jenny chuckled. "And I can tell him just how thoroughly you pursued your objectives."

She could hear the grimace in Nick's voice. "Yeah, that's just what I'd need. I'd be out selling apples on the street in a week."

"I could give you a reference as an ice cream driver, if you want."

"Thanks."

"You never asked me," Jenny said, a little while later again. Time seemed to slip so easily away in this silvered darkness. Daylight floated away and left them lying together without hurry.

"Asked you what?"

"Why I was seen at those mailboxes."

"Why *were* you seen at those mailboxes?" he echoed in his best official voice. "I was just about to ask."

"Would you believe me?"

"I'd kill dragons for you."

"Next time Mrs. Warner steals Kevin's ball, I'll be in touch."

Still they lay, entwined, peaceful, holding off the world by sheer dint of their contentment.

"Mailboxes," he nudged.

"Kevin," she explained, "has decided he wants to be a mailman when he grows up. So, to that end, he's been playing mailman."

"With other people's mail?"

Jenny nodded. "With other people's mail. I figured it out when I first found Bill Hobbs's medical bills under my bed. Kevin is on parole. I'm watching for repeat offenses."

"What about other people in the neighborhood?"

Jenny thought a moment. "No. I don't think anyone else in the neighborhood wants to be a mailman when they grow up. Buffy wants to be a stockbroker, and I want to be a cowgirl."

"I'll know where to come if I get any reports of rustling."

"Who do you think it is?"

Nick shrugged, his chest rasping against the sensitive skin of her back and sending up fresh shivers. "Hell, I don't know. The only person I'm sure it isn't is me. And that's only because I'm never far enough away from that damn truck to steal anything."

"Except when you're here."

"What about when I'm here?"

"You had enough time to steal my good sense. I'd like to know where you put it, please. It's probably time to put it back on."

For a long moment, there was no answer. Jenny felt the atmosphere shift, sensed Nick tense almost as if he were bracing for something.

"You mean you don't think it's sensible to make love to a man on your kitchen counter?"

Jenny smiled, but already it had lost some of its glow. "I mean I don't think it's sensible to make love to a man who lives to be a lawyer."

"Because you did once and look where it got you?"

The caution in his voice took the rest of her smile. She wanted to hug her arms around her belly, to curl away from him even as she burrowed more deeply into the strength of his embrace. "Something like that," she admitted.

"You're not being very reasonable about that."

"No," she admitted. "I'm not. I'm gun-shy. Especially after the three rounds I went today."

"Not everybody's like him, Jen."

"God, I hope not."

"I'm not going to apologize for what I want," he told her. "I'm sure as hell not going to give it up. I've worked too damn hard for it."

Tears stung the back of Jenny's eyes. She knew she was a hot reactor on the subject, but Nick was becoming so important to her. Too important.

Even so, she couldn't bear to hear that hurt edge to his voice. He *had* scraped a lot harder for what he had, after all. And if a desire to be a lawyer had gotten him this far, how could she argue?

"I'm sorry," she apologized, feeling the cold seep into their little nest and hating it. "It's just hard to believe."

"What, that I want to be a lawyer?"

"That you love me."

It was enough to stop the cold. In one motion Nick had her turned around to him, so she could see his eyes, so she could believe his sincerity. "You'd better believe it, lady. I don't lie naked on couches with just anybody."

Jenny matched his winsome smile. "Well, that's the most poignant testimony I've ever heard."

"I've also been spending evenings in the law library trying to figure how to get you out of your ex-husband's clutches."

That had Jenny's full attention. "How could you do that?" she demanded, pulling all the way around so that her feet hit the floor and the afghan slipped.

Nick's eyes slid to where the moonlight washed her breasts. "What?"

His fingers seemed to want to follow. Jenny took them in hand and demanded his attention. "The Jerk," she nudged.

He smiled, easily switching positions so that Jenny's hands were in his. "Easy," he assured her, dropping kisses onto her palms. "It's just a little harder to get custody if the D.A.'s been after you." Kiss. "And since I happen to be good buddies with the guys over at the D.A.'s office, and since your ex is in arrears about six months for his ridiculous excuse for child support," kiss, "with your permission, he's going to be hearing from the law in about two days."

Jenny was finding it increasingly difficult to keep her mind on child support. Nick bent to her hands again and skimmed her now-sensitive palms with his tongue, tasting all the way to the edges of her fingers. Hands again, and he was lighting the same, furious fires. Jenny just wanted to stretch, to purr like a cat and watch him consume her, bit by delicious bit.

"I was going to wait a while," he continued, testing the insides of her wrists and making her gasp. "You know, a few tickets, a little subtle harassment. . . . But I figure this custody thing warrants special attention."

"But why—" he was traveling the inside of her arms, his teeth nipping at the tender flesh, his tongue leaving a trail for the cool air to find "—why didn't somebody do this before?"

Pausing only long enough to lift a self-satisfied smile at her, Nick explored her elbows. "Because," he said, "no one else has my principles."

Jenny thought she was panting. She wasn't sure. She just knew that without even being touched, her breasts felt like splintered glass, sharp slivers of heat scattering through her. "The principles that got you on the truck?"

He nodded. "I'll have to send the chief's brother a thank-you note."

The tide was rising quickly, hot, thick lava, lapping at her toes, oozing along her calves and spilling over onto her thighs. Seeping into her belly and breasts and taking her breath. Again.

She couldn't think properly. She couldn't seem to care anymore that the Jerk was a jerk. It only mattered that Nick had cared enough to help.

"You really did that?"

Nick moved around so that he sat behind her, his legs straddling her, his lips down at her throat. "Slaved day and night."

Jenny's head came back. Nick's hands were edging around her waist. His teeth were nibbling on the tender flesh along her shoulder. She thought she was going to moan.

"I guess some lawyers aren't . . . so bad."

Nick brought his hands up so that he circled her completely, held her firmly. He was working his way up to her ear and around to her breasts.

"I hear," he said, slipping his tongue into the shell of her ear and provoking gasps, "that I'm pretty good."

"You're—" Jenny responded by sliding her hand behind her and testing his response "—okay."

He laughed, but he sounded breathless. Jenny laughed back, and sounded even more breathless than he. Nick found her breasts. He filled his hands with them, and Jenny was lost.

Nick saw the daylight edging closer and wondered if he'd stayed too long. He lay curled around Jenny on the couch, her head on his shoulder, her hands around his waist. He smelled citrus and soap, lovemaking and morning, and thought that he could live like this forever. He could survive anything if he only had the chance to have this moment each day, this fragile space of peace when Jenny slept in his arms.

She was so beautiful, her eyes closed and her lashes lying like soot against her pale skin. He wanted to run his hands through her hair and kiss her awake. He wanted to make love to her again.

But he knew better. He was on her time, now. Daylight was coming and with it waited the responsibilities, the questions she hadn't asked. The questions *he* hadn't asked.

For at least that moment when the moonlight died into mauve and the birds woke in the trees, Nick could find happiness. For that moment, he could have it all.

"Jenny?"

Her face puckered a little and she nestled closer. Nick ached to love her awake.

"Come on, little girl," he coaxed, finally giving in enough to push her hair back from her forehead.

It made her smile. "I bet you're the fairy godmother, and you're going to tell me it's midnight."

He smiled back, really feeling it take root. "Well, I figured you didn't want certain elves to find you here when they came down for cereal."

Opening her eyes, she nodded. "I appreciate the forethought." For a moment Jenny just watched him, her eyes languid and dark in the half-light, like a deep spring in the woods. "Problem is, I just don't want to move."

Nick ran a finger along the tip of her nose. "See what happens when you let your imagination get out of hand?"

She stretched against him, and Nick knew what the word frustration meant. He could hardly suppress his immediate reaction, but he knew better than to think he could enjoy it. He had business to discuss with Jenny, and it wasn't the kind you could pursue with a sleek, full, warm body nestled in your arms.

"Come on," he urged, moving faster than he should have. "There's something I have to talk to you about."

Jenny obviously didn't wake as quickly as he. When Nick eased her up to a sitting position, she sat there swaying and shivering for a minute, her hair in delightful disarray, her eyes wide and soft. Nick gritted his teeth. It was only getting worse. He had to get back into his jeans before he couldn't.

"It's okay," she assured him with a vague smile. "I still respect you."

Realizing that Jenny wasn't ready to fend for herself just yet, Nick wrapped her in the afghan and turned for his jeans. He didn't miss the fact that the one thing Jenny had definitely noticed in her half-alert state was his state of full alert.

"Isn't nonverbal communication a wonderful thing?" she offered with a much too wicked grin.

"Knock it off," he warned, already yanking on what he knew would be his most uncomfortable pair of pants. "I can't make sense when you look like that. Get some clothes on."

The sound of her giggle was like bells on the wind. "I think you make perfect sense. I'm just sorry we don't have time to . . . pursue the subject."

The rasp of a zipper was loud in the quiet room. "Get dressed, Jen."

Jenny offered a peculiarly girlish grimace. "Fairy god-mothers just aren't as much fun as they used to be."

This godmother responded by hitting her in the face with her nightgown.

"All right," Nick said a few minutes later while the cof-fee perked and the birds came to raucous life outside the windows. "I need to ask a big favor, Jen."

Perching on a chair opposite him, Jenny offered that sleepy half-smile that was doing such damage to his seams. "Pancakes are out of the question, Nick. I don't cook breakfast."

He scowled. "I'm serious."

"I know," she nodded, refusing to give up her smile. "You're always serious. Gives you frown lines."

For a moment he could do no more than stare at her, his head tilted in consideration. "Well, at least I know you're not crabby in the morning. You're not there, at all."

She just smiled. When the coffee gurgled its last, she got up to pour.

"Jenny, I need to maintain my cover."

He thought she'd object, that she'd anticipate what he was going to ask. Instead, unbelievably, she giggled. "Your cover," she echoed. "It sounds so desperate, like you're running guns for the Godfather or something. I guess an ice cream man was just never my idea of a dangerous situa-tion."

He couldn't help but grin back at her lilting observation. "You've never gotten between a seven-year-old and a bombpop on a hot day," he retorted.

Setting his cup down, she slipped back into her chair and eased her chin down onto her hands, that smile still lighting her sleep-softened features. "You want me to help keep the Godfather in the dark."

Nick was going to take a sip of coffee. With the cup halfway up, he scowled. "Something like that."

"Am I undercover, too, then?" she asked. "Do I have an alias and a secret-decoder ring?"

"Jenny."

She smiled again and finally brought herself to upright attention. Somewhere in that odd little conversation, the alert intelligence had returned to her expression, and Nick found himself missing the gamine inside.

"The least I can do for the man who has made it his mission to personally harass my ex-husband is help him catch less despicable crooks. What can I do?"

He stopped, faced her with even consideration. "Keep seeing me."

For a moment Jenny just considered him in return. "And how do you ask for dates?" she countered.

Nick shook his head a little, the coffee back on the table as he leaned closer to convince her. "It has nothing to do with last night. I need to finish this assignment, and the only way I'm going to do it is if you don't report me to your friend the detective and the neighbors."

Jenny's eyebrows lifted. "Nobody?"

"Nobody. Not even Barby and Bill Bailey. Not even your family. For the next few days until I can find something, you have to pretend that I'm still the neighborhood drug dealer."

"And keep inviting you over."

"It would give me greater mobility."

Jenny spent a moment facing her tablecloth. Her gaze shifted a little to find the papers and books Nick had swept onto her floor. Without thinking, she got up to pick them up before the kids had a chance to ask. It seemed important somehow that they didn't stumble upon the traces of her lovemaking.

"Was this what was on your mind when you showed up last night?" she asked, fighting inexplicable tears. Stupid that his question had changed the flavor of his promises. Dumb that she should be looking for hidden agendas everywhere.

But then at one time she had been too obtuse to look for hidden agendas, and they'd jumped out to bite her. Jenny didn't want that to happen again.

Bent over the cups and cookbooks she was trying to gather into her arms, she didn't hear Nick scrape his chair back. She didn't notice his approach. Suddenly he was there on the floor next to her, pulling the little pile from her arms, turning her toward him.

"I didn't come here last night for the sole purpose of convincing you," he told her, eye-to-eye, his hand on her arm, his voice intense. "I came to ask. I forgot to do it the minute I saw the tears on your cheeks." Pulling her to her feet, he set down the books and took Jenny into his arms, barring flight and doubt with just the strength of his arms. "I was as surprised as you were, Jen," he said. "I still am. But I'm not sorry. In fact—" how could a smile be so suddenly devastating? she wondered seeing his "—I'm selfish enough to admit that for the first time since I set foot on that damn ice cream wagon, I can really look forward to this assignment."

"I'm not recess," she warned, terrified by the way his eyes sapped her resolve. Exhilarated by the conviction she saw there.

"I never said you were," he countered. "All I'm asking is that the department pick up some of the expenses of this courtship. In return, we wait until I've caught the forger before you reveal my secret identity."

"If I didn't think we had real problems," she answered, "I'd say it sounded like a lot of fun."

"Problems are to be worked out," he said. "We can do that."

For a moment Jenny's challenge was a silent one. She couldn't bear to go forward, couldn't bear to slip back. "Are you sure?" she asked, knowing that there was no more important question in her life.

"I'm sure."

Jenny would have been a lot happier if Nick's eyes were as convinced as his words. Even so, she could still feel the warm musky aftertaste of love. She could still see the flashes of passion in Nick's eyes when he'd come to her last night. And she still saw the small, lonely boy who refused to let himself believe. For that, she nodded her head.

"All right," she allowed. "I'll give it a try."

It was only later when she sat once again alone at her table and heard the first stirrings of her children that Jenny began to doubt her decision.

Chapter 13

It didn't take Nick much longer.

When he left Jenny's, he headed back to the station. The drive was a quiet one, the streets still empty of rush-hour traffic, the summer morning just beginning to take shape. Nick spent the drive wondering at the events of the night before. He hadn't lied to Jen. He was still amazed that either of them had shown such uncharacteristic abandon. He was awed that she had given so much, known him so well, grown so quickly comfortable with him.

Nick wasn't usually comfortable with anyone. He'd never been relaxed enough with a woman to want to wake up alongside her in the morning. Nick's idea of a relationship had always been marked by the boundaries imposed by a lifetime of distrust. If he left first, she wouldn't get a chance to.

Suddenly, all that was different. Nick was the one who wanted to stay. He wanted to walk into that tumbled, raucous house and never see sunlight again. He wanted to curl up on Jenny's couch like a contented cat and just soak in the love in her eyes. The taste of her the night before had finally convinced him of that. She had felt so right in his arms, so alive, so vital. She had felt as if she belonged there.

As Nick sped down the interstate toward Clayton, he finally admitted that for the first time in his life, he felt as if he belonged, too.

The Corps had been his home, and then the force. Manetti had been a kind of mentor, and Baker the obnoxious surrogate kid sister. The other cops had become his friends. But none of them had needed him. None of them had made him feel as if he made a big enough difference to matter a damn.

Of course, it would take something special to give him that feeling. Dora had seen to that. But finally, after thirty-five years of wandering, Nick knew what it felt like to see home. He saw it every time he looked at Jenny.

When he walked into his office, though, the silver lining showed its cloud. The room was empty for a change, the night guy evidently down exchanging outrageous propositions with the dispatcher. There was paperwork everywhere, and a couple of new files on Nick's desk. On top of the files was the box of crayons. By the lamp sat the lumpy blue figure of Papa Smurf. Without thinking, Nick walked over and picked it up.

Toys. Kids. Why did the mere thought unsettle him? Nick had to admit that he really enjoyed Emma and Kevin, but he had never been forced to be the bad guy around them. He'd never had to disappoint them or obstruct them. They were nice kids, but every time Nick thought of having kids he thought of the homes where he was raised, the kids other people imposed on him as brothers and sisters.

There had never been privacy, never any fun. Kids had been a never-ending, mind-numbing responsibility. They had never been quiet. Never friendly. Nick couldn't think of Jenny holding that newborn without picturing a ten-year-old boy having to monitor a toddler right alongside. Never an escape, never any help, never a meal or private moment without interruptions.

Never, never any freedom.

Was this something Nick could dive back into, even for Jenny? Could he assume responsibility for Emma and

Kevin, overseeing homework and doling out allowances, attending Boy Scouts and father-daughter banquets? Could he anticipate children of his own and keep from resenting their intrusion in his life? Or on his relationship with Jenny?

Marriage. He'd never really considered anything else. He wanted Jenny for his own. He loved her. He thought he loved her children. But he couldn't only *think* that, if he wanted Jenny. He had to *know*. He had to find out one way or another or Jenny wouldn't so much as let him in the door.

He'd never wanted anything so much in his life. He'd never been so afraid that he couldn't get it. Flipping the Smurf over in his hands, Nick shook his head. He'd promised her he'd work through their problems. He just hoped he could.

"I think it's time to call this all to a halt."

The meeting had reconvened, all parties present. Detective Richards slouched in Barb's blue-flowered armchair, and Lauren and Miss Lucy shared the couch. Barb paced and Jenny sat swinging her leg from the other armchair. Barb had just had the floor.

Studying the beaded moisture on her glass of lemonade (freshly squeezed), Jenny fought a smile. It was obvious that Nick hadn't quite escaped unnoticed yesterday morning. Barb was appointing herself Jen's guardian in the neighborhood meeting.

"We still haven't caught the dealer," Richards allowed, his eyes considering Jenny rather than Barb.

Jenny shrugged. "I'd really hate to let somebody like that get away with it."

Barb came to an unhappy halt. "You can't allow him to keep showing up at your house like that, either, Jen. Think of what it'll do to the kids."

"He hasn't done anything to hurt the kids."

So far Lauren and Miss Lucy watched much like a tennis match. Miss Lucy had worn her best straw hat for the occasion and Lauren came decked out in her best designer sweat suit. Jenny, as ever, was in her brown polyester uniform. She could hardly wait to get back to school just for the chance to wear old dresses.

"He seems such a delightful young man," Miss Lucy offered, her gloved hands folded in her lap. "He even knows what kind of ice cream I want before I get to his stand on my walks." A scan of her audience didn't seem to encourage her. "Dreamsicle," she offered with a definite nod, as if that would settle the matter.

Then Jenny did smile. "Have you been able to connect him to the sales in any way?" she asked the detective.

"Not yet. We still don't have that kid who's in Europe, and nobody else claims to know anything. We've made a couple of arrests since then, but the information's even more vague."

Jenny just nodded.

"Seems amazing to me," the detective went on, "that you've spent so much time with him to not find anything out."

"Well, let's see," Jenny answered, eyes up. "We've discussed the state of my car, the state of the Cards, the state of the nation and the state of ice cream."

The detective wasn't impressed. "Lady..."

Jenny faced him. "Detective, I'm not going to ask the man to marry me just to get his phone number."

His short laugh was offensive. "I didn't say anything about marriage..."

Jenny lifted a finger. "Say another word and you'll not only lose my cooperation but your suspect. I'll walk right up to that truck and tell him just who owns that blue Plymouth in the driveway."

At least she got a smile out of Barb on that one. Jenny really didn't enjoy deceiving Barb. After all, Barb only wanted to help. But she had to admit that the double-life situation piqued her imagination just a little. There was something a bit heady about playing one role for your neighbors and another in private.

"I'll make you a promise, Detective," she offered finally. "The minute I get his phone number, I'll call. Any time, day or night. Will that make you happy?"

Losing his patience, he shambled to his feet. "Lady, I haven't been happy since high school. You call me when you get *anything*."

Looking up at him, Jenny just nodded. "Absolutely."

It seemed he couldn't leave without at least one moralization. "And don't let yourself forget," he added, finger pointed threateningly, "just who that is you're dealing with out there."

"Oh, I don't think there's any chance of forgetting that, Detective." God, how she wanted to be there when he found out.

"I don't like him much," Miss Lucy announced after the detective had made his exit. She was settling her purse over her arm in preparation of making her own departure. "He has no manners. At least young Nick has manners."

"Well, that's certainly a redeeming feature on a drug dealer," Lauren muttered under her breath.

Miss Lucy never heard. "Time for my stroll, my dears. Do you all have your papers?"

They answered in chorus. "Oh, yes."

"Fine," she smiled. "Fine."

She never quite remembered to say goodbye. But then, by the time she strolled out the door, she was humming "The Toreador Song" from *Carmen*. Jenny grinned. Lauren shook her head. Barb collected glasses and emptied ashtrays.

"Jenny, you can't jeopardize yourself just to spite that policeman."

Jenny couldn't help but see the real concern in Barb's eyes. "I'm not jeopardizing anybody, Barb," she insisted, not knowing what else she could say. She stood up. "You know you can trust me."

Barb came to a sudden halt, ashtray in hand, and faced Jenny. "No, I don't," she argued, sincerely upset. "Not anymore."

"Not anymore?" Lauren echoed from where she sat on the couch. "Since when?" Her head was back on a swivel between the two friends, but it seemed she couldn't see anything.

Jenny didn't waste any attention on her. "Barb..."

Barb shook her head. "You just look too...too content, all of a sudden."

"And that's wrong?"

"With Nick it is. You *know* that, Jenny." Jenny could see her reaching for logic and failing, desperate to turn Jenny away from what she thought was a course to disaster. Barb ended up just shaking her head. "You know better."

All Jenny could do was sigh, because without knowing it Barb had hit a bull's-eye. "Maybe I don't," she admitted.

There was so much she wanted to talk to Barb about. She wanted to carry on her personal debate vocally, exposing each side for flaws, like a jeweler holding a gem up to the light. She wanted to know why she was so excited and so afraid at the same time. She wanted to know why she wanted so very much to believe Nick when she should have known better, just like Barb said. But until Nick found his thief, she couldn't say anything. She couldn't do more than pretend she was falling in love with a suspected drug dealer, and in doing so, suffer the frustrated concern of her friend.

For Barb, on the other hand, it was easy. She knew Jenny had already made one mistake, just by the look in her eyes. She was terrified she was going to compound it out of loneliness and frustration and longing. And Jenny couldn't tell her she was wrong. She couldn't tell her she was wrong on any count. Because even though Nick wasn't the person Barb thought he was, he could still be as dangerous as she feared. And Jenny could still make mistakes she couldn't take back.

She just couldn't talk about them.

"I don't care if he's selling drugs to Buffy," Barb said, her eyes eloquent as she shook the glass in her hand until the ice cubes rattled. "I don't want you hurt. Call Detective Richards. Tell him you quit."

"I can't," Jen said, finally turning away because she couldn't stand the hurt in Barb's eyes any longer. "Nick's going with me to pick up the car this afternoon."

"*I'll* do it," she argued, a hand to Jen's arm.

Jen whirled on her. "No, you won't," she snapped. "Now, I have to go, Barb."

Lauren just lifted an eyebrow at the sudden lightning that sparked between the two neighbors. "I'm glad *I* don't look so content."

Nick did his very best not to say anything about the chocolate candy bar Kevin was dragging into his back seat. That upholstery was original, after all, in pristine condition. Nick had spent the last Saturday afternoon washing it down again just to make sure. And they were climbing in out of ninety-degree heat. Nick was under no illusions about what that did to chocolate.

"Finish it," Jenny snapped economically. "Seat belts."

Nick stared. Kevin immediately backed out before the candy bar got near to a seat, and swallowed the rest of the bar in a gulp and a grin. Licking his fingers absolutely clean, he crawled back in after Emma who was arranging her dress around her knees like a princess on a carriage ride. Both of the kids snapped into their seat belts without help or fuss.

Nick really wasn't going to say anything. It was obvious from the look on Jenny's face that he hadn't looked as unconcerned as he'd thought.

"I'm sure Barby has about ten different ways to get melted chocolate out of upholstery," she assured him with a grin. "But prevention is nine-tenths of the solution."

Nick didn't quite keep the response from his expression. He was surprised when Jenny grinned again.

"My house is a mess," she said. "Not dirty. There's a difference."

"One I bet Barby can't see," he retorted with a like grin.

Jenny chuckled. "Buffy lives to build forts in my playroom. She never knew all the ways you could use cookbooks and blankets before."

If only it had stayed that pleasant. Jenny relaxed in the front seat. Nick geared down through the afternoon traffic and the kids played paper, rocks, scissors in the back seat. After the upheavals in Barb's kitchen, Jenny had actually begun to ache for her days to settle into a peace as comfortable as the one in this car. She wanted to believe it could be like Nick promised, that she could talk to Nick about his day and tell him about the funny things the kids had done. She could bask in the peace, the support, the camaraderie.

Then, inevitably, paper tried to beat out scissors, and the competition in the back seat came to blows.

"She's cheating! Mom, she's cheating!"

"No, I'm not. I win . . . ow, he pushed me!"

"But she's cheating!"

Jenny heaved a sigh. She could see the sudden tension in Nick's jaw. The decibel level put Iron Maiden to shame, and it showed no promise of peace without direct intervention.

"Sit on your own sides."

"But she bit me!"

Jenny had to turn around for that. She found Kevin waving the offended finger, which he'd obviously stuck right under Emma's nose, and Emma sitting primly with that smug little cat-in-the-cream smile that said that yes, she had cheated and had bitten Kevin and expected to come out unscathed. Jenny gave her a swipe across the knees.

Tears erupted on that side of the seat, too.

"You know how I feel about biting," she warned. "Now, if you can't play together, you won't need to come out of your rooms at all when we get home." Home was a long way off, at best, and Nick's fingers were white around the steering wheel.

"I find that rock and roll helps sometimes," she offered, turning back around.

He didn't seem to hear her.

Jenny sighed and rubbed at her tightening forehead. And she'd been looking forward to spending time with Nick, even on the way to the car dealership. Somehow, she should have known this would get in the way. But then, if he wanted to see children at their worst, this was definitely the time to partake. He was certainly getting the full treatment.

Of course, once they arrived, it didn't get any better. Emma slipped and fell into the only puddle of grease on the parking lot. Kevin wasted no time delighting over it, which infuriated Emma even more. Nick grew even more quiet as Jenny shepherded her little flock into the claustrophobic waiting room, sat Emma on a plastic chair that wouldn't notice a little more grease and gave her a *Sports Illustrated* to read.

"Thank you, Nick," Jenny said, preparing to formally let him off the hook. She couldn't bear to see a grown man suffer, and he had all the earmarks. He stood against the front door like a sane man who'd wandered into the locked ward, and his forehead had tightened to headache levels. And that was making her suffer. "I'm sure you have someplace to be. We'll be fine now."

He nodded, not taking his eyes from where Kevin persisted in blaming Emma for his troubles. "When you get the car."

Jenny couldn't think of anything to do but shrug. Emma was sticking her tongue out at Kevin, who was making dive-bomber noises with a Matchbox ambulance in her general direction. It didn't take much imagination to guess what he was hoping to annihilate with his latest strategic weapon. Jenny thought the day was about as miserable as it was going to get.

By that time in her life, she should have known how stupid that kind of thinking was.

"You want me to pay how much?"

The cashier stared at her through the window with fish eyes and popped a bubble. "That's what it comes to."

Jenny took a very deep breath. "And what about the estimate I got three days ago? The one that came in two hundred fifty dollars cheaper?"

The girl, obviously not working her way through a graduate-school degree, shrugged and popped her gum. "Dunno."

Jenny leveled her best attention-getting glare. "Then find someone who does."

Another shrug brought out the mechanic, a man who reminded Jenny very much of Detective Richards on his better days. This man was wiping his hands on a grease rag and also popping gum. And smiling.

"Now, Ms. Lake," he offered, unaware that the slightly scruffy-looking man perusing his *Field and Stream* was with the customer, "you couldn't very well drive off without a working water pump."

"You didn't say anything about it on the estimate," she objected, millimeters from losing control.

He liked his shrug as much as his cashier. "Nothin' much I could do. It needed to be fixed."

Jenny felt Nick approach from behind, and knew that he was about to come to her defense. Not even bothering to look around, she raised a hand to silence him. This one was hers. She had waited a long time to have the nerve to finish this little scenario out to her satisfaction.

"I didn't ask for a water pump," she said with such deadly calm that even the kids looked up. They were well acquainted with that tone of voice. "You didn't mention a water pump in the estimate. I—am—not—paying—for a water pump."

Another shrug, this replete with regret. "I don't know about the estimate, ma'am. I just know what was fixed. And if you can't pay for it, then I can't let you have it."

Jenny's smile was not a pretty sight. "I do know about the estimate," she answered quietly. "I have it on tape. On my answering machine. Now, I'd much rather not have to involve the Better Business Bureau and the District Attorney in this little misunderstanding. I don't even want to call my lawyer. I'll either wait here until you take it back out and put in the old one, or you can include it at the original cost for my goodwill since I didn't ask for it, anyhow."

"You want me to take it out?"

She nodded. "I'll wait." Before he could answer, she turned to her children. "I'm afraid we can't go to McDonald's until this man finishes the car. It might be *hours*."

Jenny should have felt worse about what she'd programmed her children to do. The fact that she felt herself at a distinct disadvantage in situations like this propelled her to use every conceivable weapon at her disposal to help even the score. And her children were a powerful motivator.

Within moments, it was highly uncomfortable for anyone else in the tiny waiting room. Jenny had thought the noise level in the car was bad. Now, it was unbearable. And what made it worse, was that Emma was a master whiner. No sane person could stand it for more than a few moments without running screaming into the night.

And Nick, much to Jenny's surprise, joined right in, complaining about the kids and the wait he'd anticipated when he'd brought his car in and the way this company was treating this nice lady. Jenny almost laughed aloud when he stalked back out the door.

Jenny didn't know whether it was her logic or her coercion, but she had her car back in under fifteen minutes. When she saw it rattle out of the bay, she realized she should have held out for something better. Even with its new parts, it was still a bit embarrassing to drive. The windshield was cracked and what wasn't rusted was dented.

As she pulled to the edge of the parking lot, she slowed next to the midnight-blue GTO that sat there, its driver slouching alongside with an impossibly huge grin on his face.

"I say," he said in his best Etonian accent as he headed over to assess the condition of her poor, beaten-up car. "Have you been in a terrorist attack?"

"Held hostage by a greasy man with a monkey wrench," she retorted, grinning up at him.

Nick leaned down, resting an arm on the hood over her window and shaking his head at her. "I had my hand on my badge, you know."

Jenny nodded, the exhilaration of her small victory still bubbling in her. "I appreciate it, Nick. But if you'd come to my rescue, that guy would have figured he could get away with that every time a single woman came in. I had to get out of my own jam."

He was still shaking his head. "Well, he'll never make that mistake with you again."

"He'll probably never let me in his parking lot as long as I live."

She felt so flushed with her small victory. So brave and intrepid, as if she'd just won a round with the Jerk and all his lawyers. A stupid little joy, a minor daily battle. But one she'd never quite won to her satisfaction before. It was the first time she could remember having walked away from an uncomfortable situation without feeling a residue of shame and guilt for somehow not conducting it better, not having more control, not being somehow taken advantage of. That man would sure as hell know she'd been there. And she wanted to celebrate.

"I have a date tonight," she said, squinting up to where she could see a fresh sheen of sweat glisten on Nick's upper lip. "Me, some kids and a big clown with a hamburger. I'm free for dinner tomorrow night, though. Interested?"

She wanted to see the silly exhilaration echoed in his eyes. She wanted, perversely, to see pride there. It made a difference to her that Nick would celebrate her successes along with her.

Instead, she saw strain. The tension was back in his forehead, that tight line between his eyes that reflected more than glare from a summer sun. He looked up for a moment, as if assessing the traffic that whistled and rumbled past. As if consulting a calendar, checking for room, for interest. Jenny saw the way he held on to the rim of her car with a tight hand and wondered why it hurt her that he was bothered.

"How about the day after?" he countered, looking back, but not really seeing her somehow.

The kids were getting restless in the back without air-conditioning. The promise of hamburgers had not been lightly given, and they wanted payment. Suddenly Jenny felt the heat, too. She felt the humidity closing in on her, closing off her air, her room. She saw the flat glint in Nick's eyes and thought for the first time not of windows but mirrors. Closed off, separate, distant. She saw the street, the cars chasing along after the clock, the rows of shiny new cars lined up behind her. She didn't see Nick anymore.

It didn't make sense. It just hurt.

"No," she answered, not knowing why, just knowing that she had to restrain the sudden urge to beg, to plead, to grab on to him and not let go until he explained his sudden retreat. "I'm afraid I have a teacher's meeting."

"Mo-o-o-o-m!"

Nick started like he'd been slapped. "They're hungry, Jen. I'll call."

"Nick?"

He'd already straightened. Pulling his sunglasses from his pocket he slipped them on. "When you get home from dinner tonight,'' he said with a sudden smile that seemed to beg patience. "I'll call."

And then he was gone.

The restaurant was noisy. The kids added their own voices, jumping unnoticed in the plastic booth and chasing imaginary foes through paper mazes and slurping shakes to the very bottom of paper cups. Jenny sat alongside picking at the junk food she usually craved on a par with chocolates and good wine, and fought the urge to cry.

It didn't make any sense. He'd helped her in that garage, playing the game like one of the kids. And then, when they'd made it safely outside he'd stepped back, as if to say, that's enough. I've come too close and I don't like it there. Jenny had known he would reach that place sooner or later, but still she couldn't accept it. She couldn't understand it.

She couldn't abide by it.

She wanted Nick there. She wanted him in her house, in her arms, in her dreams. She wanted him by her side to bolster her courage and celebrate her advances, to cushion the retreats and forgive the mistakes. She wanted him to open his private doors to her, to let out the musty secrets that darkened those seductive eyes and set his brakes so quickly. She wanted him to trust her.

She wanted to be able to trust him.

She loved him. Dammit, she'd forgotten how much that hurt.

Jenny refused to answer on the first ring. Let him think that she wasn't sitting right by the phone with a gin and tonic at hand waiting for him to call. Let him think she didn't care whether she ever heard from him again or not.

What an absolutely sophomoric reaction. She *must* be in love.

"Hello?"

"I'm sorry."

Two words, and the stuffings went right out of her knees. She sank onto the playroom floor, glass in hand, nightgown cool against freshly bathed skin, floor solid and reassuring. Still she was suddenly hot.

"You're forgiven. What did you do?"

She heard a chuckle, and it raced down her spine. Jenny found that she was lying, her head propped on a throw, the glass on her stomach, her eyes closed.

"I bet you're not that lenient with your kids."

Jenny smiled to herself. "Kids need a lot more intimidation than adults. That's because, generally, they're smarter."

"They sure had me outgunned today."

Jenny did her best to hide the leap her heart took. If he couldn't take the kids today...

"Kids get noisy sometimes, Nick."

"I'm not talking about that. I'm talking about the garage. They weren't in the least surprised by what you did. Shows they were smarter than I was. I was stunned."

Pleasure seeped into her like sunlight. "Why? Because I held my own?"

"Held your own?" he countered with sincere astonishment. "You nearly showed him his head on a platter. *I* was getting ready to take out that water pump." There was the slightest of pauses, a redirection. "And here I thought you might need help."

Jenny's eyes popped open. What had she heard just then? Not just amazement. Not just the grudging admiration, or the humor. Something... deeper. Something that sounded like her own voice when she'd called out to him on that parking lot.

She was sure Nick didn't realize himself that it had slipped out. Jenny was just such an expert at need that the slightest trace of it kindled a like reaction in her. She saw the taut line of his forehead again, the rigid distance in his eyes, and thought, suddenly, of disappointment.

Disappointment? Why?

"Jenny?"

"Oh, I'm sorry. I'm here." She closed her eyes again, soaking in the sound of his voice like water, trying to see him, his face, his movements, the subtle shadings of those whiskey-brown eyes. Trying to understand what it was he'd been looking for that afternoon that he hadn't found.

"What are you wearing?"

Jenny let her own chuckle roll down the wires. "Is this turning into an obscene phone call?"

"Depends. What are you wearing?"

"Oh, just an old yellow cotton nightgown."

She actually heard a groan. The satisfaction of it settled into her toes and turned them to curling. Need again, pleasure that he'd sought her out. That he sang his desire in unsaid sentences.

"Tell me something," she said, setting her own screen to receive. "Do you have a wood floor?"

"A what? What does that matter?"

She smiled and knew that it looked wicked. It felt wicked. "Just tell me."

"Sure. Yeah, it's wood."

"Cool?"

"Yeah. I'm lying on it right now. Feels pretty good."

Jenny's eyes were closed again, the images sharp and tantalizing. She nodded, her tongue searching out the dry edges of her lips. "I know. What are you wearing?"

"Gym shorts."

It was her turn to groan. She could see it so easily. His back, so lean, so taut and smooth like the torso of a well-caressed statue, stretched out against the gleam of oak. The lamp by his window casting little pools of light like spilled milk over the floor, the rest of the room in darkness, the breeze licking hot over his chest, skimming through the glisten of sweat.

She could see him, a drink on his chest, his arm behind his head, a knee bent. She could taste the salt, could feel the sensation of marble and velvet. Just the image sent shafts of pure pleasure through her.

"Where are you?" he asked, his voice suddenly husky.

Jenny just smiled.

She could have sworn Nick heard that smile. He didn't answer, not in words. The sound of a quickly intaken breath brushed her ear almost as intimately as if he'd been lying alongside her on that cool, earthbrown floor.

He knew exactly where she was. Jenny could almost hear him construct his own images. His had the advantage, though. He'd already helped make memories on her floor.

She just had anticipation to mold. Jenny wondered if it could possibly be any more evocative.

"You're making me crazy, lady," he objected harshly, giving her his answer. "And I'm not even in the same municipality."

"Feeling's mutual," she assured him, finally sipping at the gin she'd never had the chance to drink the other night. The fire slid down her throat and approached the embers fanning in her belly. "I suddenly want to see the inside of that apartment of yours very much."

"I have the most disconcerting feeling you already can."

For a moment there was silence, a silence filled with static, with the frustrations compounded by too little privacy, too many problems, too much interference.

"I'd really like to talk," Nick said softly.

Unconsciously Jenny nodded. "Me, too. I think we need it."

"Away from the kids?"

She sighed. "Away from the neighborhood."

"We could try Coral Courts."

Jenny laughed. Coral Courts was St. Louis's most notorious landmark, the first motel with hourly rates and garages to protect anonymity. Now so venerable it had been saved the wrecking ball by concerned citizens, it still carried with it the patina of lasciviousness, the distinct air of wanton abandon.

Even at age thirty, Jenny couldn't quite gather the insouciance to patronize the Courts.

"Someplace I can give the baby-sitter a phone number, if you please."

Another pause, a gathering of innuendo and promise. "How do you feel about hardwood floors?"

Now Jenny's smile was tremulous. "I've been fantasizing about them for a week."

She heard him answer, an unintelligible sound deep in his throat and knew that she'd been right. She hadn't been the only one fantasizing. She hadn't been the only one tossing and turning in the dark. The sound heightened the tension in her, the desire that sang like ship's rigging in the wind, the fear that gestated with every unsaid word, every unanswered question. The hope that refused to be quelled, even when she saw him wince at the kids or run from the commitment.

Jenny didn't know what to say to this man to convince him that he wanted to trust himself to her. She didn't know what she wanted to hear from him that would convince her she could let him in past her defenses. She felt as if she were walking a tightrope, and that far below, just in her line of vision, the net kept growing smaller. And still, when she had the chance to get off before she fell, she didn't.

"Nick?"

"I'm here."

"What were you sorry for?"

It took him a second to answer. Coming back from his own quandary, distilling his thoughts, Jenny wasn't sure. She couldn't catch that elusive need in his voice anymore.

"For letting you get away without kissing you."

"Nick..."

"Without pulling you into my arms right out on that parking lot and making you as hungry as I was."

She gave herself a second to regain equilibrium. Jenny had never known the power of mere words before. The breadth of intimation. Deliberately seeking distance from the memory of his hot hands, his cool, sweet lips that could so sap her common sense, she opened her eyes to the shadows that collected in her house. Instead of the gentle pleasure of sleeping with Nick, she thought of the grinding loneliness of sleeping alone again. "Then it really must have been something bad to drive you away."

There didn't seem to be any answer for that. Closing her eyes against the pain that bloomed in her chest, Jenny just waited. Just wondered what it would take to open those doors. She wondered if she even had the energy left to attempt it.

"Nick?" How could her voice sound so very small? How could just his silence shatter her resolve?

"Yes, Jen."

"Why a lawyer?"

A pause, the sound only of empty air between them, of distance. "Does this have anything to do with ducks?"

Jenny would have none of it. "Why did you work so hard from the very beginning to be a lawyer?"

This time his answer was too quick. A defense. A barrier long since erected. "I liked the uniform."

More. She wanted more. She wanted to know that he wouldn't pander to the Izod god. "That's enough?"

"When you're ten and you don't have a decent pair of shoes it is."

End of discussion. The sound, somehow of a latch catching. Jenny heard it as surely as if he were in the same room. Her frustration only built. Her fear. Her determination, oddly enough. They had danced so close tonight, fingers touching in delicate ritual to appease, but not sate. She wanted satisfaction. She wanted substance.

In the end, though, she knew the limits of a phone call. It was time to call retreat. "I didn't get a chance to say thank you today."

"Thank you?"

She nodded, her eyes still closed, tears stinging but refusing to fall. "Standing up to that guy was important to me. Dumb, but important. I couldn't have done it without you being there behind me. Thanks for letting me do it alone."

Nick let another silence build to the edge of tension. "You mean you've never turned a mechanic to coleslaw before?"

"Never. You gave me the courage. I was hoping you'd share the triumph with me."

She didn't know how, but the silence changed. It became more charged, more taut, as if her words had altered the texture of the future somehow. Jenny didn't even realize she was holding her breath.

"Would tomorrow be all right, after all?"

Jenny let her breath out in a small whoosh. "Tomorrow would be fine."

She hung up smiling, and wishing she knew why. If tomorrow were so fine, why was she so scared?

Maybe because for all they'd said, they hadn't really given any answers. And she was still very afraid of the answers they would ultimately have to find.

Chapter 14

Nick, my man, you look wasted.''

Without doing much to stifle a yawn, Nick set down his *U.S. News* to face his newest buddy, Todd Sellers. As ever, the teen was decked out in the latest designer labels, with his spike haircut perfectly rakish and his sockless shoes appropriately scuffed. Today, however, Todd stood without his usual crowd of followers.

Nick made it a point to look around. "A little empty out there, isn't it, Todd?"

Todd just scowled, hands jammed in pockets. "Run into a little dry spell, they fade like suntans, ya know?"

No, Nick thought, he didn't know. He really didn't care, come to think of it, except where it connected with his case. The longer he went without sleep in that oven of an apartment, the more he wanted to wrap up this farce and get on with his life.

Of course, it probably didn't help that he'd spent the last few sleepless nights doing a spot of much too intense dreaming. Even cold showers had lost their power.

It had been particularly bad last night after getting off the phone with Jenny. It had been bad *on* the phone with Jenny.

He'd been lying on the floor in just his old shorts, with the window fan blowing that hot breeze across his chest imagining what she looked like. What she felt like. Anticipating what it would feel like on his floor instead of hers. He hadn't even moved for an hour after he'd hung up the phone, so acute had been the discomfort.

And then, because he knew damn well he wasn't about to get any sleep that night, either, he'd cleaned the place.

Oh, hell, he thought, resettling in the sticky seat, he was going to have to do something about the fit of these jeans.

"You okay?" Todd asked with a squint behind his designer shades.

Nick came very close to cursing. "I, uh, hurt my... back last night. Old war wound."

"Oh, yeah, really? Man, like you should be able to take care of that."

Nick lifted an eyebrow. "Some things just can't be taken care of."

Todd shook his head with a conspiratorial grin. "Can't make me believe that, man. Just takes the resources and the bread, ya know?"

"That's what it always comes down to."

Nick got a snort and a definite nod. "Ya got that right. Well, things are a little tight for me right now, but, you know, come see me when the waters flow again, okay? A man-to-man loan."

"Hey," Nick agreed more brightly. "You're on, man. I appreciate it. How 'bout an ice cream or two on the boss?"

Little Todd, Nick realized as he slowly climbed out of his truck, bore watching. Nothing like a spot of enterprise in the suburbs to brighten a boy's summer. Maybe the day wouldn't be quite so unbearable, after all.

"Is there a hurricane coming through tomorrow and nobody told me?" Jenny asked her bagger as she began ringing up yet another three-digit order.

"Looks to me like the city's havin' a gang barbecue," he retorted, shaking out his bag.

All Jenny wanted to do was get off her feet. Take a shower. Lie down on Nick's floor.

For the hundredth time that day she shook off the image. It certainly wasn't doing her any good. Every time she began to think of what waited for her beyond the day's duties, she began dropping vegetables and misreading labels.

But her feet did ache, even with the supports and nurse's shoes. And she couldn't quite get Nick's words from her mind. All his words, scattered over the last two weeks, tumbled around in her brain so that they aligned in different patterns according to her needs. He loved her, he'd love her children—their children. He couldn't commit, no matter what; it just wasn't in his nature.

He was going to be a lawyer for stability. He was going to be a lawyer to make up for every deprivation he'd had as a kid. To get even with the system.

She loved him. She was terrified of him.

Well, at least both of those were true. She did love him. She'd spent another sleepless night last night conjuring him to mind, trying somehow to bridge the gap between them with mental images, with wishes and silent urgings. Wanting him to know, somehow in the dark and private hours of dawn that she was the one he needed.

And she was terrified of him. Of everything he brought back into her life: the tumult, the trepidation, the uncertainty...the agonizing hope.

God, how she hated that the most. Treading from moment to moment as if maneuvering across thin ice, knowing it should crack, praying it wouldn't, your eyes desperately fixed on the far shore that should get closer but didn't.

Beep, beep, plunk. She was working on autopilot, skimming cans across the bar-code machine in smooth succession, balancing fruit on the scale, punching the computer like a typist in a speed contest, her movements agitated and choppy, her mind miles away.

Only three more hours.

She wasn't going to make it.

"One-hundred-forty-two dollars and fifty cents."

Across from her, the blousy woman in the tank top and tattoo looked up. "Oh, I don't got that much. You gotta do somethin'."

Jenny counted all the way up to forty before she managed to hold her retort in. She should have anticipated this. This particular customer did this as regularly as prickly heat in summer.

"I'll tell you what," the woman decided, checking her wallet again and eyeing the already packed groceries. "I don't really want none o' them oranges. And the Chocolate Gumby cereal. And..."

The bag boy dug, Jenny rerang and the lady picked the scant nutrition from her haul and put it back. Jenny didn't say a word. But, then, she hadn't said a word that morning when Barb had made a frontal assault on her, and she hadn't objected when Kate had tried flanking maneuvers, both in an attempt to dislodge Nick's position in the Lake household. Barb had been worried, so everyone had heard about it. And Jenny still had to face Barb when she went home for the kids. She was surprised the Jerk hadn't shown up, as well, the way this day was going.

She was surprised her customer, who was puffing on her cigarette and repacking her doughnuts, didn't say something about how Nick was going to be bad for her. She was probably just too busy complaining about the prices.

Jenny simply wasn't going to make it. Her time with Nick tonight was going to be too important, and everyone she'd come into contact with today was conspiring to sabotage it. She watched the tattooed lady grunt on out and wondered just what would be next.

"Jenny, you're closing. Take over line six."

Jenny tried to warn off her next customer. "I'm..."

She hadn't even noticed. So engrossed had she been in trying to maintain her patience in the face of the last straw, so exhausted by the sleepless night and overwhelming morning, she hadn't taken a moment to anticipate her next customer.

His smile forgave her.

"Do you think you could squeeze in just one more customer?"

"One more, Marge!" Jenny yelled without looking away. "He was already in line!"

Nick's grin broadened. Jenny faltered. Her pulse rate picked up abominably. Somehow she forgot how much her legs hurt, because suddenly her chest hurt worse. That damn hope again. She was so afraid of him, and all she wanted to do was stand there and stare at him.

"I'm proud of you," he was saying, his eyes crinkling with a humor that seemed oddly intense. "I saw you cringe at every double negative. You never said a word."

Jenny tried her best to find levity. "Just one reason a schoolteacher should never work in a store."

"After this summer, I feel for you."

She should be able to think of something amusing to say, something light and smart. She couldn't. Suddenly the sun was in his eyes and it was sapping her strength.

"Pasta?" she asked, reaching for the few packages he carried.

Never taking his eyes from hers, he nodded. "I thought I'd cook tonight. I'm having somebody over. Think she'll like it?"

Jenny had to run the tomato sauce over the scanner three times. Her hands were shaking. Mushrooms, green peppers, fresh garlic. Mouth-watering ingredients, startling anticipation. She couldn't drag her gaze from his either, crystal-green battling honey-brown. Dark, sensual attraction and terror.

In the next lane a toddler was screaming for candy. One of the baggers dashed off for a price check, and the doors swished open not ten feet from her. All she could hear was Nick. All she could smell in that crowded, noisy food store was Nick. And it unnerved her.

"I think she'll like it a lot."

Again he nodded, slowly, his eyes darkening. "Good. I can hardly wait to eat."

He lifted a head of lettuce for her. Jenny brushed against his hand when she accepted it and almost dropped it on the floor. "Hungry?" she asked breathlessly.

He steadied her hand with his own. "Starved."

Jenny felt his voice to the tips of her toes. The caress of his fingers followed right after, seriously damaging the support in her knees, wiping out hours of pressure on her feet. She still wanted to sit down, but now just because she wasn't quite sure she was still standing. It was that damn hope again. Slicing through her like lightning, sapping her strength, softening her voice as if the caution could better facilitate it. Hope. What a strange aphrodisiac. The most powerful she'd ever known.

"You still have three hours," she admonished them both.

Nick's grin settled in his eyes like heady, forbidden sin. "It'll give the sauce plenty of time to bubble."

Jenny couldn't do more than blink. "Oh."

She couldn't breathe. Her sensibility had just melted, and the bar coder was beeping at her.

Pulling away, she turned to her computer, slapped at some keys and came to a figure. Somehow she managed to relay it to him and exchange money without ever really facing him. She kept watching the display of disposable lighters at the edge of her counter as if waiting for revelation. She knew Nick smiled, and knew that that smile would do even more damage to her support structure.

"Well," he said, his voice low, intimate as he picked up his bags. "Thank you. I'll be able to start cooking now."

By the time Jenny shot him a startled look, he'd already walked away. That was when she noticed that the lines had grown quiet. She didn't hear the toddler anymore. Nobody was talking about prices or weather or vacations. Wondering, Jenny turned a little to see a row of faces turned to her. Turned to follow Nick out of the store.

She couldn't believe it. Every person down the line had been witness. Not necessarily to the conversation. Evidently that hadn't been the telling point. From the looks on every one of those faces, the look on hers had been blatant. She was mortified.

And Nick, with an absolutely nonchalant expression on his face, was carrying those bags right in front as he walked very carefully out the door.

"Have a little of that pasta for me, honey," the lady in the next lane sighed. "Looks spicy as hell."

Four other women nodded. Jenny had been right. She was going to die of embarrassment long before she ever got out of this store.

It had only gotten worse. When she got home Barb had greeted her with news that another neighborhood girl had been busted for drugs, not three blocks from the house, and as much as Jenny wanted to enlighten her she had to face all that concern and outrage with a quiet face. The kids had been wild, cornered in the house with a listless, lingering rain and not happy for it. And the mail had brought two over-due bill notices and a license renewal for the car.

The first warning should have reached the Jerk that morning. It said pay up or be visited by the man with the subpoenas. Jenny had decided to give him one more bene-fit of the doubt before hauling in the big guns. Nick hadn't agreed, but then Nick didn't have to face the Jerk on a reg-ular basis and plead for him to visit his children.

So, she figured she'd be getting a call from the law of-fices of Wellerby, Cline, Phillips and Phillips anytime now. Probably from a secretary, maybe a partner. Powerful, threatening, distant, so the Jerk wouldn't have to dirty his hands with her.

Jenny stood in the shower wondering just how the heck she thought she was going to have a good time tonight.

She got out with a churning stomach to find Emma and Spot on her bed, both of them whining. And that was how she got dressed for her big night with Nick, caught between anger, frustration and guilt.

Emma didn't want her to go. "Not *again*, Mommy," she sighed with every ounce of heart-wrenching pathos in her. "You're never here with me anymore."

Fine, Jenny thought, fastening her earrings and taking another look at her dress. This should be just about enough to bring back up that fancy dinner Nick was so busy cook-ing.

Just the thought brought her hand to her stomach. Trying to quell butterflies. She could feel the honey-thick warmth of those eyes again, the erotic promise of his whisper.

Hardwood floors and pasta dinners, and she was going to partake like a pagan at a ritual. She didn't know whether she had the courage for it.

"I'm just going to see Mr. Nick," she finally answered the accusing, instinctively manipulating eyes of her daughter. "He asked Mommy out on a date."

"A date?" Emma asked, astonished. "Again? That's a lot."

That's two, Jenny thought. Not enough to be certain and surely not enough to throw aside all her carefully compiled protections. She knew she'd likened Nick to that dangerous stranger in town, the one who seemed to consume good sense with the promise in his eyes. But Jenny wasn't the type to succumb to that kind of heat.

Was she?

"Spot doesn't want you to go," Emma tried again. "She's afraid she'll feel boring."

"Bored," Jenny immediately corrected with a smile, seeing that the cat who was so afraid of being "boring" had given up trying to get loose from the little girl and was asleep. "Have Susie play Chutes and Ladders with Spot," she suggested, sweeping the little girl into her arms and heading for the stairs. "That will keep her from being boring."

Emma nestled into Jenny's neck, cooing with contentment, which only made Jenny feel worse. Who said parents instilled guilt? she thought. Kids were the pros. Parents were just paying them back for nights like this.

The doorbell rang when Jenny was halfway down the stairs. She looked up, surprised. Susie was already ensconced in the playroom, so it must be Nick. And he was early.

Emma immediately dug in for a tighter hold. Jenny didn't bother to dislodge the girl before reaching to answer the door.

The smile she'd been working on died a painful death. It wasn't Nick. It was the Jerk. In person. In a rage.

"You want to explain this?" he demanded, waving the letter in her face.

She'd been right. The mail had been on time. Her stomach took another dive. Emma clutched tighter, whining.

"Come in, if you'd like," Jenny greeted him with a carefully even voice. "But I'd appreciate it if you'd do it civilly. Emma's having a bad day."

"Don't you—"

"She said do it civilly."

Both Jenny and the Jerk turned at the new voice. Nick had shown up, evidently right on the Jerk's heels. He was smiling now, wearing a feral expression Jenny had never seen on him before—and he was leveling it straight at her exhusband.

"Name's Nick Barnett," he greeted him, hand out, eyes flat and hard. "I'm a friend of Jenny's."

"Mr. Nick!" Emma squealed, unpeeling herself from Jenny and outstretching her arms.

Stepping in past the Jerk, Nick obliged, which didn't do much to increase his stock with Mr. Lake.

"Why don't you have a drink in the kitchen?" the Jerk grated. "I have some business to take care of with Jenny."

"No," Nick disagreed very evenly. "You have business with me. I'm the one who sent the letter. Hey, peewee, how 'bout hoppin' off for a minute? I have to talk to your Daddy."

Emma, astute as ever, did just as Nick asked. Dispatching one final look at each adult, she skipped into the playroom to join Susie.

"In here," Nick suggested in steely tones Jenny had never heard. Suddenly he was a different man, the man he'd fought so hard to grow up to be. The man was in absolute control, and he was exerting that control. It fascinated her even as much as it frightened her.

The three of them stepped into the living room, where Jenny had only left on one light. The shadows settled into Nick's features in sharp slashes, the taut line of his jaw, the deep creases along his mouth. He was furious, and he was thinking. In that moment Jenny saw the power in him she'd only imagined before: channeled, directed, keen as a laser and just as potent.

She saw, for the first time, the cop. The lawyer. And she wasn't sure she wanted to.

"Just who the hell do you think you are?" the Jerk demanded, looking, for the first time in Jenny's memory, ineffectual against Nick's power. "This is none of your damn business."

"Whatever is between you and Jenny," Nick retorted, "is one thing. But if you're going to act like an adolescent and hurt your kids over it, then other people get involved. And I'm one of them. I just can't believe Jenny's lawyer didn't do it sooner."

"You don't have any idea what's involved!"

Now Nick smiled, and it was a terrible sight. "I know what kind of man deserts his kids. Now if I were you, I'd work this out with Jenny while I'm in talking to Kevin, or I'll make your life so miserable you won't want to get up in the morning."

Then he was gone, leaving a rip in the fabric of the pulsating silence, leaving a void in Jenny's home. Where the Jerk was an intruder here, now, Nick belonged. God, Jenny thought, it's become impossible.

"Do you really think you can parade this guy around to scare me?" her ex was demanding, almost purple with rage.

Jenny shook her head, still even more stunned than the Jerk by Nick's words. Jenny knew where they'd been born; she knew their power, their conviction, the pain of their conception. Instead of standing here with a man she no longer loved, she wanted to go to Nick and soothe the child in himself he'd exposed.

"He's the first person who's given me decent advice," Jenny said, straightening to face her husband. "You want a part in your children's lives, then, by God, deserve it. I'm tired of apologizing for you. I'm tired of denying your children because their father is too damned selfish."

"Jenny," he retorted, her challenge more important to him than its content. "You know better than to push me."

Jenny shook her head again, wondering at how little he had changed in all the years she'd known him. Unable to think of any other way to deal with him, she turned back to the front door. "You don't scare me anymore. Now, get out."

Amazingly enough, he did.

It didn't improve the condition of Jenny's stomach. She stood for a long moment by the door, trembling, fighting to stave off the tears, the confusion. The challenge between the men still remained, a residue of ash in the air, a faint throb of energy. And Jenny was so tired of the taste of that ash. She just wasn't sure she could face more.

She didn't even know Nick had returned until he laid a hand on her shoulder.

"I'm sorry."

She laughed, a short, sharp sound. "You've apologized more in the last twenty-four hours than that man did in six years of marriage."

"How 'bout we get some spaghetti, lady?"

Jenny took an uneven breath. "Nick—"

Increasing his hold, he turned her to him. "No excuses. Go tell Emma that the wicked witch's friend has disappeared, and we'll leave."

She couldn't believe it. The room looked just as she'd imagined. After coming to an uncertain stop in the doorway, Jenny took a minute to take stock. Dark wood floor, polished to a gleam, white walls with a few geometric prints. Bookshelves, filled to overflowing, and bare, minimal furniture. Space and silence, a haven in the midst of a noisy city.

The front windows were bayed out onto the tree-lined street just off the college campus. In the daylight Jenny was sure she could see the crenellated towers past the trees, but now, with the sky given to clouds and the rain slicking the streets, the world was as shadowy as the room in which she stood.

The rain spattered on the windowsill outside. A fan in the window whirred softly and another was running in the tiny white kitchen to the right. That one was blowing mouth-watering smells of oregano, basil, garlic into the living room. Jenny wished the Jerk had left her with more of an appetite.

"Take off your shoes," Nick invited, closing the door and following her in. "Pull up a floor."

Jenny couldn't help but smile. "Do you mind if I do just that?"

"Gin and tonics on the way."

She sat just outside a pool of light, reading the titles on the bookshelves. Law, well-thumbed classics, mysteries. Anything, it seemed, Nick could get his hands on. A few knickknacks, a German beer stein and an old gavel. A diploma, still closed, propping one shelf of books and a framed law-enforcement citation propping another. Shoved there as if to negate their importance, the only hints into Nick's life. No pictures, no cards, no mementos of other people in his life.

It made Jenny ache. She saw stringent self-sufficiency in this room, rigid independence. She also saw the hard-won victories of a man who refused to rely on their meaning.

She saw a man alone. A man who in thirty-five years had not learned to share his life.

"Comfortable?"

Jenny looked up to see that he'd discarded his jacket. He was in pleated wheat-colored linen slacks and a hunter green T-shirt. He looked like sin personified. Jenny reached for the glass he proffered. Ice clinked. Condensation trickled over her fingertips. She hadn't realized until now how hot the room was. Nick joined her on the floor and the temperature went up another few degrees.

"I haven't been comfortable since the first time I thought about this room," she admitted, her gaze straying down. It only led to the discovery that she hadn't been the only one in that condition.

"Isn't nonverbal communication a wonderful thing?" Nick asked with a crooked grin.

Jenny couldn't quite bring her eyes back to his. There was so much roiling around in her—so many questions needing answers, so many protests born of isolation and defense, so much yearning she hadn't even known existed until two weeks ago. "Are we going to waste more gin?" she asked instead.

Nick sighed, lifting a hand to run it along the line of her jaw. "I think so."

That got her to look up. Unfortunately, the set they bumped into were already smokey with desire. "Nick, we have to talk."

He nodded. "I know. Problem is, right now there's only one thing I can think of." His hand slid lower, along her throat where it unleashed unexpected sparks.

Jenny jumped. Caught her breath. "Nick—"

He smiled again, that crooked admission of weakness, of preoccupation. "Jenny, I can't think of a better time to talk than when you're lying in my arms. Later."

He was leaning closer, his eyes narrowing, his hand flattening against her collarbone, seeking purchase.

"The sauce—"

"Is just about to boil."

She never felt him take her drink away. She only felt his breath, soft, musky, as he bent to kiss her. She felt his hand sweeping along her arm, coaxing, teasing. She felt her heart hammer against her chest and her breasts strain against the lace of her best bra. She felt the molten hammer of his touch, the dark lightning of his soft, surprised groan when he first tasted her with his tongue. She felt him ease her back onto that cool, dark floor.

Patience had been sacrificed to sleepless nights, subtlety to passion. Jenny felt the wood against her back, felt the harsh heat of Nick atop her, the rain-cooled breeze from the fan against her suddenly damp skin, and stumbled over a fierce hunger that shattered her.

She wanted to taste him, to touch him, to drive him to a frenzy like he'd done to her. He tangled his hands in her hair and she moaned, the sensation as sharp as her desire. He dropped kisses along her face, her throat, and she arched, writhed. She clutched at the material at his shoulders and yanked it from the waistband of his slacks. Her lips skimming the freshly shaven smoothness of his chin, she reached to unbutton, to seek her own purchase.

Nick could taste it on her. Desire, hunger, as harsh and sudden as his own, as consuming. She fought him tonight, dancing against him as if mere touch would not satisfy her. As if she meant to devour him whole. The ferocity of her little moans stirred him, incited him. Throbbed in him like molten iron. He gasped when she raked his chest, her fingernails sharp and chill, her fingers so deliciously soft in their wake. He bent to taste the sweat on her skin, to fill his hands with the sweet fullness of her breasts only to find them already taut for him.

He added his own groans to hers, deep throated and urgent, the throb an ache that urged unbearably. A heat that called for communion. How he wanted to sate himself with her, the soft, tender places, the dark secrets, the bold promises. He saw the wild light in those forest green eyes and wanted to follow it to his death.

The floor was already slick. Jenny felt it against her naked skin and thought that nothing could be more provocative. Nothing, maybe except the tumescent beauty of Nick's body. The light revered him, caressing the broad planes of his chest, slicing along the sharp tendons and well-defined muscles of his limbs. Kissing his face with the gentlest of fingers so that his eyes glowed and the dimple in his chin begged to be tasted.

Jenny did. She tasted that dimple and the ones on either side of his mouth when he smiled at her hunger. She drank the tang from his glowing skin and nestled against the whisper-rough hair on his chest. She gave herself up to his touch and demanded her own. The fan cooled the perspiration on her skin. The rain kept them company in that silent, hot room. The floor cradled them.

Nick spiraled in her like a tornado, hot and urgent, faster and faster until she was caught in his vortex. Gasping, writhing, the lightning taking her, shuddering through her, drawing him closer, closer. Provoking cries, pleas from them both, until Nick met her, until he drowned himself in her, dancing in that same bright, fierce wind, that same fiery sky, breaking through to the sun and finally falling again.

And in the aftermath, the rain. The breeze, humid and cool against sweat-sheened bodies. The night, quiet and dark.

"Some day," Jenny sighed as she watched her fingers winnow through the hair on Nick's chest, "I'm going to have to make love with you on a bed. Just to see what it's like."

Nick groaned. "Give me a few minutes."

Jenny chuckled, trying to understand why tears should threaten when she felt so content. Nick was stroking her hair. She could hear his heart trying to slow, felt the still-ragged slant of his breathing. He was so warm against her, so solid and strong. Lying there in the safe silence of his apartment, she should have wanted nothing more than to stay where she was. She shouldn't have still been afraid.

"I am going to have to get to that spaghetti sooner or later," he admitted with a desultory yawn.

"Later," she voted, doing her best not to tense up. If only she could hold on to this moment a little longer. This perfect little island of peace in her life.

"I did promise some conversation," he admitted, slipping his other arm beneath his head.

Jenny closed her eyes, fighting the tight stinging in her throat. "Later."

"No," he said quietly, his hand stilling against her. "I think I owe it to you to finish it now."

"Finish is such a . . . final word." Damn, those tears were closing in fast.

Was he smiling? Jenny thought she could hear it in his voice. "You wanted to know why I was sorry yesterday."

"You told me."

He shook his head. "No, I didn't. I didn't explain it. Hell, I didn't even understand it until we talked on the phone last night."

"Understand what?"

For a moment, all Jenny heard was the fizzle of rain, the whir of the fan, the swish of traffic two stories down. She kept her eyes on the line of Nick's chest, as if fortifying herself with his reality.

He was so beautiful. So gentle.

And, she knew now, so ferocious. It didn't make her feel any better.

"You surprised me yesterday. When I saw you handle that guy like a top sergeant, I thought... I thought you didn't need me."

Jenny went perfectly still. She couldn't quite breathe. If there was an admission she hadn't prepared herself for, that was the one. Knowing that she couldn't hide any longer, she turned in Nick's arms. She pulled herself up on an elbow and faced him. The shadows settled deeply into his eyes, protecting him, distancing him. For once, she thought it wouldn't help.

"That matters?" she asked very quietly.

His smile was wry, admitting more than any words could. "Yeah," he said. "It does." In those three words, Jenny heard the sum of all those years of disappointment. Of his fears, not meaning enough to the people he cared for. Not counting. Not existing.

That took care of the tears. They welled up and slid down Jenny's cheeks unheeded. "If I didn't need you so very much," she admitted so softly that the rain danced through her words, "I would have been able to sleep this week. Much as I'd like to say I'm a wild woman, I don't lie naked with any man on his floor just because he has an unforgettable tush."

Jenny wasn't sure, but she saw a glint in his eyes as well, as if the shadows there had collected and swollen.

"I love you, Nick," she said, a hand up to his face. "I need you. But loving and needing aren't the problem here, I think."

"You're still worried about my job?"

She shook her head, unable to express just what seeing him faced off with the Jerk had done to her that evening. "I married a man who liked the uniform. One who thrived on the control and the power."

"Who says I—?"

Jenny shot him a look.

Nick had the good sense to grin. "I am not a barracuda, Jen. I can give you references, if you want. Go talk to Manetti. Hell, I couldn't even steal hubcaps."

"Neither could the Jerk. But he's the best legal thief in the business."

He took a moment, his eyes assessing, his hand still against her back. "And just what kind of law do you think I'm going into?"

"Law is law," Jenny retorted from instinct, even knowing how unfair it sounded—how unfair it was.

"The only office I'll have in Clayton is in the County Courts Building," he said. "I've applied for the District Attorney's office, Jen."

"The..."

He nodded. "I'm not a policeman because I get off on badges. I like the work. Why would I spend all these years walking an undercover tightrope and then close myself into a corporate law office?"

Jenny didn't even hesitate. "Security."

He thought about it. Then he nodded a little. "Granted. Security. Success. But there is more than one kind of success."

"Are you sure?" she asked. "I saw you in there with my ex-husband tonight. No offense, Nick, but I could hardly tell you apart. Are you sure you're not telling me what I want to hear?"

"Yes."

"And my children? *All* my children? I can't back down on that, even for you. It's too important a part of my marriage."

"I got through yesterday better than I thought."

Jenny sighed. "Yesterday is one day. The Jerk told me he'd agree to children. And then he told me he'd made that promise because he thought that's what I wanted to hear. Well, I don't want you to tell me what I want to hear. I want you to tell me what you feel."

She saw her own turmoil mirrored in his eyes. "I'll try," he promised, and she knew he meant it.

"Nick," she said with a sad little shake of her head. "I'm almost nuts with this after two weeks. How much longer am I supposed to hang on before you know?"

"Jenny, that's unfair."

"Dammit, I *know* it's unfair. But I'm not talking justice here, I'm talking survival. I just can't last much longer the way it is."

Nick came up, pulled Jenny to him, held her to him as if afraid she would run before he got a chance to change her mind. "I need you, Jenny. I love you."

Jenny curled right into his lap, her face into his neck, her arms around his shoulders. She'd never felt so wonderfully alive. She'd never felt so lost and frightened. "Nick, I don't know what to do."

"Marry me."

Jenny's tears fell harder, harder than the rain, spilling down Nick's chest. "No. I can't. I just can't."

The phone shattered their little pool of silence. Nick ignored it, his head against Jenny's, his arms tight enough around her to reassure him.

It kept ringing.

"Nick—"

Abruptly he let her go. Jenny stayed where she was, huddled on the floor, just beyond the light as he stalked over to the phone. She wanted to run after him. She wanted to run away. Sobs collected in her chest and threatened to break free.

"It's for you."

Her head shot up. Quickly swiping tears away with a hand, she got to her feet. Her baby-sitters always had her number, but they rarely used it. Jenny picked them on the basis of their self-sufficiency. God, she hoped the Jerk hadn't come back and stirred up the kids.

"Susie?"

"I'm sorry, Mrs. Lake. I didn't want to bother you—"

"What's wrong, hon?"

"Kevin. I thought you'd want to know. He's upstairs throwing up. And he has a fever. I thought he was pretty crabby... Oh, no, Emma!"

The sounds were unmistakable. Jenny wanted to laugh. She wanted to scream. Of all the times for her children to come down with the flu, it had to be while she was standing naked in a man's apartment talking about their future together.

"I'll be home right away, Susie."

Nick was already pulling on his pants. "What's wrong?"

"The flu," Jenny said with a watery grin. "My children have picked this of all nights to decorate my bathrooms."

She bent to pick up her things.

"Is there anything I can do? Do you want me to stay with you when you get home?"

"No," she answered instinctively, trying to spare him the unpleasant details of her family life. She'd just pulled her dress over her head when it occurred to her. She straightened, reconsidered, nodded. Nick still looked confused.

"Yes," she changed her mind instead, and stepped into shoes. "I would like you to stay. If you want to know what it's like, this is it. You're going to get the full family treatment, Nick. You are going to participate in the Flu Follies."

Nick wasn't sure whether he'd meant the offer. By the time he followed Jenny out the door, he was sure. He hadn't.

But it was too late now.

Chapter 15

Nick had thought it was going to be bad. He had no idea.

By the time they reached Jenny's house, several bedrooms were ruined, and both kids were wailing at the tops of their lungs up in the bathroom. The baby-sitter looked as if she'd just been through an Indian uprising.

"Will you take Susie home, Nick?" Jenny asked, heading right upstairs.

Nick was more than happy to oblige.

Things weren't much better by the time he got back. He found the Lake family firmly ensconced in the main upstairs bathroom. Both Emma and Kevin were flushed and whining, their nightclothes stained and wet. Jenny was bent over them, running a bath.

"What can I...do?" Nick asked, praying she wouldn't have any suggestions. The room was already pretty piquant, and these kids looked like they weren't finished yet.

"I have to strip beds," she said without turning around. "If you'd just get them into the tub and start rinsing, it'd help. I have to get their fevers down."

Nick tried to maintain his nonchalance. "What about Tylenol?"

Jenny straightened with a scowl and pointed to the definite pink tinge on both pajama tops and bathroom wall. "That," she said evenly, "is the Tylenol."

Nick gulped. "Oh."

"Out of those clothes, my babies," she sang, dropping a kiss on each head as she scooted out of the room. "God, this house is too cold."

Nick looked from one kid to another. It wasn't as if he'd had practice in a while, and as a child he'd always been really good at being somewhere else when something like this was going on. He wasn't sure whether he should help peel those clothes, or just pick up a rag. His first thought was just to dunk them both like doughnuts and get that stuff off them.

"Mr...Nick," Emma sobbed, hands up for help. "I throwed...up."

"Yeah, peewee," he agreed, finally unbending enough to help her. "I can tell."

"I don't want to sit in there with her," Kevin whined, his eyes glassy and cross.

"Looks like that's the only option, pal," Nick said. He'd just gathered all the pajamas when Jenny swept through and collected them.

"It's not a pretty sight out there," she warned with a wry smile.

Nick scowled. "It's not a pretty sight in here."

"I'll bring up drinks."

"Jen—"

She stopped, her arms loaded with linen, completely oblivious to the fact that the sheets would soil her good dress. Nick felt like an idiot. Worse, he felt a coward. But just the smell was churning his stomach.

"I'm not...uh, good at this."

"You're a cop," she retorted, surprised somehow.

"And as a cop," he answered as evenly as possible, "I've never been stuck in a small, smelly room with *sick* kids." He invested those four letters with every nuance of the word.

Jenny's smile didn't make Nick feel much better.

"They didn't make me a mother because I aced the course in flu," she said. "If you're serious about family life, this is where it starts."

And then she left.

Cruel, Nick thought with a scowl. Heartless. Then Emma started gasping and he was in business.

Jenny returned with large gin and tonics. Nick accepted his gratefully, already tired. He had both kids in the tub, and neither of them was happy about it. Emma cried and Kevin complained in a high, tremulous voice that grated on Nick's nerves. What was worse, the only place to sit was ground zero. He had the feeling he was going to be up and down a lot.

Jenny sat on the floor by the tub.

"Not bad, Barnes," she grinned wearily. "Might make a mother out of you yet."

Nick snorted into his drink. "The night is yet young."

"I have to clean in here, too," she noted, not moving, her face already flushed. "God, I hate the smell of pine cleaner."

"Can I make a bed or something?"

Her smile was dry. "Already done. Although, you'll probably get your chance before we're finished."

Emma began whining to get out. Kevin echoed in a higher register. Nick thought their voices reverberated like a high-caliber rifle shot around the room.

"You're still sick, babies," Jenny soothed, reaching over the edge of the tub to soak a rag and squeeze water over Emma's back. That didn't make Emma any happier. "Let's get these old fevers down, honey. Then Mr. Nick'll read you a wonderful bedtime story."

Nick raised his eyebrow. Emma, however, was appeased—at least for the moment.

"I'm sorry, Nick," Jenny said a minute later, pushing her hair back from her forehead. "It's too hot in here. I turned the air-conditioning down too far."

"It's fine," he answered, beguiled by the way the humidity curled her hair. She was leaning against the wall, her arm stretched out to encourage Kevin to keep rinsing.

"You do this often?"

Jenny shot Nick a quizzical look.

He lifted the glass. "You seem so prepared."

She smiled. "Enough times in six years to know how to get through it the easiest. When Kevin used to get the croup, we'd camp out in the bathroom for two days. I had special bathroom bedrolls for us."

Nick just shook his head. "A lot goes into it, doesn't it?"

"What?"

"Motherhood. Children."

Jenny gave her own children a considering gaze that grew very soft. "Best job in the world."

"M-o-o-o-m...!"

Nick was up, and Jenny had Kevin out of the water in one fluid movement. They spent the next hour repeating the procedure.

The kids' fevers came down, but unfortunately the rest of the flu refused to abate. Jenny dressed Emma while Nick dressed Kevin, and then they traded for stories. Buckets were strategically placed for accidents and the bathroom given its full cleaning. Nick was all for heading back down to the playroom for some rest, but Jenny held him off.

"Let's not push our luck," she suggested. "Stay in with Emma for a bit?"

Finally, exhausted just from the calisthenics in the bathroom, Nick agreed. He took up his position on the floor at the foot of the little girl's bed and leaned against the wall. Emma slept, her blond hair wet and tousled against the pillow. Nick watched her for a while, amazed at the beauty of a sleeping child. Stunned by how small she really was. It wasn't something he thought about when Emma was awake. She always seemed so old. Such an adult. But now, asleep, her pale lashes fanned out on freckled cheeks, she looked like a tiny porcelain doll.

If only she could stay like this, he could handle her. Nick had serious reservations about whether he was really cut out for the bathroom patrol. He couldn't believe Jenny did it with such aplomb, sailing around to clean and then dispatching kisses and hugs and not seeming to notice that she was getting wet or dirty or ragged. She really didn't seem to care.

He'd never met anyone like her. Never known a hand on his forehead when he was sick, or a soothing word to help the medicine go down. Maybe most mothers were like this. Maybe he really hadn't seen life like it was. Or maybe Jenny was just special.

"Mommy?"

Nick was up in a flash. Unfortunately, his reflexes were the wrong kind. He wasn't quick enough. Jenny had been right. He was going to get his chance to change a bed tonight.

"Okay, peewee," he soothed, an uncertain hand to the little blond head. "You sit in your rocker for a minute. I'll ask Mom where to find the sheets. Deal?"

"I'm . . . I'm sorry, Mr. Nick."

"Hey—" He crouched down to smile for that tearstained little face. "Tell you what. You can take care of me when I'm sick. Then we're even. Okay?"

That seemed to appeal to her. "You'd look silly in the bathtub."

He got back to his feet with a grin. "Don't let that get around."

He'd thought Jenny would be in with Kevin. When he stepped into the boy's room it was quiet. Kevin was curled into a fetal position, his vast collection of invasion toys cluttered over bed and floor. Jenny was nowhere to be seen.

Then he heard a funny whimpering sound, and turned back for the bathroom.

He opened the door and came to a halt.

"Oh, Jen . . ."

"And I . . . just cleaned . . . the . . . bathroom . . ."

Nick stood frozen in the doorway, unsure whether to go in or go out. She was crouched over the bowl, hair limp and face pasty. Here Nick had thought she'd been in with Kevin, when all along she'd been trying to keep this from him.

Her body convulsed again and Nick's decision was made. He crouched down next to her and pulled her hair gently back. "You're burning up," he protested, not knowing how else to tell her how much it hurt him to see her so sick. "Why didn't you say something?"

She wiped her mouth on the rag she held and shook her head. "You've been such a help with the kids. I couldn't...couldn't ask you to..."

That sentence wasn't finished, either.

Jenny couldn't believe it. Her big night. Her wonderful date, and here she was retching in the bathroom while Nick ran relay between the kids. She could hardly get her head up anymore from where she rested it against the cool tub rim. She was just so exhausted, so hot, so shaky. And Nick was still in Kevin's room changing sheets.

Well, if this night didn't cure him, nothing would. She wanted to cry. She probably would have if she'd had any moisture left in her anywhere. She felt like a squeezed lemon. She felt like stale bread—hot stale bread.

Then Nick came back. She could smell him first, cool like a summer night, his footsteps quiet and hesitant like he wasn't sure what to do with her. That was all right, she thought. She wasn't sure what to do with her anymore.

"I found your nightgown," he was saying, crouching close enough to run the back of his hand down her cheek. That felt cool, too. Cool and life-giving. Sweet. From some hidden well tears sprang up and stung her eyes. "Why don't I help you get it on and get you into bed, Jen? Maybe you'll feel better."

"I'm sorry, Nick," she apologized yet again. "This isn't fair."

"You're right," he answered with a soft grin. "It isn't. An entire pot of spaghetti sauce went to waste, I've changed more beds than a hotel maid and when I get the flu I'm going to have to let Emma take care of me. Now come on, let's get you to bed."

He lifted her. Jenny couldn't think of a sweeter thing anyone had ever done for her. He carried her into bed, and helped her get undressed and then covered her. And when he wasn't checking on the kids, he sat right by her through the night.

*   *   *

By the time the sun came up, Nick felt as if he'd been awake for a week. Everybody was finally asleep in the house, all foreheads reasonably cool, all stomachs quiet. To say he'd never been through anything like that in his life would have been an understatement. He'd survived a thousand firefights in Nam, drug busts, gang fights, union negotiations. In all his thirty-five years, he'd never fought a siege like the one he had last night. He hoped like hell he never would again.

Finally crawling off to the couch downstairs, he put in a couple of hours of sleep and then stumbled awake for the day.

Coffee. That sounded like a good idea. Shuffling around the kitchen in bare feet, he ran a hand through tumbled hair and brewed a pot. Looked for cream and settled for skim milk. He still hadn't eaten since last night, when he'd spent so much time testing his spaghetti sauce so that it would be just right for Jenny.

His spaghetti sauce was probably a congealed mass by now. It served him right for courting a mother. He should have just picked out a stewardess or a bank clerk like normal men. On their dates they went to the movies, maybe a club. On his, he worked the wards.

Well, he thought, pouring off a preliminary sample and adding the milk, at least it gave him a chance to finally decide. Jenny had said if he wanted to know about family life, last night would be it. Well, it was.

He'd been dumped headfirst back into the responsibility, the backbreaking work. He'd waded in tedium and fought revulsion. And somewhere in the small hours of the night, the answer to all Jenny's questions had finally come to him.

He looked up, wondering how she was doing. He wasn't about to wake her. She'd looked so exhausted lying there, her face almost translucent, her eyes huge and dark. He'd ached again, just like before. It hurt too much, sometimes, he realized. Too much to see someone you loved hurting. The flip side of living, the caring too much, the wanting too much. The ache when you couldn't do more.

He'd never known that before. He'd never been given that. He didn't know how to deal with it. Would Jenny hurt as much if he'd been the one racked like that? Yes, he realized, remembering the pain she hadn't been able to keep from her eyes when he'd told her about his childhood. She would. She'd stroke his cheek and murmur to him, straightening his sheets and aching with her eyes.

God, he thought, with a frustrated shake of the head. That was such a small thing last night. What about the big things? The big hurts and aches? How did you survive bearing that for someone else? Wishing for their pain and dying a little when you couldn't take it from them? How did you share?

Did he have the ability? Did he have the strength?

He did have the love. But, as Jenny said, was that enough? It scared the hell out of him.

Nick had begun to pace, walking through silent rooms without seeing them, picking things up, putting them down, straightening. He reached the front window and saw that unbelievably enough it was a nice day out: fresh, clear, storm-swept. Distracted, he pulled the curtains back a little.

Suddenly, his attention was completely caught. Completely, fatally caught. Not now. Aw, hell, not now!

He leaned in a little, trying to make sure, following progress, watching hands and pockets. Following the sleight of hand that made envelopes disappear from Barb Bailey's mailbox.

"Aw, dammit. Now I'll *never* get off that damn truck!"

Jenny wasn't sure what she'd expected. She knew what she'd hoped for. She'd hoped that she'd wake to find Nick right there, sitting in the rocking chair or curled up alongside her...even curled up downstairs. He wasn't. He was gone.

Making sure the kids were still asleep, she trudged downstairs. Still hoping. Still wishing for at least a note—*something* that would promise a return.

There was nothing, just cold coffee in the pot and silence. Spot rubbed up against her leg looking for food, the church bells were ringing noon Angelus. Half the day gone. Half the day left.

What for? The hope that had seen her down the steps was fading fast, folding in on itself like a dying flower. She'd made it a point to drag Nick over last night to force his hand. Well, she sure had. She'd dumped him right in the river to see if he'd swim, and it looked like he hadn't made it to the other bank.

His hand had been so cool against her cheek, though. He'd carried her into bed. No one had ever done that for her. No one but her mother had held her head when she'd been sick. How could he stay through the worst and then just take off? It didn't make any sense.

It made perfect sense. He'd reached his decision. She'd sure seen to that. Now she had to face getting through the rest of the day alone, and then the night, and then the next day. She had to survive, just as she had the last two years.

She'd thought she hadn't any tears left. Somehow they rose again, sliding down her cheeks and spilling onto the table. So what if he was going to be a lawyer? He was Nick. He was gentle and funny and pragmatic. He was the sound of gulls and fast engines, the wind in her hair and the sun in her eyes. He was freedom and security, and it didn't matter if he decided to be a bank robber, he would still be the man she loved.

Damn him. He had to listen to her and come along last night. He had to let himself be talked into the test. She could have fooled him a while longer, long enough to...

To what? To marry him? To have more children? To show him just what it was he'd locked himself into, just like the Jerk? She couldn't do that and she knew it. She couldn't cage him just because she couldn't bear to lose him. Better to make it a clean cut. Better to leave now.

If it was better, it should have been easier to stop the tears.

Emma and Kevin got up after a while and ambled in to sit in the playroom. Barb came over and prescribed chicken soup. Kate called and asked again about going to tea. Each asked what was wrong with Jenny, and she used the flu for an excuse. Then each asked if there was anything else to be done. Nothing, Jenny said each time. Nothing, at all.

And she sat at the table, knowing she should do something but without the energy to move. Listening to the silence in her house and hating it. Gathering her children to her for hugs and reassuring her family that everything was all right. She watched the sun slide past her kitchen window and settle against the horizon in crimson slashes. She heard the birds, the neighborhood dogs, the television, and still she couldn't quite decide to move.

She didn't want to go forward, because it would mean admitting she had to go on without Nick. She had to face that endless succession of days again, of frustrations and responsibilities, of lonely, silent nights when there was no one to share the small minutes of darkness with her, no one to create something new with.

In the end, she knew she couldn't stay where she was. She still had two children who didn't deserve to be neglected. She had a family, and she had a life. And she damn well had to get on with it.

At the time she usually began talking the kids into getting into pajamas, Jenny changed out of her nightgown. She showered and dressed and straightened up her room. She could still smell him there, so that if she closed her eyes he was still there, his eyes like gems, his voice a hush of concern.

But he wasn't there, so she went back downstairs.

And there she found him, sitting at her kitchen table.

Jenny came to a stop. For a moment she blamed it on dehydration, or residual fever. On wishful thinking. She'd spent the day mourning him and, just like a genie, he was back.

"I thought you'd taken the noon train out of town," Jenny offered hesitantly.

Nick flashed a smile that was equal parts apology and triumph. "I'm sorry I wasn't here when you woke up. How are you feeling?"

Jenny shook her head. "Confused."

"I know." Taking another assessing glance that seemed to mean something special, he launched himself to his feet. "Can we talk?"

Jenny almost found herself stepping back. She didn't want him too close. She didn't want to feel that hope resurrecting in her chest, inflating like a balloon threatening to burst free. She didn't want to be disappointed again.

But he was here. "You did a good job on Kevin and Emma," she said, still so very unnerved. "Thanks."

"Yeah," he nodded a little. "I was talking to them. They're watching TV. Want to sit in the living room? I need to talk to you before the neighborhood breaks in."

Instinctively Jenny looked around. This wasn't exactly the center of neighborhood activity. "Why?"

He flashed a sudden smile. "Explanations come with the talk."

She followed him back in, easing down onto her couch as if in a stranger's home, unsure what she wanted him to say, afraid of what he would.

For a long moment, Nick just stared at his hands. "First of all, the reason I left so abruptly. I didn't want to wake you. You'd been through . . . a lot."

Jenny couldn't help but smile. "Childbirth," she amended, "is a lot. The flu is survivable."

Nick smiled, and in it betrayed the insecurities he'd brought with him the night before. "Yeah, well, I'm not a good judge of that stuff. Anyway, the long and short of it is that our secret is out. My cover is blown."

Jenny straightened. "How?"

Another smile, this one pure satisfaction. "Case is closed, suspect apprehended."

"You're off the ice cream truck?"

This seemed to deserve a grimace. "Well, that remains to be seen."

"Why?"

"Because the suspect is the chief of police's aunt."

Jenny sat back, stunned, trying to ingest the information. "Mrs. Warner? Mrs. Warner was stealing checks?"

Nick shook his head with another wince. "Miss Lucy."

That brought Jenny to her feet. "You *arrested* Miss Lucy?"

"Sit down, Jen," Nick urged, taking her hand. When she did—albeit reluctantly—he continued. "It's not all that bad.

She's turned state's evidence. Her lawn crew got her involved. Seems it's a bit more expensive to live across your street than the old ladies thought. When the 'nice young gentlemen' came to her with the idea, Miss Lucy decided to pad the Social Security a little.''

Jenny couldn't get past the bald truth. "Miss *Lucy*?"

Nick grinned. "Quite a savvy old lady. She sure had me fooled. When I laid it out to the chief, he got hold of her and she admitted it right away. Said she figured nobody would arrest a nice old lady like her. They certainly wouldn't sentence her.''

"They won't, will they?"

Nick shrugged. "She'll probably get a suspended sentence.''

Jenny just kept shaking her head. "Miss Lucy."

Nick nodded. "She was delighted I arrested her. Said she was thrilled I wasn't a drug runner, after all.''

"Well, then," she said, still trying to assimilate the easy stuff. "It's all settled.''

"Not," Nick objected, "quite."

Jenny looked up. "What?"

"There *was* a drug dealer in the neighborhood. They picked him up this afternoon.''

Jenny was beginning to anticipate now. "Him?"

Nick nodded. "Todd Sellers. I figured it out yesterday. We were able to link it all up. Oh, and by the way, I met your lovely Detective Richards. I'm surprised that guy can find the rest room most days.''

"I bet he was thrilled when you told him."

"He did refer to the legitimacy of my birth once or twice.''

"Todd," Jenny murmured, frowning. "Poor Lauren." Ideas, assistance for both households formed in her mind, and then she turned back to Nick. "Anything else?"

"Well, yes."

She sighed. "What?"

"Marry me."

This time Jenny went very still. "Pardon?"

Nick smiled then, his face lighting, his eyes bright with delight. "You have a pretty mean boot camp, lady. But I think I passed."

"You think?"

He took her hand. Jenny let him. She couldn't seem to think, to feel. To hope. Time came to a standstill and the world held its silence for the answer.

Nick looked briefly at where he held her hand, as if considering what he had. Then he returned his gaze to her. "I went back to the apartment this afternoon," he said. "After being here and then running around with all this. I thought I could use a little peace and quiet before I came back here. Know what I found?"

Jenny could do no more than shake her head.

"Emptiness. It wasn't quiet there. It was just empty. I kept waiting for the sound of your voice, for Emma and Kevin to bolt through the door." He took a breath, discovering even as he spoke. "I missed this house. Jenny, I don't know how I'll do with a big family. I've never tried it before. But I realized today that I damn well want to try. I've lived in an empty place too long. Fill my life for me."

Jenny should have grown tired of the tears. They betrayed her again, even before she could speak. "Whiffle-ball games, and all?"

"Pink houses and tuna-noodle casserole and soccer games."

"Yes," Jenny said, and thought she'd never said anything that sounded so right before. "Yes. I'll marry you."

It was summer again. The days still stretched in languid succession to a close-approaching autumn. School would start at the end of the weekend. For now, the house was filled with the noise of a family picnic. Horseshoes were being played out in the backyard and whiffle ball in the street. Amanda scooted in her walker and Jessie gurgled as he bounced on his grandmother's knee.

In the kitchen Jenny and Claire were doing dishes and sampling leftover potato salad.

"All right," Claire admitted. "You win."

Pushing wet black hair back from her forehead, Jenny turned from the sink. "Why?"

Claire delivered a sisterly glare that grudgingly admitted defeat. "You look happier than I've ever seen you in your life."

Jenny grinned. "Probably because I am."

"I have to admit he cleaned up real well, didn't he?"

Jenny took a look through to the picture of Nick and her on their wedding day. He'd pulled out what he referred to as his yuppie wardrobe, all pinstripes and power ties. She had worn an ivory dress and hat.

"Actually," she admitted, wistfully, "there are times when I miss that ponytail."

Claire rolled her eyes. "You still have the tattoo."

Jenny grinned. "Yeah. Sometimes we get in his GTO and play the rock and roll really loud, and he wears those T-shirts..."

"And those ripped jeans?"

"I saved them."

"Probably shouldn't let the D.A.'s office know about that."

"Oh, they know. He's been begging to go undercover again."

Immediately Claire bristled. "Now?"

Jenny smiled. "Back in the high rises. He's been asked to help Kevin crack an insider-trading scandal."

"Kevin? You mean the Jer—"

"The same, much to his chagrin." A partial victory there—money for the children, but no change in attention. It just didn't seem to be in her ex, especially with his new family to consider. On the other hand, a very colicky first baby had rid him of the custody notions.

They had, in the end, come to a more manageable truce.

"Where is he?"

Startled, Jenny looked up. The door slammed right behind a bear of a man. He'd been on the heels of her father, who was in the process of going for another beer.

"Hello, Marco," Jenny greeted the ice cream magnate. "I see you've met my dad."

Marco proceeded to slap her dad on the back and almost send him over on his nose. "I like your family."

"Thanks," Jenny acknowledged. "I like yours. Now, if you'll take your loud lungs out into the yard, I'll go find Nick."

"He should be out there defending the Barnes honor."

Jenny just smiled. "You know darn well where he is. Now, go on."

"You will not allow me to witness this miracle all the police bet would never happen?"

"I'll take pictures," she promised. "He might spook if someone approached too suddenly."

Marco's laugh should have awakened Miss Lucy from her nap across the street.

Jenny made sure the two men had taken their evidently in-progress discussion of city politics outside before tossing her towel at Claire. "Finish these, will you? I have to see a man."

Claire's smile gave away her affection for her new brother-in-law. "I think it's cute."

"Yeah," Jenny agreed with an even sillier grin. "So do I."

The noise receded as she climbed the stairs. It always seemed so much quieter up here. Especially late, when the kids were in bed and she and Nick lay together talking over the day. A haven. Her home had become full and noisy and safe. And finally whole.

She always knew where to find him these days. Jenny pushed the door open a little. The room was a little cleaner, the bed emptied of clutter. It was easier to do now that Jenny was just substitute teaching. Of course, Nick refused to keep his books out of the bedroom, but she didn't mind. There was something so settling about reading together.

The rocking chair was still in front of the window, right where the morning sun would find it. The morning light was long gone, but the sky glowed softly behind him, casting him in a kind of halo, a soft light of welcome.

He'd changed in the last year. Grown, she thought, into his position, into his family. His face looked more mature, more authoritative. His hair was precisely cut now, full and just beginning to gray at the temples, and he'd recovered the mustache that seemed so important to him. He wore polo shirts instead of his favorite Grateful Dead shirts, but Jenny could still see that tattoo. The wild side of him still peeked out when she wanted it to.

Today, though, there was just peace. Wonder. Nick was rocking slowly back and forth, his eyes down on the tiny bundle in his arms. Jenny watched him and fought the sting of new tears. It never failed to break her heart all over again to see this man with his tiny new daughter and see the joy in his eyes.

He knew she was there, of course.

"I thought I heard her crying."

Jenny grinned. "Amazing. Two weeks old, and she already has all your buttons pushed. This kid is going to be a pro."

"Hey," he objected, even though his eyes still held that strange peace. "Don't talk about my daughter that way. I'm just getting in my time while I can. It's only gonna be a few years before she's gone."

"I doubt it," Jenny assured him. "I have a feeling Maggie's going to be thirty before you even let her date."

"You'd better believe it."

"I'll tell Emma, too."

"Emma's *already* thirty."

"Marco needs your help at horseshoes," she said. "And Emma is waiting for you to swing her."

The plus, the special bonus Jenny couldn't have dreamed of if she'd tried. The only person more protective, more loving, more devoted to her children than she, was Nick. He was a champion Chutes-and-Ladders player, a rabid soccer fan, an attentive escort to tea. Maggie's arrival had just cemented the growing family.

"How many more do you want?" he asked again, their little game, their special bond.

"Five," Jenny answered. "To form an even number."

"Six," Nick countered. "Then we'll have a baseball team."

"Oh, I don't know," Jen demurred. "Kids are so demanding."

Slowly getting to his feet, Nick brought Maggie over to her mother. "It's different when they're yours," he informed her archly.

They stood there for a moment, together, sharing the small silence in the house, the small life they held between them.

"Thank you," Nick finally said, his eyes warmer than any summer sun.

Jenny lifted her face to bask in his gaze. "For what?" she asked, knowing. Never hearing it enough.

"For my new family," he said, motioning to include the noise still drifting up from outside. "All of it."

Jenny couldn't offer any words that would contain the love she felt for her husband. She just smiled and reached up to kiss him, their new daughter caught between them.

Nick reached out a hand to her. Jenny saw the truth in his eyes, heard the wonder in his voice, and was content.

"Thank you," he said. "For filling my life."

*   *   *   *   *

Silhouette Intimate Moments®

COMING
NEXT MONTH

#313 TIME WAS—Nora Roberts
When Caleb Hornblower comes to after the craft he was piloting crashes, he doesn't understand how very far from home he is. He has traveled not only through space, but through time, only to discover that home is what he finds in Libby Stone's arms.

#314 TENDER OFFER—
Paula Detmer Riggs
Alex Torres returned to southwestern Ohio to help his ex-wife, Casey O'Neill, fight the takeover of her company. But in the ruthless corporate world, it was not the only battle to be waged—he also had to regain the respect and trust of the woman he'd never stopped loving.

#315 LOVE IS A LONG SHOT—
Joanna Marks
Laura Reynolds's testimony had been crucial in sending Quinton Jones to prison for a crime he didn't commit. Now Quint was back, and Laura desperately wanted to set the record straight. But she knew that once he found out who she really was, he would be bound to break her heart.

#316 FLIRTING WITH DANGER—
Linda Turner
Someone was trying to drive beautiful heiress Gabriella Winters insane. So she fled her family mansion—only to run headlong into the arms of Austin LePort. There was more to this handsome hobo than met the eye, and soon Gabriella found herself truly mad . . . madly in love.

AVAILABLE NOW:

#309 THE ICE CREAM MAN
Kathleen Korbel

#310 SOMEBODY'S BABY
Marilyn Pappano

#311 MAGIC IN THE AIR
Marilyn Tracy

**#312 MISTRESS OF
FOXGROVE**
Lee Magner

You'll flip . . . your pages won't!
Read paperbacks *hands-free* with

Book Mate · I

The perfect "mate" for all your romance paperbacks

Traveling • Vacationing • At Work • In Bed • Studying • Cooking • Eating

Perfect size for all standard paperbacks, this wonderful invention makes reading a pure pleasure! Ingenious design holds paperback books OPEN and FLAT so even wind can't ruffle pages – leaves your hands free to do other things. Reinforced, wipe-clean vinyl-covered holder flexes to let you turn pages without undoing the strap... supports paperbacks so well, they have the strength of hardcovers!

Pages turn WITHOUT opening the strap.

SEE-THROUGH STRAP

Reinforced back stays flat.

Built in bookmark.

BOOK MARK

BACK COVER HOLDING STRIP

10˝ x 7¼˝, opened.
Snaps closed for easy carrying, too.

Available now. Send your name, address, and zip code, along with a check or money order for just $5.95 + .75¢ for postage & handling (for a total of $6.70) payable to Reader Service to:

> Reader Service
> Bookmate Offer
> 901 Fuhrmann Blvd.
> P.O. Box 1396
> Buffalo, N.Y. 14269-1396

Offer not available in Canada
*New York and Iowa residents add appropriate sales tax.

BM-G

SILHOUETTE DESIRE™
presents
AUNT EUGENIA'S TREASURES
by CELESTE HAMILTON

Liz, Cassandra and Maggie are the honored recipients of Aunt Eugenia's heirloom jewels...but Eugenia knows the real prizes are the young women themselves. Every other month from December to April in Silhouette Desire, read about Aunt Eugenia's quest to find them worthy men and a treasure more valuable than diamonds, rubies or pearls—lasting love.

Coming in December: THE DIAMOND'S SPARKLE

Altruistic attorney Liz Patterson balks at Aunt Eugenia's attempt at matchmaking. Clearly, a shrewd PR man isn't her type. Nathan Hollister, after all, likes fast cars and fast times, but, as he tells Liz, love is something he's willing to take *very* slowly.

In February: RUBY FIRE

Passionate Cassandra Martin has always been driven by impulse. After traveling from city to city, seeking new opportunities, Cassandra returns home...ready to re-kindle the flame of young love with the man she never forgot, Daniel O'Grady.

In April: THE HIDDEN PEARL

Maggie O'Grady loved and lost early in life. Since then caution has been her guide. But when brazen Jonah Pendleton moves into the apartment next door, gentle Maggie comes out of her shell and glows in the precious warmth of love.

Aunt Eugenia's Treasures
Each book shines on its own, but together they're priceless

SD-AET-1

Wonderful, luxurious gifts can be yours with proofs-of-purchase from any specially marked "Indulge A Little" Harlequin or Silhouette book with the Offer Certificate properly completed, plus a check or money order (do not send cash) to cover postage and handling payable to Harlequin/Silhouette "Indulge A Little, Give A Lot" Offer. We will send you the specified gift.

Mail-in-Offer

OFFER CERTIFICATE

Item:	A. Collector's Doll	B. Soaps in a Basket	C. Potpourri Sachet	D. Scented Hangers
# of Proofs-of -Purchase	18	12	6	4
Postage & Handling	$3.25	$2.75	$2.25	$2.00
Check One				

Name _____

Address _____ Apt. # _____

City _____ State _____ Zip _____

ONE PROOF OF PURCHASE

To collect your free gift by mail you must include the necessary number of proofs-of-purchase plus postage and handling with offer certificate.

SIM-2

Harlequin®/Silhouette®

Mail this certificate, designated number of proofs-of-purchase and check or money order for postage and handling to:

INDULGE A LITTLE
P.O. Box 9055
Buffalo, N.Y. 14269-9055